DRAINED

A NOVEL

MARC DANIEL ACRICHE

Printed in the United States of America
Print ISBN: 9781735816104
E-Book ISBN: 9781735816111

Sunken Island Books
443 East 6th Street, Suite 3
New York, NY 10009

Interior formatting by DartFrog Books

Cover design by David Litman

To Dina

CONTENTS

JENNIFER'S
BROWNSTONE

CASEY'S
APARTMENT

CENTRAL
PARK

NEW
YORK
CITY
2048

ROOSEVELT
PREP

BROADWAY

LIGHT
BORDER

UNION
SQUARE

EAST
VILLAGE

MARTIN'S
APARTMENT

E. HOUSTON ST

TOMPKINS
SQUARE
PARK

LUDLOW
GARAGE

TODT HILL
ACADEMY

STATEN ISLAND

CHAPTER ONE | LOST AND FOUND

|

"**Bags open, people**. Power's down. We're doing it the old-fashioned way."

A collective grumble roiled the line. About forty kids stretched along the New York City, Upper East Side street, waiting to get into school. Casey Parker, stuck about midway, raised her hands in a what-the-fuck gesture to the security guard pacing the line. He smiled at her and shrugged. She had already missed first period, and now she was going to miss Lab. Casey sighed. This was not good. She was failing Chem, her first time ever failing anything. She needed to get inside, she needed to get to lab, and she needed the power to stay on. Lifting her sunglasses, she checked her screen to see if she'd missed any notifications about the outage. There was a curt message from her mom about dinner, but otherwise nothing. She jockeyed to see what was up at the front of the line, but she was too short and the guy's head in front of her too big. The guy, Jonas, she knew from English Lit. Casey stood on her toes and put a hand on his shoulder. It was damp from sweat.

Jonas turned and looked at her hand, then at her. "I could give you a boost."

Casey stood down, wiping her hand across her tank top. "You calling me short?"

"Never, Parker. You are tall in every way except height."

"Good," she said. "You know I'm sensitive."

Jonas grinned at her, then went back to his business.

The line moved but not fast enough. The blistering hot morning wasn't making things any easier; Casey tugged at her top, hoping for a breeze. It was October, it was well over ninety degrees, and it had been like this for days. Another step, then two, and she was almost at the front of the line. A school guard checked bags behind a folding table. Behind him, a full-body scanner—good for guns, knives, and illicit substances—loomed, lifeless and frustrated.

"Great," Casey said, frustrated as well.

"What's great?"

She turned. Jennifer, her best friend, was standing next to her, smiling. In a sleeveless blouse and ponytail, Jennifer looked fresh, rested even. She looked the exact opposite of how Casey felt; that was usually the case, though. Her best friend had a politician's way of pulling herself together. It ran in the family.

"What's great?" Jennifer repeated.

"The power outage . . . the line . . . one guard checking all of us." Casey waved at the teenagers in line behind them.

"What's the rush? Sirota's got us in assembly anyway."

Casey stepped to the inspection table. "All of us?" she asked, lowering her bag from her shoulder. She flinched when its strap scraped against her sunburnt skin.

"No. Just the seniors."

"Don't tell me it's a fucking Recruiting thing." Casey put her bag on the table.

"I won't . . . but it's a fucking Recruiting thing."

The guard looked at them sideways.

Casey's stomach, already in knots thanks to being late, tightened some more. She was not a fan of Recruiting or the wars it helped fuel.

The guard, after poking around in Casey's bag, slid it back to her. She grabbed it, but he held on. "Is there a problem?" she asked, surprised.

The guard eyed them both. "You two should watch what you say."

"Excuse me," Jennifer said. "Do you know—"

The guard cut her off. "I do know, Ms. Hargrove. But still." He let go of the bag.

"No offense meant," Casey said, grabbing the bag and slinging it over her shoulder. He was right, after all. You never knew who was listening, and speaking poorly of Recruiting could get you in trouble.

The guard ordered her around the table. "Arms out," he said, a metal-detecting wand in his beefy hand.

Casey spread her arms out as directed, and the guard gave her a perfunctory once-over. Wearing shorts and a tank, it wasn't as if she could hide much. The scanner silently agreed, and the guard waved her along. She waited as he checked Jennifer next.

"Where's your stuff?" Casey asked, realizing Jennifer didn't have her bag.

"In my locker." Jennifer held her arms out to the side. "I came back out after first period. I was looking for Martin."

"You mean your boyfriend?"

Jennifer smiled as the guard let her through. She lowered her eyes. "He's not my boyfriend."

"Right. After last night, I'd say he was. You were practically glowing."

In front of them, Jonas had his arm behind him, holding open the door.

"Where were you this morning, anyway?" Jennifer asked.

Casey thanked Jonas, and they followed him inside. "I was up late after I left you guys at the bar. We fought again." She pushed her sunglasses up over her forehead, forcing her dark curly hair to fall in line and away from her face.

"You fought about Bruce?"

Bruce was her mom's new boyfriend, and Casey was having a

hard time accepting that her mom was dating again. That Bruce was a douche didn't help any. "Bruce. My grades. Fake IDs. Same shit."

"Fucking Bruce," Jennifer said.

"Fucking Bruce," Casey agreed.

Climbing a short stack of stairs, Casey watched her footing as her eyes adjusted to the dim interior lighting. Her high-tops squeaked on the polished floor. Once past another set of doors, they were confronted with a bottleneck of students. As Jennifer had said, it was just the seniors, and they were being herded into the auditorium.

Jennifer searched the line forward and back. With about a foot on Casey, she had a mostly unobstructed view.

"Anything?" Casey asked.

"No. It's just not like him. He'd at least message me."

"And you tried him?" The line inched forward. A freshman, judging by his small size, excused himself and slid between them. His sweaty forearm brushed against Casey's.

"Of course. But I'm trying to play it cool. I don't want to seem desperate."

"You? Desperate? Never." Casey wiped her arm on her shorts. "He should be flying a banner letting you know where he is. You're Jennifer fucking Hargrove."

"Stop." Jennifer blushed. "It's different with Martin. He's different."

"You think he joined up?" Casey pointed toward the auditorium doors. "A Recruiting assembly . . . could mean another Recruiting list."

"Never. Not Martin. He would have told me."

Casey shrugged. She didn't know Martin well enough to know what he'd do. The line continued to inch along as her frustration spread like a rash she couldn't scratch. "Who calls an assembly during a blackout?" she huffed.

"It's better than class."

"Not when you're failing."

"You'll be fine. You always are."

The way things were going this semester, she wasn't so sure.

They reached the auditorium. Beyond the double-door entrance, Brian Jasper—who had graduated the year before—was handing out screens. Brian had been crushing on Casey since junior high. He was sweet, and they used to be friends—or, at least, friendly—but Brian's military allegiance had become too much for her, and they had drifted apart. She nudged Jennifer. "What's he doing here?"

"He works in the Recruiting office. You knew that."

She guessed she knew that, but she hadn't been expecting to see him now. "I can't . . ."

"Come on. You could do a lot worse. Look at him in that uniform."

"Stop," Casey said. Whether guy or girl, good-looking or not, the uniform, and the violence it represented, was the problem.

Brian spotted her, and his face brightened. He smiled, and it was so genuine that Casey didn't know how to react. How could anyone be so enamored with her? She forced a smile in return, hoping it came off as genuine. He was too nice a guy to hurt. She put her hand on Jennifer's back and guided her in first.

"Jennifer Hargrove," Brian said, handing her a screen.

"Colonel," Jennifer said, saluting.

"The election's looking good for your father," he said, ignoring her teasing.

"That's what I hear."

Jennifer's father was Michael Hargrove, head of the Independent Coalition Party and most likely the city's next mayor.

"Well, the ICP is lucky to have him, and the city will be, too."

Jennifer turned to Casey. "You hear that, Case? You are lucky to have him." She took a backward step away, and then another. "As long as you're not black, or Latino," she continued to rant as she turned and headed down the nearest aisle, "or Asian, or live downtown."

"She never changes," Brian said.

"She is pretty consistent."

He handed Casey a screen. "You should come out to one of the orientations this month."

She took the screen. "You know that's not me."

"You'd be surprised."

No . . . I *wouldn't*, she thought. The last thing Casey could imagine doing was signing on the dotted line as an ICP recruit. If the ICP hadn't been hounding her police-officer father with corruption charges—charges he had vehemently denied—then maybe he wouldn't have felt the need to leave. "Sorry, but no," she said, caring a bit less now about being genuine. She took a tentative step toward the aisle and tried to spot Jennifer in the crowd.

"Okay," Brian said. "You know where to find me if you change your mind."

She half-waved and hurried away, agitated by the hard sell. After a few steps, she glanced back. Dude was still smiling. He was so fucking earnest.

Casey weaved down the aisle, dodging students as she went. Jennifer, sitting toward the front and to the side, was talking to Greg. The auditorium was hot, and the kids passing her were even hotter. She kept her arms close to her side to avoid any inadvertent rubbing. Jennifer turned and gestured for her to hurry on up. She pointed at the empty seat next to her.

"Fuckin' Sirota," Casey said, still mad that he'd called this assembly in the first place. She dropped into the saved seat, putting her bag between her feet on the floor.

Jennifer turned. "I blame Recruiting," she said, a bit too loudly, seemingly undeterred by the mild rebuke they'd just received outside. She held up the screen Brian had given her. "You'd think they had enough bodies by now."

There were never enough bodies.

Between the occupation forces along the southern border and the hot wars across the Middle East, the ICP was always in need of recruits. Still, Jennifer needed to keep her voice down. Questioning the ICP could get you in trouble. Glancing around, most of the seniors within earshot were their friends—ones who, for the most part, could be trusted.

"You're extra 'anti' today," Casey said.

Jennifer scowled. "I was fine until Soldier Boy up there. Not to mention the rent-a-cop outside."

"Brian likes your father . . . you can't blame him. He's practically brainwashed to like him."

"Well, my brainwashing wore off a while ago. I don't have to like him."

Casey slid down into her seat until her bare knees touched the row in front. She felt bad for her friend. Jennifer's father was absent for the most part, and when he was present he was indifferent at best. In truth, she felt sorry for herself, too. Whether mentally or physically absent, a lost father was something they both had to deal with.

From the row in front of them, Tanya turned, her hand shading her eyes. "Can't we close them?" she asked, pointing in the direction of the windows behind them.

"The curtains don't work without power," Greg answered. His hair was mussed, and he was in the same T-shirt he'd worn to the bar last night. "We tried."

"Great," Tanya said, turning back.

Greg leaned forward, and waved at Casey. "You made it?"

She rolled her eyes. "Is everyone keeping tabs?"

"Spreadsheets," Greg answered. "We plug in everything you do."

Casey sneered. "Nice T-shirt, by the way," she said. "Is this day two or three?"

Greg looked down. He lowered his nose to his armpit and took a deep, exaggerated breath. "Three," he said. "Just how you like it."

Casey sat back. *Boys*, she thought, looking to Jennifer for affirmation. But Jennifer wasn't paying attention. She was holding herself up by her seat's armrests, looking around the auditorium. After a moment, she lowered herself back down and leaned toward Casey. "I still don't see him."

"I'm sure he's fine. Martin's a downtowner like me. We're a tough breed."

"It's the downtown part that concerns me. They were scheduled for an outage last night, and he was worried about getting home."

"That's like the third night this week."

"Fourth," Jennifer said. "I don't know how they do it."

Casey scanned the auditorium. It was a full house. Despite the heat, the seniors gabbed, fidgeted, and generally carried on. Brian had made his way to the front of the auditorium and was standing at attention next to the stage. Sitting in the first row were the science and math geeks Martin usually hung out with. But Jennifer was right; Martin wasn't with them. On the stage, Vice Principal Sirota appeared from the wings, his tie loosened and off-center, his dress shirt stained with perspiration. He had a bullhorn in his hand and was flanked by two uniformed ICP officers. He shuffled to the center of the stage, shoulders slumping. His companions walked tall.

The rowdy crowd finally hushed.

"Thank you, seniors," he said. Sirota's voice was more nasal than usual. He held up the bullhorn, exposing his unsightly pits. "Can everyone hear me all right without this? I really don't want to use it." Hearing no objections, he continued. "You should all have received screens from Recruiting on your way in. Please make sure to fill them out before you leave, and bring them to Recruit Jasper." He pointed to Brian below him. "If you see any of your classmates who aren't here, let them know they must report to Recruiting and fill one out before Thanksgiving break."

Jennifer leaned in. "Glad you're here now?"

"Thrilled," Casey said. And it was true. Any chance to avoid a trip to Recruiting was appreciated.

As Vice Principal Sirota bleated on, Casey tuned him out. She slipped her screen from her bag and made the rounds of her music sites. Domino Falls was playing the Beacon on New Year's Eve. She had seen them a few weeks back and would sacrifice a foot to see them again.

Looking up, Sirota had moved to the side as one of the uniformed men took over. After a well-worn spiel about ICP loyalty, respect, and sacrifice, he began reading the latest Recruiting list. Publicly announcing the names was meant to honor the recruits and their families—an exercise in patriotism—but Casey dreaded the reading. The recruitment process seemed so random and opaque. Kids like Brian would sign up, and that was understandable. But, increasingly, kids she never thought of as ICP material were suddenly joining, and it made no sense. Still, you never questioned the ICP. If you were seventeen, you were eligible, and that's all anyone needed to know.

Today, Jonah Carson led the list of new recruits. Jonah joining up made sense. He was as deep into the hive mind as Brian.

Casey didn't recognize the next two names, but someone behind her gasped after the second one was read. She turned to see who had slipped, but it was no one she knew. The girl, maybe a sister or a girlfriend of the new recruit, had her hand over her mouth and tears in her eyes. Casey felt terrible, but Recruiting was like that—it was random, it was sudden, and, nine times out of ten, it sucked.

Lost in thought, Casey wasn't paying attention when the next name was called. However, she did hear Jennifer gasp. Casey turned to her friend. "Jen . . ." she began to say, then things slowly registered: They had called Martin's name. Jennifer's almost-boyfriend hadn't been late or cutting class; he was gone because he'd been recruited. Casey's casual suggestion had been right. Casey looked to the stage; Sirota was glaring in their direction. Jennifer started to stand. She was about to say something that could not be taken back, and Casey could not let that happen.

Grabbing Jennifer by the arm, Casey forced her to sit back down. Jennifer looked at her, stunned. "Jen, no," Casey said.

Jennifer sat back, shaking off Casey's hand. With her eyes glued to the stage, she whispered, "No way. There is no fucking way."

Casey didn't know if there was a way or not, but that was irrelevant. Her best friend would not take this lightly. But lightly was the only choice they had. Jennifer sat stiffly in her seat, her eyes red and wet. One tear, then another rolled down her cheek. Casey knew she'd have to get her friend out of the auditorium and find a safe place for her to vent. The rest of the school day, if not the week, was shot for sure, and she could kiss her Chemistry grade goodbye.

Strangely enough, she felt relieved, glad for the excuse not to try.

2

"You're not supposed to be here!" Casey yelled. She slammed her bedroom door behind her.

Casey and Jennifer were in Casey's apartment, only a few blocks from school. With her mom at work, it had seemed like a good place to just let Jennifer be. But she had been wrong. Bruce was in the apartment. Alone. This infuriated her. He had no right to be.

Casey tiptoed toward the door and put her ear up against it. She closed her eyes, trying to hear better.

"You really think he's listening?" Jennifer asked. She was sitting on Casey's bed, a couple of feet behind her.

Casey waved for her to be quiet, then leaned into the door. She pressed her ear as flat as it would go and covered her other ear with her hand. She listened. She waited. But it was no use. If Bruce was on the other side, she couldn't hear him. Turning, she joined Jennifer on the unmade bed. Her tiny bedroom felt more claustrophobic than ever. Band posters papered the walls behind them. They both stared at the door. "Fucking Bruce," Casey said. "Did I tell you she gave him the key code to the apartment?"

"After a month?"

"After a month. She thinks she's in love."

"What does she even see in him?"

That her mom had turned her attention from a cop—one who cared deeply about the community he served—to a stockbroker whose main concern seemed to be enriching himself made no sense. And the more she tried to make sense of it, the more frustrated with her mom she became. "Maybe it's his hair," Casey said, grasping.

"He does have nice hair."

Leaning back, she pulled her screen from the front pocket of her shorts. "I'm messaging my mom. This is not right that he's here." She started typing.

"It's not right," Jennifer said.

Casey stopped typing and studied her friend for a moment. Gone was the put-together girl she had been so impressed with earlier. Jennifer's hair had fallen from its ponytail, and her eyes were red from crying. Casey lowered her screen. She hadn't meant to get distracted; she wanted to be present for her friend. Right now, Bruce was irrelevant.

"Don't stop," Jennifer said. "Your mom needs to know."

"Later. My Bruce issues aren't going anywhere." She pointed at the screen in her best friend's hand. "Anything?"

"Nothing."

"It could be the blackout."

"The blackout doesn't explain his recruitment."

Casey nodded. She knew it didn't, but she was at a loss.

"It's not like him. He would have said something."

"You said he rarely went out. Maybe last night was his way of saying goodbye."

"He told me that I'd see him tomorrow. He would have said something."

They debated their options. They needed to know more, but it was hard to know whom to trust. There was talk of asking Jennifer's father, but questioning the man who was basically in charge of Recruiting didn't seem like the wisest move. After some discussion, they decided that contacting Martin's mom would be their best bet. The problem was Jennifer didn't know her name or their address. She knew they lived downtown, in the East Village near the park, but that was it. Casey slipped off the bed, took a Twister-like step over Jennifer, and sat at the desk that abutted the bed. On the desk was a tablet-sized screen lying face down.

Jennifer put a knee on the bed and turned to face Casey. "What are you thinking?" she asked.

"There's got to be something about them." Casey flipped over the screen and started searching for anything on Martin. Pages of hits came up. Who knew there were so many guys named Martin Santos in New York City? Casey positioned the screen so they both could see. Together they scanned, but none of the links were relevant. On the third page, Casey spotted something. "There," she said, pointing to a photo that looked like Martin toward the bottom of the screen. She tapped at the link under it. The picture was from The Villager, a downtown news site, and the headline above it read: Moving On Up. The caption below identified the family as Martin, his mom, and his grandmother. Martin was in the middle, towering over the two women. They were all smiling, and they all shared the same slim nose and expressive eyes. The article praised "one of their own" for getting accepted into Roosevelt Prep for his junior year.

"He looks like a baby," Jennifer said, smiling, maybe for the first time since hearing the news.

"Yeah. He definitely filled out." Martin's mom had her arms wrapped around one of his. Martin had his other arm wrapped around his grandmother's shoulders. "They look close."

"Ridiculously so. He worships both of them."

"No dad?"

Jennifer shook her head. "Died when was he was little. I don't think he really knew him."

"Maybe for the best," Casey said. "Having all the good memories makes it harder."

Jennifer touched her arm. "You don't mean that."

She shrugged. No, she didn't mean it, but sometimes she felt it.

"But you see what I mean?" Jennifer questioned. "He worked hard, real hard, to get into Roosevelt Prep. Why would he throw that away?"

Casey nodded in agreement. Jennifer was making sense. Having gone to a downtown school until sixth grade, Casey knew how dysfunctional they could be. She had liked her teachers well enough, but her elementary school building had been decrepit, blackouts had been common there, and her classrooms were always jampacked. Of course, as any kid would, she had fought the move uptown, but now she knew how lucky she was that her parents had summoned the wherewithal to do it. Not everyone's parents did. The fact that they both kept working downtown and had a long commute each day made their sacrifice even more commendable. Casey sighed, feeling bad about her maybe-it's-for-the-best quip about Martin's dead dad. It wasn't for the best. Even a father like hers—one who had disappeared off the face of the Earth—deserved credit for the good stuff. She needed to remember that.

"You think maybe being at Roosevelt was too much pressure for him?" Casey asked.

"No. He was breezing through . . . would've graduated with honors." Jennifer tapped at the picture, zooming in on Martin's mom.

"She would understand what I'm going through. I can't imagine she's taking this lightly."

Casey took the screen and searched for Martin's mom, then his grandmother, hoping for some personal information—maybe a workplace or an address. But their names were just as common. After a minute, she gave up. "I got nothing," she said.

Jennifer stood. She paced the tight pass between the bed and the dresser. She picked her bag up from the floor and tossed it on the bed. She ran her fingers through her hair and mumbled something about finding people they could trust. Casey had never seen her friend so distraught. She knew Jennifer liked Martin, even liked him a lot, but Jennifer had liked loads of boys over the years, some quite a bit. How had she missed her friend's growing attachment? Really, though, it wasn't much of a mystery. She'd been too absorbed in her own life and her own problems. She knew her grades had suffered since her father left, she knew her relationship with her mom was in the toilet, and now, Casey realized, she had to add her relationship with Jennifer to that list.

"Fuck it," Casey said. "Let's trust people." She pointed to Jennifer's bag on the bed. The screens Brian had handed them were peeking out the top. In their rush to leave the auditorium, they hadn't filled them out. "I could give Brian a shot. His Recruiting database has got to have an address or a phone number."

Jennifer stopped pacing. She looked at the screens. Her face ticked up a notch toward hopeful. "You'd go to Recruiting?"

Casey shrugged. "Sure."

"You hate Recruiting."

"For you, I'll go to Recruiting."

"No," Jennifer said. "There's got to be another way."

"What about Stan?" Casey asked. Stan was Casey's calculus tutor and one of Martin's friends.

Jennifer tilted her head from side to side. "Better," she said. "But doesn't his father run the ICP Science Division?"

Casey grabbed the tablet again and searched for Stan's dad. Jennifer was right. He was a bigwig. "Everyone's going to be related somehow," Casey said. "The ICP have their hands in everything."

Jennifer agreed, but they kept trying. They discussed talking to everyone from the assistants in the admin office to the school nurse to the lunch lady who served them food. But in the end, they came back to Stan and Brian. With Stan being the safer bet, and much to Casey's relief, they decided to track him down first. Brian and a trip to Recruiting would be their backup plan.

As they gathered their stuff to head back to school, Jennifer stopped her. "Can you send me that picture?" She nodded to the screen on Casey's desk.

"Sure," Casey said, grabbing the screen. "It is a good picture."

"No," Jennifer said. "I want to use it."

"For . . ."

"If this doesn't work, I'm going downtown and showing it to everyone I can."

"I don't know," Casey said. "The soon-to-be mayor's daughter, wandering around downtown? That's not very wise."

"Well, what if the infamous-downtown-detective's daughter came with me? Then would it be okay?" Jennifer smiled.

"Still dumb . . . but of course I'm coming with you." Casey gestured at the door. "After dinner, though. Asshole out there is invited, and I promised my mom I'd play nice."

3

Casey and Jennifer were in the school's cafeteria, circling the tables, looking for Stan. Despite the end to this morning's power outage, the cafeteria simmered thanks to an abundance of windows. Kids strolled by, balancing trays, some glancing at Jennifer as they passed.

"I don't feel comfortable," Jennifer said, a small quake in her voice. She lowered her sunglasses over her eyes.

Casey touched Jennifer's shoulder, then pointed to an empty table in the corner. "I'll find him."

"Thanks," Jennifer said.

Before Jennifer could step away, Greg appeared in front of them, seemingly from out of nowhere. "Where the hell did you guys run off to?" he asked, running his hand through his unkempt hair.

"Just needed some air," Casey said.

"Crazy about Martin, right?" He slid into place next to Casey. "Nice guy. Didn't think him the soldier type."

"I can't," Jennifer mumbled, and she walked away.

Casey turned to Greg. "Dude . . . way to read a room."

"What?" He raised his hands. "Aren't we happy for him?"

She looked over at Jennifer, who'd settled in at the open table. "Sure," she said, turning back. "It's just that he didn't tell her, and they were getting close."

"Shit," he said, grasping the gravity. "He was one of those."

Casey nodded, then continued to scan the room. "You see Stan?"

"Little guy? Martin's friend?"

"Yeah."

Greg pointed to the far end of the cafeteria. Stan had his back to them, but his hair, an overgrown bowl cut, gave him away. He was sitting at a table with a bunch of kids she knew only by face; a spirited conversation was in progress. "Thanks," she said, and started to walk away.

"Wait," Greg said. "Why Stan?"

Casey stopped, glanced in Jennifer's direction, then stepped back. "Jennifer wants to talk to Martin's mom. We think she can help. We need a way to get to her."

Greg put his hand up to his chin, stroking the wisps of hair he called a beard. "You know his father's ICP, right?"

"Whose isn't?"

"True," Greg said. "But tread lightly. You never know."

"I will. Thanks."

Casey walked away again, a little more nervous than she was before.

Greg was right. A deft touch was called for, but only to a degree. Stan had been tutoring her this semester, and, while he was excitable and a bit too talkative, she saw nothing in him that would make him a snitch. As she headed toward his table, one of his friends pointed at her. Stan turned. His face slipped from congenial to sour. He stood up from the table, pushed his glasses up the bridge of his nose, then gestured to his friends to give him a minute.

He and Casey met halfway.

"This isn't about calculus, is it?" he asked.

Casey shook her head.

"C'mon, Parker." He looked around the cafeteria. "You know we can't do this here."

She moved closer. "She just wants to talk to you."

"I can't. Besides, I don't know anything. He blindsided me, too."

"And that's not strange?"

"Of course it's strange, but we can't fuckin' talk about it."

Casey was taken aback; she'd never heard Stan curse before. "Can you at least tell me where he lives? We'll figure out the rest."

"Downtown."

"No shit. Where?"

"I don't know. He never invited me over. I think he was embarrassed."

This Casey understood. While she did live uptown, her apartment, with its measly two bedrooms and one bathroom, was a far cry from the mansion-like homes of some of her Roosevelt Prep classmates. "All right," she said. "Sorry to put you on the spot."

"It's okay. But be careful. People talk."

Dejected, Casey turned away. Jennifer was still at the table; Greg was now sitting with her. They were talking. He looked to be trying to console her.

"Parker . . ." Stan said before she could walk away.

She turned back to him.

"Tell Jennifer I'm sorry. If I hear anything, I'll get in touch."

"Thanks," she said. "It's appreciated."

4

Casey walked the third-floor hallway. With fifth period in full swing, the hallway was mostly empty. After striking out with Stan, she'd left Jennifer behind and headed upstairs to the Recruiting office. Her mind raced with what-ifs as she tried to reassure herself that she was just going to have a chat with Brian. She was just getting an address; it was no big deal. Shushing her overactive mind, she stopped a few feet before the office to gather herself. There was a poster-sized screen on the wall. A sharp-looking officer promised character growth, leadership skills, and a reason for being. Casey wanted none of these things. If she had to think about the big picture, all she really wanted was to be unstuck. Yes, time had ticked forward, but her life had not. She blamed her father's abrupt exit for that.

From her bag, Casey gathered the screen from this morning's assembly. She held it to her chest and took the last few steps to the office. Brian was at the intake desk, but he wasn't alone. A girl was sitting next to the desk with her back to the door. From behind, the girl could have been Karla from AP History. Her broad shoulders and buzzed nape seemed familiar. Brian talked while looking at a screen in his hands. He hadn't yet noticed Casey standing outside the glass door. That he was busy had her debating whether to come back later. But before the pros and cons had a chance to make their case, Brian looked up, smiled at her, and waved for her to come inside. Shit. She wasn't ready, but she grabbed the door's handle and pulled anyway. The girl turned, now confirmed as Karla, and watched her enter. Brian pointed Casey toward a row of plastic chairs to the right of the doors.

"I'll be with you in a second," he said.

Casey acknowledged him and sat, putting her bag down on the empty chair next to her. Sunlight poured in from two open, apparently empty offices behind him. She rested the screen on her lap. The rough plastic of the chair scratched at her bare legs. She squirmed, pulling the legs of her shorts as far down as possible. While her casual attire was a relief from the heat, here it had her feeling exposed. A minute or two passed before Brian wrapped things up. They stood. Karla enthusiastically shook his hand, then turned to leave. She gave Casey a half-hearted "hey" on her way out the door.

Brian called Casey over. Her anxiety inched up a notch. She still wasn't sure how to broach the Martin subject. She grabbed her bag and stepped to the desk. Brian motioned for her to sit. She did. The seat was warm. She tugged at her shorts again. Heatwave or not, tomorrow she was wearing jeans.

"Karla seemed eager," she said, handing Brian the screen.

"She's feeling it out . . . that's more than most." He considered Casey for a moment. "I'm guessing you're not here out of eagerness."

"Well," she began. "The thing is . . ."

Casey tried to stay as close to the truth as possible. She told him about Jennifer's dismay over Martin's recruitment and explained that the two had gotten close. She relayed how Jennifer understood that recruits couldn't talk of their plans. However, Jennifer still wanted to say goodbye, and she hoped contacting Martin's mother would help. Casey steered away from any talk that could be interpreted as questioning the system or the ICP. Jennifer's need to reach out was about unrequited love. That was all. The longer Casey babbled on, the worse she felt, but Brian nodded at all the right points and seemed receptive. She suspected he knew she was holding back. Everyone held back a little when it came to the ICP. It was the way things worked. When she was done, he sat back slowly in his chair.

"Jennifer Hargrove in love," he said. "Go figure."

"Crazy, right?"

"Can't she just go to her father?"

"I'm sure she will eventually, but he's busy with the election and all."

"You know I'm not supposed to give that kind of information out."

"I know," she said. "But I promised I would try." Casey looked down. She studied her fidgeting fingers. She thought she was losing him. She didn't want to lead him on but decided to throw out a carrot. "Besides," she continued. "It gave me an excuse to stop by."

"You never need an excuse, Casey."

If she hadn't felt bad about the idea of using him before, she certainly did now.

Brian took her completed Recruiting screen and tossed it into a bin behind his desk. Judging by the size of the pile, most of the seniors had already returned theirs. "Recruiting's complicated," he said, scanning his own screen. He stopped and took a quick look towards the office entrance behind her. "Once someone is in the system, it's all black-box kind of stuff." He swiped at the screen. "At least let me see what's public and what's not. I don't think we processed Martin yet."

"I owe you one," Casey said.

"I'm going to hold you to that," he said, smiling.

Brian checked the doors behind her one more time. He did a double take, then abruptly stood and saluted. Casey turned. The two ICP officers from the auditorium had sauntered in. They had their hats under their arms, and their ties were loosened. Smiling freely, they seemed much more relaxed than they had been on stage. Still, Casey's anxiety spiked, flushing her cheeks. The two men casually returned Brian's salute, walked past him, then retired to their respective offices. Casey smelled alcohol as they went by.

Brian sat. He studied her. "You're red," he said.

She felt her face flush even more. "Nerves, I guess."

"They're not monsters, you know."

Casey wasn't so sure about that, but now was not the time for a discussion on the merits of the ICP. "I know," she said. "Maybe it's the uniforms."

Brian looked down at his own formal attire.

"No. It's different with you," she lied. "I know you."

He smiled, flashing a bit of the earnestness she'd seen in the auditorium this morning. "Good," he said. "There's nothing to fear from me . . . or the ICP, for that matter."

Again, she was not so sure, but she nodded anyway.

Getting back to business, Brian swiped and tapped at his screen. A puzzled looked spread across his face. "Huh," he said, tapping some more. "Martin's file is locked." He showed her the screen. On it, a window with Martin's name flashed red. Layered over that, a message box read: Level III Access Only.

"And that's unusual?"

"It is for me, at least." He looked at her, lowering the screen. "I'm sorry, Casey," he said. "I can't help you."

Fuck.

After thanking him profusely, Casey left. She was at a loss. Pulling her screen from her pocket, she messaged as much to Jennifer.

"Downtown after dinner then!" Jennifer messaged back.

Casey sighed. There was no point in arguing, but another night away from her studies was the last thing Casey needed. She checked her Outage app. Downtown was scheduled to go dark at eight tonight. She corrected herself: Another night of not studying and trekking into a blackout was the last thing she needed. But she messaged Jennifer back, "Of course!" and headed, completely unprepared, to her sixth-period class.

5

The routine was familiar.

Casey pulled three plates from a cabinet above the sink in the kitchen. From the drawers below, she counted out three placemats and three cutlery sets. Tonight's third setting was for Bruce. The last thing she wanted today was more Bruce, but she was too frazzled to protest, and she had too much on her mind.

Casey brought the plates, mats, and silverware to a small dining table nestled between the kitchen and living room. Instinctively, she began by placing a mat at the head of the table. No, she thought, Bruce doesn't get to sit there. Instead, she put Bruce and her mom on one side and herself opposite them.

Casey went back into the kitchen to get the glasses. Her mom was at the stove. An untied apron hung from her neck, protecting a dress shirt and a pencil skirt underneath. Casey thought her mom looked too skinny, but the same could be said about herself. Casey settled in by her side. With a wooden spoon, her mom stirred a bundle of baby spinach. The spinach wilted and mixed with the olive oil and garlic at the bottom of the pot. Casey leaned over the stove and inhaled deeply. "Smells great," she said.

"Not too much garlic?" her mom asked.

"What? Are we vampires?"

Her mom smiled and nudged Casey with her elbow. In the Parker household, there could never be too much garlic. Casey leaned her shoulder into her mom's and noticed she was slouching. Usually, their shoulders matched up. Casey thought she must have had a hard day and felt a little guilty. Plus, the way they had fought last night couldn't have been helping. "I can take over if you want to freshen up."

"Oh, Casey, that would be great. I haven't stopped all day," she said, handing Casey the spoon.

"Court was okay?" Casey asked.

"No, not really. The judge handed us our asses." She lifted the apron from her neck.

"Were there kids involved?"

"Two," she said, passing Casey the apron. "Ages three and six."

"So young," Casey said, waving off the apron. She was still dressed in her tank and shorts, and they were in no need of protection.

Her mom shrugged. "We don't get much sympathy from the judges these days." She draped the apron over the breakfast counter. "Their mother's been clean for a year, and still that's not enough."

"Was the father from uptown?"

"Uptown and well connected. She never stood a chance." Her mom tapped the counter, turned, then left the kitchen.

Casey watched her go. She again noted the slump in her shoulders and straightened her own in response. She was proud of her mom. Keeping her law practice up and running downtown was no easy task, but she was trying to make a difference. It meant less money, it meant days working without power, and it meant some pretty horrible commutes. But it also meant being an advocate for the powerless—which, as her mom was quick to point out, was always a worthy cause.

Casey gave the spinach one more turn, then lowered the flame on the burner. She bent and waved a hand in front of the oven window. The window turned clear to reveal a casserole dish inside. She studied the baking tilapia; there was a nice breadcrumb crust forming on top. She stood and took note of the oven's timer. The dish would be ready in two more minutes. Casey pulled her screen from her pocket and checked for messages. There were two from Jennifer, who was trying to gauge when she'd be finished with supper; and one from Greg, who fancied himself an expert on all things downtown, offering his help with their quest. Casey was grateful for the offer. She couldn't remember the last time she was downtown, let alone in a blackout, and having a guide would be great. But not knowing how Jennifer felt about company, she would leave the decision to her.

With a series of short beeps, the oven's timer ended. Casey turned off the timer and the burner. She gave the spinach another stir, then took a side step over to the fridge. Inside, she found a salad that her mom had already prepared. Dark green romaine leaves peeked above the bowl's rim. She stole a cherry tomato from the top before taking it out. "Do you want me to dress the salad?" she yelled.

But before her mom could answer, the screen by the apartment door began to buzz.

"Shit," Casey muttered. She did not want alone time with Bruce. If she was being honest, she actually felt a little embarrassed about how she had reacted earlier that afternoon. Bruce shouldn't have been in the apartment alone, but yelling and slamming doors was not the answer.

"Can you get that?" her mom called out.

Casey's jaw clenched. "I thought he had the code?" she called back, placing the salad on the counter next to the fridge.

"Emergencies only . . . I told you that."

Exasperated, Casey took a deep breath. Before heading for the door, she checked the burner once more. It was off. She stood at the doorway to the kitchen, waiting a moment with the hope that her mom would appear, but that wasn't happening. Resigned, she went to answer the door. She tapped the adjacent glowing screen, and it came to life with a flicker. Derek, the overnight doorman, was talking to someone off screen, nodding. His face was turned away. Casey liked Derek. He'd been the overnight doorman for about two years and wasn't much older than her. He had come to New York from Texas before the last round of travel restrictions were passed.

"Derek," she tried to interrupt. It worked; he turned to face her.

"It's Bruce," Derek said, his southern drawl dragging. "He's on his way up." He glanced off screen again, then turned back and continued. "Since when does he have the code?"

"A few days now," she said, leaning in close to the screen. "She didn't even ask me first."

"You talk to her about it?"

"If yelling counts, then yes."

Casey knew Derek disapproved of the yelling. Over the past year, she had spent more than a few nights talking with Derek about her mom. This was usually after a fight prompted her to storm out of the apartment and camp out in the lobby until she cooled off.

There was a knock on the door.

"Shit. I gotta go," Casey whispered, filing a mental note to make sure Derek knew she was going downtown tonight.

The screen went dark. She tapped it again, and a number pad appeared. She entered the apartment's code. With a click, the door's lock released. She hesitated for one more moment, then opened the door. Bruce stood tall in the doorway, smiling. But as soon as he realized it wasn't her mom answering the door, his smile sagged.

"Bruce," she said with a slight head nod.

"Casey," he responded in kind.

She waved him inside. Bruce was wearing the same suit and tie from their morning encounter. She was surprised he could wear all that in this heat, but he was not one for casual dress. In fact, Casey couldn't recall ever seeing him in anything less than a jacket, dress shirt, and tie.

She closed the door behind him. "Mom's getting changed."

"Smells great," he said. He took off his jacket and hung it on the back of one of the dining room chairs.

Casey returned to the kitchen while Bruce hovered on the dining room side of the breakfast counter. She purposefully kept busy with her back to him. Turning the burner on underneath the spinach, she double-checked the flame to make sure it was as low as it could go. She gave the mixture a few perfunctory twirls. She hoped Bruce wouldn't recognize the stalling.

"Casey," he said.

No . . . please, no small talk. She wished her mom would hurry the hell up. Reluctantly, she leaned her head back and partially turned her shoulders. She continued to stir. "Bruce," she said.

"I'm sorry for surprising you this afternoon."

She stopped mid-stir. Huh—not quite small talk, and an apology no less. She fought the urge to turn around. Without seeing his face, she couldn't gauge his sincerity. "Ah, okay," she said.

"No, seriously. I was here after having breakfast with your mom. I got hung up with a call before she left for court. Then the blackout started, and I decided to wait it out."

Casey was at a loss for a response. She fiddled some. She turned the burner off. She gave the spinach one more stir. She wanted to be mad, but his excuse was solid. It wasn't the explanation that was the problem; her anger stemmed from the fact that there was a Bruce in the first place. She tapped the wooden spoon against the cast-iron skillet. A lingering clump of dark spinach slipped off the spoon and back into the pan. She placed the spoon on a plate next to the stove, then grabbed an oven mitt hanging from a magnet on the side of the fridge. She put the mitt on, then opened the oven door, releasing an aroma of oregano and lemon that mixed deliciously with that of the spinach's garlic. Removing the tilapia main course from the oven, she placed it on the stovetop next to the spinach. With that, she decided to cut Bruce some slack. She turned to face him. "You don't have to explain. It's fi—"

But Bruce wasn't listening. He was smiling widely and facing the hallway that led to the bedrooms. From the hallway, her mom strode to him, smiling just the same. On her tiptoes, she kissed him gently on the lips. Bruce's hands came to rest on her waist, her mom's hand rested on his chest, and Casey's heart sank. She had never seen them like this. A wave of contradiction swept over her. This was real: her mom, Bruce, the relationship, their happiness. Fuck.

She didn't want it to be true. It's not that she didn't want her mom to be happy. She did. She really did. It was just that it pushed her dad, and her delusional hopes for a happy reunion, farther away.

Casey's denial—once her pillar—crumbled.

She turned to the stove. She couldn't watch. Looking for a distraction, she spotted the salad bowl she had left on the counter. Her hands trembled as she went to grab it. She was surprised at her own visceral reaction.

"You okay?" her mom asked from behind.

Casey steadied her hands, grabbed the salad bowl, then turned. Her mom and Bruce were standing side by side. They didn't look horrible together. She hated herself for having a hard time with the truth. "All good, Mom," she said. "Oil and vinegar?"

Her mom slipped past Bruce and into the kitchen. She cocked her head. "You sure you're okay?"

"Yeah, just the heat."

She felt Casey's forehead with the back of her hand. "You are warm," she said.

"I'm fine, Mom."

"Okay, sit." She took the salad from her. "I'll finish."

As Casey turned to leave the kitchen, she caught Bruce's eye. She looked away. She still didn't know how to deal with him, but at this moment she was willing to try. When she reached the table, Bruce pulled her chair out. She sat as he pushed the chair beneath her. She wished he weren't being nice. It made it harder to hate him.

"Thanks," Casey said.

In her shorts pocket, her screen vibrated. A message had come in, probably another one from Jennifer. She resisted the temptation to look, determined to be as present as possible for her mom. She deserved at least that.

6

With dinner wrapped up, Casey, Jennifer, and Greg were on the subway heading downtown. In keeping with the downtown theme, Jennifer had dressed for the occasion by going all black: black T-shirt, black shorts, and black Doc Martens. Jennifer was up and optimistic, glad that some action was being taken. Casey, on the other hand, was skeptical. They knew Martin lived along Avenue A, near Tompkins Square Park, but the park and most of the streets to the east were condemned thanks to a bloated East River and the flooding that came with it. Plus, she couldn't imagine finding residents out and about on a night with the power down. It seemed like a fruitless endeavor, if not a dangerous one. But she kept her doubts to herself, not wanting to bring her best friend down.

As the train pulled out of the Twenty-Third Street station, they were the last people left in the car. Casey looked through to the next subway car; only a few stragglers remained there as well. Greg nudged her, pointing at the screen above the seats across from them.

"Last stop is Fourteenth," he said. "Tunnels are all shut down after that."

"Since when?"

"A couple of storms back."

"Remember?" Jennifer chimed in. "We had my father's car take us to that lecture in Brooklyn."

Casey nodded. "I thought we were just being lazy."

"Sure . . . there was that. And no subway."

The train slowed, pulling into the Fourteenth Street station. Jennifer was first to the doors, eager to get going. Casey and Greg joined her as the train screeched to a stop.

"Hold your nose, and move fast," Greg said, fidgeting to adjust his knapsack.

"Because?" Casey asked as the movable grills that bridged the gap between the train and platform thumped into place.

Greg pointed toward the front of the train. "Drowned rats in the tunnel. It does not smell pretty."

Casey and Jennifer glanced at each other, then back at Greg.

"Your idea . . . remember?" he said, taking a deep breath and pinching his nose.

They did the same as the doors opened. Even with the precautions taken, Greg was right—the platform did not smell pretty. Having had a mouse or two die in her apartment's floorboards, Casey knew the sickly-sweet, sulfurous smell well.

The trio rushed from the car, down the platform, up its stairs, then up another set of stairs until they hit the street and fresh air.

"That was not just rats," Casey said, between heavy breaths.

"Yeah," Greg said, catching his own. He turned to Jennifer, pointing down the station's stairs. "Your father should pledge to clean that up."

Jennifer scoffed. "Move Wall Street back downtown, and I'm sure he'll get right on it." She leaned her hand on his shoulder.

Casey turned to orient herself. They had emerged on the north side of Fourteenth Street facing downtown. Union Square Park was behind them. She checked her screen; it was a couple of minutes past eight o'clock. The lights downtown should have been out already. "It's late," she said.

"Good," Greg said, waving them toward the curb. "Crossing the border with the lights on always helps."

"Border?" Casey asked.

"Light border," Greg said, pointing to his left and right.

"Fourteenth Street . . ." Jennifer added. "Martin called it that, too."

And then Casey saw why.

With a snap, across the busy street, a black curtain fell. Buildings, defined by light a moment ago, now loomed shapeless in the dark. Casey looked left and right, east to west, and it was the same on either side: a border of light and dark separating the city—the haves and the have-nots defined. Casey turned uptown. A statue of George Washington on horseback gleamed. Tree-lined paths extended uptown, weaving well-lit trails through the park. Past all this, above the trees and rooftops, the Empire State Building dominated the sky. Its uppermost reaches and tip-top spire were lit in brilliant red, white, and blue.

At the curb, they stopped to chart a path. Crossing without traffic lights proved to be tricky. Horns blared as the traffic became a tangled mess. A chorus of shop gates rattled closed, signaling that the businesses along the border were calling it quits for the night. A police car pulled up at the curb, and two cops got out. They didn't seem to be in much of a rush as they donned orange vests and lumbered into the street. They split up, with one officer staying near them to cover Broadway and the other walking east along the double yellow lines toward Fourth Avenue. The officer on Broadway stopped the confused traffic, waving Casey's group and a few other pedestrians across. Once safely on the dark side of Fourteenth, Greg slid his knapsack off his back, then pulled a long-necked flashlight from it. It looked heavy in his hand.

"Are you going to light the way or hit people with that?" Jennifer asked.

"Light the way," he said, turning it on and testing its weight in his hand. "But it's good to be prepared."

They walked along Broadway with Greg's beam and pseudo–billy club leading the way. The farther south they went, the quieter and darker it became. A few people hurried past, heading uptown. A car or two, high beams on, headed downtown. The quiet was more akin to an early Sunday morning than a late Thursday night. Up ahead, a church loomed. Its stone facade and gothic spires reflected the lingering light on its north, uptown-facing side. Greg's beam caught a plaque mounted next to its arched wooden door. Grace Church, it read.

"This is Martin's church," Jennifer said. "He wanted to take me one day."

Casey looked at her. "You . . . in church?"

"It's not crazy. I used to go."

"Your father would be ecstatic," Casey said.

"He could make a campaign ad out of it," Greg said.

"Better than the gossip pages," Jennifer said, and they all agreed.

It wasn't that Jennifer was a celebrity or anything, but she was known. There'd been pictures published of her doing teenage stuff: kissing boys, smoking, drinking. That they were scandalous at all was because of who she was, nothing more. She didn't give a shit, but her father sure did. When a new picture would crop up, he'd emerge from his indifference and give her a talking-to. But what should have been about parenting was more about public relations. The soon-to-be mayor didn't necessarily care about what his daughter was doing, just that she'd been photographed doing it. This made Jennifer rebel even more. Until this morning, Casey had thought Martin was just another form of rebellion. But she had been wrong—that they were downtown, trying to track down Martin's mom, was proof of that.

After the church they made a left, heading east on Tenth Street. They zigzagged some, going a few blocks south on Fourth Avenue, then a few east on Eighth. The streets were eerily quiet until they hit Second Avenue. There, thanks to a generator-powered bodega and a bunch of food trucks, some of the downtown bustle returned. It was an oasis in an otherwise dark town. They checked the traffic on the avenue and waited as a yellow cab passed by. Dodging potholes, they dashed across. Greg swung his backpack forward and put his flashlight away. Jennifer smiled, taking out her screen. "This is where we start asking."

"Great," Greg said. "You guys start there." He pointed to the people charging their screens on a communal mat in front of the bodega. "I'm going to see if that guy knows something." He pointed to the man behind the counter of the Taco Taco truck parked at the corner.

In front of the brightly lit bodega, Jennifer circulated among the gathered crowd. If any of them recognized her, they weren't letting on. She showed the family picture of Martin around. An older man opposite her started nodding. "That's Martin," he said. "Nice kid."

"Do you know his family or where he lives, by any chance?" Jennifer asked.

The man pointed behind him. "I've seen him on Avenue A quite a lot, but that's it."

Jennifer thanked him and the people generally, then she and

Casey joined Greg at the taco truck. The truck had chili-pepper lights strung around its windows, adding an element of festivity to the dark night. Inside, a mustachioed man wearing a stained apron was busy putting together the fixings for a burrito. A scoop of cubed pork landed on a bed of yellow rice and pinto beans. A stray bit of pork rolled off and onto the surrounding tortilla; it glistened under the truck's bright lights. Casey, although not at all hungry, was tempted by it. "Is that for you?" she asked Greg.

"A boy's gotta eat."

"A boy's gotta share, too."

Greg stared at her. "What's my only rule?"

Casey rolled her eyes. "Greg does not share food."

"That's right," he said. "But since I already had dinner, I'll consider it."

"So big of you."

Meanwhile, Jennifer was showing the burrito guy her screen. "Yeah. I've seen him," he said. "I served him last night."

Jennifer's eyes lit up as the man tucked and folded Greg's burrito into shape. "It was weird, too," the man continued. "A couple of dark tourists were asking him questions. They were French, I think."

"Dark tourists?" Jennifer asked.

"Yeah, you know . . . foreigners, usually. They come down here looking for danger or something." He put the now foil-wrapped tube on the counter in front of Greg.

"What were they asking him?"

Greg waved his screen at the truck's pay terminal.

"They were asking if he was local, about the blackouts, if life was difficult. Things like that." The man looked around, then leaned in close. "They even asked about the ICP. Called them tough men or something."

"And Martin?" Jennifer pointed to her screen. "The guy you served . . . did he answer?"

"No," the man said. "He knew better. Clammed up right away." It was then that a glint of recognition swept over his face. He straightened, wiped his hands on his apron, and took a step back. "You're . . ."

Jennifer nodded. "Don't worry. My politics are not his."

Casey, appreciating the man's discomfort, put her arm around Jennifer's shoulder. "Thanks," she said to him. "Did you see which way he went?"

The man directed them east toward Avenue A.

Casey thanked him again and led Jennifer away.

"What was that about?" Jennifer asked.

"You spooked him."

"My father spooked him . . . I'm not my father."

"He doesn't know that."

"In Jen's defense," Greg said, "he's the one who brought up the ICP." Greg pulled back the foil from the top of his burrito, then offered Casey the first bite.

"Yeah," Jennifer said. "And what's with the couple asking about the ICP? Who does that?"

Casey took the burrito from Greg and helped herself to a decent bite from the corner. It was hot, savory, and delicious.

"They were tourists," Greg said, pulling the flashlight from his bag. "They don't get it."

After Greg was set, Casey handed him back the burrito.

Walking east, they passed a bar with its windows and doors open. A group of people drank by candlelight. The street was quiet enough to hear the clink of dishes inside. At Avenue A, they stopped. Tompkins Square Park was across the street. A barbed-wired fence blocked the Eighth Street entrance. After checking both ways of the narrow two-way avenue, they crossed.

At the entrance, Greg flashed his light on a sign attached to the fence. The sign warned of trespassing and its consequences. It was a warning that had clearly gone ignored, as evidenced by the tents, the lights, and the people milling about inside.

"All these streets," Greg said, shining the flashlight north toward the street corner, "from Avenue A back to the river are condemned." He shined his light into the park. "A lot of people who couldn't afford to move landed here."

"You sound like one of those dark tourists," Jennifer said.

"I've dabbled." Turning, Greg pointed to the corner. "People," he said, then headed toward them with Jennifer close behind.

Casey lingered by the fence for a moment before following.

"What's up?" Jennifer asked, a step ahead but slowing.

"I used to play in this park." Casey glanced back at the entrance. "I'd ride my bike down that path." She got in step with Jennifer. "And now people live in there. That's fucked up."

"That's my father for you."

Casey grimaced, but her best friend wasn't wrong.

At the corner, a group of about five people were hanging out. Most looked to be Casey's age if not slightly older. They were vaping, maybe drinking, and generally carrying on. They looked like they could be up to no good, but the same could be said about the three of them. As they got closer, Casey saw they were standing around and leaning on a traffic barrier that stretched from sidewalk to sidewalk. The thigh-high concrete slab was covered with graffiti. A lantern, sitting on top, provided some light.

Approaching the group, Greg killed his flashlight, and Jennifer politely interrupted their conversation. Passing around the picture of Martin, the sideways looks and stares began. This time, however, it wasn't Jennifer they were recognizing. It was Casey. Ignoring Jennifer, a girl jumped from her perch on the barrier. She was pretty, with a long afro that swayed with her strides. Coming right up to Casey, she said, "I know you."

Casey was clueless, but it was not out of the question that they knew each other, maybe from childhood. "I did grow up around here," Casey said.

"No, no," the girl said. "You're Detective Parker's daughter. Shit . . . that's right. He had your picture on his desk."

"You knew my father?"

"Knew your father? Fuck . . . I loved your father." She put out her hand. "Darcy," she said.

Casey took it and introduced herself in return.

Darcy turned. "Bill," she called. "This is Detective Parker's daughter."

Bill lumbered over. He was big—easily six-five—with a sweet, generous smile. "No way," he said, giving her the once-over. "Detective Parker was the best." He held out his large hand. "I can't tell you how much we miss him around here. Man's a legend."

Casey was floored. She knew her father's commitment to the community was endless; she knew he was well-liked . . . but revered? This was unexpected. For a few minutes, they regaled her with stories of her father donating his time and helping their friends, their families, and the community at large. When Jennifer and Greg joined the clique, Casey introduced them. They recognized Jennifer, but, unlike the taco guy, they were unfazed by her presence. It seemed being friends with Detective Joe Parker's daughter outweighed any baggage Jennifer carried from being the daughter of the soon-to-be mayor. After a few more pleasantries, Jennifer showed Martin's photo to Darcy and Bill.

"Lanky dude?" Darcy said. "Yeah. I saw him. He walked by here last night." She pointed toward Eighth Street and then past the barrier where they were on Seventh. "He stopped here," she patted the concrete barrier, "and left some food for the dogs."

"Dogs?" Casey asked.

"Stray dogs," Bill said. "They are all over down here. Families move away, and some leave their pets behind. Fuckin' travesty."

They all nodded in agreement at the travesty.

Bill turned to Darcy. "Didn't the van go by last night?"

"Yeah," Darcy said. "Shit. That was right after I saw him."

"What van?" Jennifer asked. "Why is that a problem?"

Bill and Darcy exchanged looks.

"You guys really are from uptown," Darcy said. "Black vans? Blacked-out windows? All mysterious and shit?"

Casey, Jennifer, and Greg all shook their heads no.

"Rumor is when you see a van, you miss a person," Bill said. "They get tossed in the back like garbage."

Deflated, Jennifer trudged to the barrier and sat.

Casey followed her. "It doesn't mean anything," she said, sitting next to her and putting her arm around Jennifer's shoulders. She looked up at Darcy. "You didn't see our friend get put in the van . . . did you?"

"No. Just saw him go by, leave the food, and head off in that direction." She pointed farther downtown, south on Avenue A.

"C'mon," Greg said, waving his flashlight in the direction Darcy had pointed. "We go that way, and we keep asking questions. This is not over."

"He's right," Casey said. "I'll admit, I thought we'd be chasing our tails here, but we're three for three. Someone may know more."

Jennifer agreed, then resolved to keep going.

Casey and Darcy exchanged information, including sending her the picture of Martin and his family. Darcy promised to keep a lookout and let Casey know if anything came up. After thanking the rest of the group, Greg fired up the flashlight, and they continued on their way.

"Did you notice the tattoos?" Greg asked when they were a few feet away.

"No," Jennifer said.

"Which ones?" Casey asked.

"They both had the circle with the two lines inside."

"And?" Jennifer asked.

"That's a Resistance symbol. It's supposed to be an electrical outlet—something about their fight for power, literally and figuratively, I guess. I saw it mixed in with the graffiti on the barrier, too. It's everywhere down here once you start looking."

"You're saying there's an actual resistance movement against the ICP?" Jenifer asked. "Against my father? And you think they are part of it?"

"That's the rumor, and I'm guessing they are."

"Damn," Jennifer said. "Where do I sign up?"

7

In the end, three for three was as good as it was going to get with the Martin sightings. After making a few more rounds and stopping a few more people, Greg, Jennifer, and Casey gave up the quest a little before eleven. They split at the Eighty-Sixth Street station, with Casey heading home. She had a small skip in her step. Never one to let a feeling go unexamined, she tried to pinpoint why she felt lighter than usual. As best she could tell, it was due to meeting Darcy and Bill. Here were two people who so loved her father that even after the ICP had dragged his reputation through the mud, they still believed in him. It was more than she could say for herself, and it was a much-needed change in perspective after a year of anger over his absence.

In her hand, her screen vibrated. Jennifer had messaged her thanks and an apology for being so down about their trip. While her best friend was glad Darcy and Bill were on the case, the talk of dark tourists, black vans, and abductions had her fearing the worst. Casey didn't blame her. She messaged back that they could try again tomorrow, right after school, while the lights were still on and the sun was still up.

At the corner of Seventy-Ninth Street, a block from home, Casey stopped for the light. At the curb to her left was an elderly woman hunched over a shopping cart filled with redeemable bottles and cans. On her right was a youngish guy dressed in a suit and tie, furtively trying to check her out. The guy reminded her of Bruce—stiff and all buttoned up. A box truck rumbled past. On its side, an ad for arthritis medicine flipped to one for acne cream and then to a smiling, larger-than-life image of Jennifer's father. His round face and shiny bald head were more sinister than jolly. Casey felt sick at the sight of him. Next to her, the old woman sneered, and the guy grinned. He was clearly part of the ad's target audience. Thanks to the election, Michael Hargrove's face was everywhere, and it was all so unnecessary. No one expected the opposition to win. Half the city didn't know his challenger's name or even care that there was an election.

The old woman looked at Casey and then towards the guy. She waved Casey closer. "He's going to fuck us like the rest of them," she whispered, pointing an arthritic middle finger in the direction of the truck.

Casey smirked at her saltiness and nodded her agreement. She glanced at the guy to see if he had noticed the impromptu show of resistance. If he had, he wasn't letting on. As the traffic slowed, the guy stepped off the curb and crossed. After waiting for the light to change, Casey started to cross but stopped abruptly when she heard the old woman curse again. Casey turned to see that this time it wasn't ideology she was struggling with; it was her shopping cart. A crack in the pavement had trapped one of its front wheels. As the cart began to tip over, Casey rushed and grabbed it before it could topple. At the same time, she glimpsed the guy turn, then snicker at their misfortune.

"Fuck you," she said under her breath.

"Excuse me?" the woman said.

"No—sorry, not you. The dick in the suit there."

"Him? Yes. Fuck him."

Casey smiled again, lifting the front of the cart to free the stuck wheel.

"Thank you," the woman said. "At least some people still care."

Casey wasn't so sure she'd put herself in the people-who-care category, but she wasn't as bad as some. "No problem," she said.

With the shopping cart free, Casey checked the light. They still had time to cross. She extended her elbow. The old woman grinned; she had a full set of shiny, white teeth. Casey had expected more wear and tear. As the woman hooked her hand in the crook of Casey's arm, she noticed her blouse. Its floral pattern was faded, but otherwise the blouse was in good shape. It had to be expensive, too. Without touching it, she thought it could be silk. The same held true for the rest of the woman's outfit: although old and worn, it was still classy. She'd obviously had money at some point. Casey contemplated how a seemingly comfortable life could end up being such a struggle. How had someone who was clearly from uptown become so down? Her father and Jennifer would have blamed the ICP. Casey tended to agree. Having seen the rot downtown firsthand, it was hard not to think otherwise. Now, it seemed, that rot was spreading.

Together, they pushed the cart across the street, exchanging gripes about the heat. "All set," Casey said as they reached the sidewalk. The woman let go of her arm, and Casey wished her a good night.

At the next corner, she turned left. Her building was about a quarter of the way up the block. Its green awning extended from the entrance to the curb. After a few oblivious steps, Casey froze. Double-parked, a car length or two before her building, was a black van, its windows blacked out. *Well, that's strange,* she thought, but she chalked up the coincidence to paranoia. Shaking it off, she continued forward only to stop again after a couple of steps. A man and a woman had exited from the back of the van. They were both well dressed, with the woman in high heels and the man in a sports jacket and a colorful collared shirt. Casey's pulse quickened as they stepped from the van to the sidewalk. The man checked a screen in his hand against her building's address. Then he saw Casey. He rechecked his screen, looked at her, and then showed the screen to the woman next to him. The woman scrutinized Casey, nodded, and together they marched toward her. The man gestured for Casey to come closer, but she instinctively moved backward.

Whatever this was, it was not good.

She turned, started to walk fast, then began to sprint as shouts and heavy footfalls followed her. When she reached First Avenue, she made a sharp right, maybe too sharp, as her feet went out from under her. "Shit," she gasped, starting to go down. She extended her arm. Her palm hit the rough concrete and slid. She felt her skin tear, but it was enough to stop her momentum. She righted herself, glanced at her wounded palm, and then looked behind her. The man was in pursuit and only steps away. On solid footing once again, she shifted into high gear. There were more shouts from behind her to stop.

Wondering if her pursuer was armed, Casey peeked behind her again. She didn't see a gun, but everything was happening too fast to be sure. Casey turned back, running hard. Just as she did, her knee slammed into something. From the clanking sound of bottles and cans, she knew she had hit the old woman's shopping cart. She was spun around by the sudden impact. The woman reached out a frail hand to help as, for the second time in a matter of minutes, the cart began to tip. However, this time, the woman kept the cart upright. Coming out of her spin, Casey also regained her balance, but now she was slowed by a limp to her stride.

Casey looked over her shoulder again. Shopping Cart Lady must have figured out what was going on faster than she had, because now the old woman was purposely spilling the contents of her cart across the sidewalk. Casey turned back, smiling. She was glad for the ally. After another couple of strides, she peeked behind her one more time. She wished the guy had slipped, rolled, or fallen, but instead, he had stopped, stepped over the mess, and then kept on coming. He lost only a step or two while keeping his focus on her. But what did he want with her? Could they have known she'd been downtown? Had speaking to Darcy and Bill doomed her? Or, worse, had this all come up because she'd been talking to Brian or Stan?

As she reached the corner, she had the light and kept on running. Glancing behind, she saw her pursuer about twenty, maybe thirty feet away. She wasn't losing ground, but she wasn't making progress either. At the next corner she had a decision to make. Staying on First Avenue was an option, since she still had the light. But instead she made a hard right, hoping a side street would have more places to hide. She spotted an open kitchen door. Inside, a cook stood next to a sizzling grill, fanning himself with a spatula. Just as she was about to make a run for the open door, a car screeched to a stop a few feet ahead of her. A bearded man burst out from the passenger side, slamming the door against the bumper of the car parked beside it.

Casey stood her ground. She looked behind her. The man from the van had stopped at the corner. When he saw her, he took off again in her direction. In front of her, the other man was reaching into his waistband as he slipped between the parked cars. He had a gun holstered just beyond his outstretched fingers. A tie flapped at his shoulder. He hopped the curb, his gun leading the way and pointing in her direction. The footfalls behind her stopped. She started to duck but then realized he wasn't pointing the gun at her—he was pointing it at the man behind her. As the man with the gun got closer, she couldn't believe her eyes. He had a beard, and he had gained some weight, but it was definitely him.

"Dad?" she questioned.

"Casey!" her father yelled as he ran toward her.

She had no idea what was happening but suspected that this was what being rescued looked like. Someone behind her yelled, "Gun!" She turned. A handful of pedestrians scattered out of the way. Her pursuer had stopped. He took a step back, and then another. He had his hands up near his chest.

Her father's arm reached around her shoulders and draped her in safety. She smelled his deodorant; it was the same powdered scent he'd always used. The smell was comforting. She thought of crying, but her adrenaline was running too high.

With his gun still drawn, her father whisked her towards the waiting car. She saw a woman inside reach over from the driver's side and throw open the rear passenger door.

"Keep your head down," he said, guiding her into the backseat.

She slid inside, keeping her shoulders slumped and her head below window level. Her father's clean scent was replaced by the stale smell of old car. After a moment, he dropped into the seat next to her.

"Go!" he shouted to the driver.

Casey took that to mean she could sit up. But, as she started to rise, he stopped her with a firm hand on her shoulder.

"No, Casey, the cameras will pick you up."

"Here," the driver said.

Casey glimpsed a jacket being passed back. She knew it was her father's coat by the worn patches at the elbows. He was never one for an updated wardrobe. She was glad to see that hadn't changed.

"Keep this over you just to be safe," he said.

She was enveloped in darkness.

Casey felt her father's weight shift again. This time his hand reached under her arm, guiding her into a sitting position. He kept his arm around her shoulder and the jacket over her head. With its collar drawn just past her forehead, she could see out the front. She leaned into his chest. His arm tightened around her. Her breathing settled. This wasn't the father-daughter reunion she had imagined a million times over. She had expected more tears, more yelling, and little to no gunplay.

But she didn't care. Her father was back.

She couldn't wait to tell her mom.

CHAPTER TWO | SPY GAMES

CASEY SAT QUIETLY IN THE BACK SEAT. Her father's sports jacket was folded on her lap. Her hand—scraped from its clash with the sidewalk—throbbed. The old sedan, speeding along, rattled with each bump in the road. Her father sat next to her, leaning forward, his arm propped on the seat in front of him. He was talking to someone named Dan on the dashboard's screen.

"Second Avenue camera's down. You're clear," Dan said.

Dan sounded young.

Her father nodded to the driver, who then made a left turn onto Second Avenue. They were headed downtown.

"You want me to loop you out of the feed at Eightieth?" Dan asked.

"No point," her father answered. "The guy saw us."

As Casey watched her dad, she realized her emotions were a mess. She was happy to see him, she was relieved to be safe, and yet she was angry just the same. He didn't get to waltz back into her life as suddenly as he'd waltzed out.

"Stay on Second," he said.

The driver—sporting a stylish sharp bob with sharp cheekbones to match—nodded in reply. She looked young, but from the crow's feet around her eyes, Casey pegged her as closer to her father's age.

"Is downtown dark tonight?" he asked the driver.

"Since eight o'clock," she said.

"Good. Dan, clean us out as we go. We should be good once past the border. I want no trace tonight."

"You mean no other trace," Dan said.

"Time and place, Dan," the driver chastised—now sounding, as well as looking, closer to her father's age.

"It's okay," her father said, touching the driver's shoulder.

"Dad, what's going on?"

"One more second, Case." He squeezed her hand gently.

She studied the back of his hand. It was familiar and strange all at the same time. She still couldn't believe it was him.

"And, Dan—fry her screen."

"My screen?"

"No choice. They'll track it."

"Who's 'they,' Dad? Seriously, enough."

He turned to her.

"What's going on? Why are you here?"

He hesitated, glancing toward the front of the car.

Casey did the same. In the reflection of the rearview mirror, the driver raised an eyebrow.

Her father took a deep breath. "Listen," he said, sitting back in the seat. "I'm here because you're in danger."

"No shit, Dad."

"Language, Casey."

It was her turn to raise an eyebrow. "Really? I was chased for blocks by some dude who wanted to throw me into a fuckin' van. I don't think cursing is my biggest problem."

2

Casey tried to hold her injured hand still, but the pain was making it difficult. She sat facing her father, her knee on the car's seat. With a tissue, he was cleaning her palm. The gravel had left a trail of scraped skin from the bottom of her fingers to the pad of her thumb. He tended to her hand and tried to explain the situation. It was a lot to take in. He talked about a list—a list the ICP kept of people they judged traitorous, if not dangerous. He said his team had access to this list and that she had appeared on it. He also said it was his job to help people who topped the list, and that he and his team pulled people to safety, as a last resort, before the ICP could make them disappear.

"These people you pull . . . they disappear? Like you?" she asked.

"They have to." He dabbed at her wound.

Despite the craziness that had led her here, his doting on her was nice. She felt safe in his presence. She always had. It dawned on her then that she hadn't felt safe, truly safe, since he'd left. She had explained away the past year with words like *anger*, *betrayal*—even *loneliness*. And, while those feelings still held, *fear* needed to be part of the mix.

Casey nodded toward the front seat. "She was pulled?"

"Beth? Yes. All of my team were."

"She can't see or talk to her family? Nothing?"

"Too dangerous."

"And you?"

"I'd most certainly be dead or locked away to rot."

Despite her anger, she didn't want him dead or rotting.

Up ahead, they were about to cross Fourteenth Street, or the "light border," as Greg had called it. Once they drove past, the darkness swallowed them. Casey turned to look out the back window. The farther they drove into the dark, the sharper the light border became. Around them, a different city emerged: one where mailboxes looked like hunchbacks, fire hydrants looked like trolls, and light posts ruled them all as giants. It was not at all quaint, as the walkthrough earlier in the night had been. It was disquieting, though not any more so than the conversation she was having with her dad.

Casey turned to face him. "And this list tells you who's in danger?"

"We're tapped right into their system. When the list gets updated, we know."

"The ICP makes people disappear?"

He nodded.

"And you guys are what? The Resistance?"

He smiled. "Some people call us that." He closed her fingers around the tissue in her palm. "We'll fix that up better once we get inside."

"Inside?"

"Sure, our headquarters."

"You have a headquarters?"

The car stopped at a concrete barrier at Avenue A and Twelfth Street. The street past it was clearly condemned, without a car or person in sight. Outside the passenger window, uptown, a sunrise-like glow mocked the darkness around them. Beth got out of the car and walked to the barrier. Judging from her silhouette outlined by the car's headlights, she looked in excellent shape. Beth bent down, then passed her hand along the bottom of the barrier.

"What's she doing?"

"Getting us home."

Beth stood, placed her hands at the top of the barrier, and pushed.

"She can't move that," Casey said.

"Watch."

Sure enough, the barrier began to move. As soon as there was enough room for a vehicle to pass, Beth returned to the car.

"Wheels," he said.

"Wheels," Casey repeated. "Does the city know you did that?"

It was a dumb question. The city was controlled by the ICP; of course they didn't know. She was starting to catch on.

3

Casey stepped from the car. She stood with the door open, resting her arm on the window frame. In front of her was her father's headquarters. Through the darkness, she saw what looked like a beat-up but historic New York City tenement building. She had grown up in one of these only a few blocks south. Counting fire escapes, it looked to be about five or six stories. It was probably a walk-up—these old tenements usually were. The whole thing couldn't have been any wider than a car length or two. It had a boarded-up entrance flanked by boarded-up windows; its brick facade was cracked and crumbling. The same went for the almost identical buildings attached on either side.

Beth got out from the driver's side and closed the door behind her. She had a flashlight in hand and pointed it toward the building.

"It doesn't look like much," Casey said, stepping out from behind her door.

"It's nicer on the inside," Beth said.

In the distance, Casey heard what sounded like water lapping on concrete. "That's Avenue B right there?" she asked, pointing to her right.

"It is," Beth said.

"And the river?"

Beth started for the building. "A half-block past."

"Wait . . . I read that the river was just at Avenue C."

"That was before the last storm," Beth said from over her shoulder.

Casey's father came around the front of the car. He had a flashlight in hand as well.

At the building's entrance, Beth picked at a piece of plywood, opening a hidden panel next to the door. She placed her hand inside. A light below her hand lit green, and the boarded-up door next to her snapped open. Casey watched, her mouth open, amazed by the spycraft.

"Watch the dogs," her father said, settling in protectively at her side. He shined his flashlight toward the building, catching two pairs of glowing eyes in its beam. "We feed them, care for them, but you never know."

Casey closed the car door behind her. The cry of its rusty hinges echoed through the street. "It fits," she said, stepping toward the building.

"What fits?"

"The crappy car . . . it fits nicely into your neighborhood." She gestured around her.

"It has its charm." Her father stopped and turned to face her. He put his hand on her shoulder.

She stopped as well, looking up at him. The gray in his dark hair reflected what little light there was. His eyes, large and dark like hers, reflected more.

"Are we okay?" he asked.

"Are you kidding? How could we possibly be okay, Dad?"

He dropped his hand from her shoulder.

"You walked out on us with no explanation . . . with no fucking forwarding address."

"I had no choice."

"There's always a choice."

"Not always. I was protecting you and your mom."

"By tearing us apart?"

He shrugged. "I don't know what to say."

"You don't have to say anything." She gestured between them. "You suddenly coming back into my life is hard, and all this—a secret headquarters, the Resistance—is just batshit insane. You can't just show up, save the day, and think that suddenly everything is okay."

He took a step back. His eyes were wet. "I get it. I'm sorry."

"Me too," she said. "Me too."

4

With Beth leading the way, they climbed the stairs of the aban-doned-looking building. At the fourth-floor landing, they stopped. This floor was different. After near-total darkness on the way up, this floor had light pooling underneath the apartment doors. Beth turned off her flashlight and opened the door across from the stairs. Once open, the light behind it flooded into the hallway. Beth walked inside, and they followed. With each footfall, the old build-ing's floorboards groaned in protest.

Inside the narrow room, colorful graffiti littered most of the surfaces. Behind the graffiti, the walls were yellowed with age. On Casey's left were two tall, thin windows, its panes blacked out—for privacy, she assumed. A floor-standing air conditioner blew cool air into the room. Along the far wall was the kitchen, or what passed for a kitchen in these old, tiny apartments. The counter-height refrigerator was missing its door. There was a half-sink, a minia-ture four-burner stove, and a row of open cabinets hanging—by a thread, it seemed—from the wall.

"This is your headquarters?" Casey asked.

Beth, a few steps ahead, turned and smiled.

"Wait," her father answered.

From an open doorway to Casey's right, a dog—its tail wagging and nails tapping—strolled into the room.

"Who is this? Casey asked, thrilled by the intrusion.

The dog was medium size and could've been some kind of Retriever mix.

"That's Bart," her father said. "Beth had him from before."

Beth went down on one knee as Bart moved slowly but deliberately toward her. Once together, Beth lavished him with kisses and head scratches until he dropped, rolled, and offered her his belly.

Watching the lovefest, it dawned on Casey that she was, to her father, from before. But, unlike Beth and Bart, he didn't get to keep her around. She thought this sad, realizing then that his self-imposed isolation was starting to get to her and that staying mad at him would be impossible to sustain.

Casey joined Beth on the floor and put out her hand. "He's gorgeous," she said.

"Yeah. I don't know what I would do without him around."

Bart smelled Casey's hand. When she was sure of his trust, she joined in with the belly rubs.

"Your dad made sure I could keep him when they pulled me. He didn't have to do that."

Casey looked up at her father. Unsustainable, she concluded again. His disappearance was turning out to be way more complicated than she had ever thought—and she had thought about it a lot.

After a few more rubs, Beth stood. Casey and Bart followed suit.

"Time to get to work," Beth said, and she started into the small room from which Bart had emerged. Bart went with her, staying close by her side.

Her father followed and motioned for Casey to come along.

As they entered the room, the word *headquarters* began to make more sense. What Casey had assumed was a small bedroom was, in fact, anything but. The room opened into another room and what looked like another room after that. There were jagged archways cut into the walls between the rooms. Windows, blacked out like the others, dominated the wall to Casey's left. A couch with mismatched cushions—one striped and one solid—sat below them. On the opposite wall was a worn wooden desk. Above the desk, mounted on the wall, were screens. She counted six of them, each one streaming a different feed. Casey stopped to study them. One of the feeds was of the entrance to her apartment building uptown. She leaned in close to get a better look. She saw her favorite doorman, Derek, sitting at the front desk. "You watch us?" she asked.

"As best we can."

Casey didn't bother probing further. She couldn't be sure if the intrusion made her feel comfortable or creeped-out. For now, she was going with comfortable. Moving on, she ran her fingers over the back of the desk's empty chair, noting the threadbare fabric across the seat.

"We have all four apartments on this floor and the floor above, and the same in the building next door," her father said, pointing all the while. "It's tight, but when we need room, we just bust through another wall."

Together they stepped through one of these busted walls and into the next room. A wooden board nailed to the floor bridged the gap between rooms. The double layer of exposed brick had Casey guessing they were stepping into the building next door. Inside, there were more desks, all beat up, each against a wall; Beth sat at one of them with Bart stretched out on the floor next to her, chewing on a bone. The other two desks were empty. There was a table set in the middle of the room with six chairs around it. Along the far wall, next to Beth, was another dilapidated kitchen. This one was L-shaped, complete with a breakfast bar like the one Casey had at home.

"Don't you guys eat?" she asked her father.

"The real kitchen is upstairs, in the living area," he said as they settled in behind Beth. "We'll get you up there next, clean out that hand, maybe get some food. You hungry?"

But Casey wasn't listening. She was looking at herself on one of Beth's screens. Her stomach knotted. It was an image from the chase, right before she'd scraped her hand. "How do you have this?"

"We're tapped into the street and traffic cameras. What the ICP sees, we see," Beth said, zooming in on the man chasing her. With his jacket flowing and his colored shirt showing, he looked breezy, as if he should have been drinking fancy cocktails on a rooftop bar. Beth zoomed in farther, focusing on what looked like a shiny tube of lipstick palmed in his hand.

"What is that?" Casey asked.

"We think it's a paralyzing agent, some kind of tranquilizer, but we can't be sure," Beth said. "Whatever it is, it's pretty effective. We've seen it take down guys three times your size in an instant."

Casey found it all so hard to believe. She studied her father. He had saved her—from what, exactly, she didn't know, but he'd been there when she needed him. Casey felt terrible for being short with him. While he didn't get to declare that they were okay, in her heart she knew they were. Casey hoped when she got home tonight, she could convince her mother of the same.

5

Casey sat on the floor next to Bart. She had a new bandage taped to the palm of her hand. After bringing her down from their living quarters, her father had excused himself to answer a call. He did not look happy when he left. And, from the sound of his raised voice, he still wasn't. In the meantime, Bring Your Daughter to Work Day continued with Beth introducing her to Dan and Garrett.

Casey immediately liked Dan. He was young, wore combat boots and plastic-framed glasses, and kept his hair stylishly messy. He seemed hip but understatedly so. Beth explained that Dan was their computer guy and was fond of hacking into the ICP's systems.

Garrett was a tougher sell. He grunted his way through their hello. He was tall, barrel-chested, bearded, and bald. Casey detected some charm behind his rough exterior, but he hid it well. Beth explained that Garrett got them things. He had worked for the city as a civil engineer and had access to a deep supply chain. At the moment, Garrett was working on getting a boiler for a local youth center. As Beth praised him, he blushed and mumbled something about hearts and minds and how it was the least he could do. As Beth explained, it wasn't just Garrett getting a boiler to help some kids. It was Dan hacking into the banks. It was Beth gaming the paperwork. And it was them giving back to a community that had been screwed over, time and time again. She was impressed, concluding that her father's team was made up of true Robin Hoods.

As the team got back to work, Casey pulled her screen from her pocket. It was still dead, and she was itching to message her mom. "Do I get this back?" she asked Beth, holding the screen for her to see.

Beth looked over. "That's a good question, and one I'll leave for your dad."

Casey didn't appreciate the non-answer, but she understood. The whole lot of them seemed to be holding something back, but she was in no position to push, and she wasn't too sure she wanted to anyway.

Her father walked into the room, scowling. He exchanged glances with Beth, then turned to Casey. "It's time to talk, Case," he said, motioning for her to follow.

It seemed she'd be getting her answers sooner rather than later. She gave Bart a kiss on the head and got to her feet. Her legs felt heavy. Dan turned from his desk to watch. Garrett came down a set of stairs, stopping before the last step. He looked at her father and then over to her.

"What?" Casey asked, holding her hands up in front of her. The less the team talked, the more frustrated she became. "It's not like you can pull me, right? I get to go home . . . right?"

He didn't answer, which was more of an answer than she wanted.

He waved for Casey to follow him.

"I have a life," she said, regretting it right off. Everyone in the room had a life once—she knew that.

Beth and Dan turned back to their screens while Garrett went to his desk. Casey followed her father down a short hallway. With each step, inevitability sunk in. There was no going back. If she did return home, she would end up being abducted by the ICP. There would be no more dinners with her mom, no more concerts with Jennifer, and no more needling from Greg. She would be gone—vanished, like Martin—leaving only questions behind.

6

Her father's office was tiny. There was room for a desk and two chairs, and that was it. There was a small blacked-out window behind the desk, and, of course, graffiti covered the walls. Her dad offered up his desk chair and Casey sat. The first thing she noticed was the picture on his desk. She smiled. It was a family picture from before he'd left.

"You remember that day?" he asked, kneeling beside her.

"Sure," she said.

Casey remembered it very well. They were at her cousin Michael's wedding, standing in a gazebo, soaking wet. She was in the foreground, taking the selfie, with her parents—mom, then dad—next to her. They were disheveled, but they were smiling and happy.

"We walked away for five minutes," he said.

"And the sky opened."

He put his hand on her arm. "I never saw your mom run so fast."

She looked at his hand, then his face. His eyes were red.

"We were happy," he said.

She nodded but sensed there was something else. "Dad, what is it?"

"Who's Bruce Johnson?"

Fuck. How did he know about Bruce? Then Casey realized that while he may have been out of their lives, they had not been out of his. Still, she hesitated. Maybe he didn't know about the boyfriend part. She certainly didn't want to hurt him; he seemed so broken already. She had no idea what to say, so she decided on the truth. "Mom's seeing him."

He was silent. Maybe he hadn't known.

"If it helps, Mom waited. She waited a long time."

He let out a small laugh. "It doesn't. But knowing that makes this next part harder."

She didn't like where this was going.

"He's the one who turned you in, Casey. He's why you're on the list."

Amazing. Fucking Bruce. He had been listening at her bedroom door. She should have trusted her instincts. Her father let go of her arm and swiped at the screen closest to him. On it was a list with her name at the very top, flashing red. He tapped her name, and a small window opened. He pointed to Bruce's name. There was a timestamp next to it. He had called in to report Casey soon after she and Jennifer had left the apartment. The bastard had sat through dinner, all the while knowing what he had done.

"So, what is he? Some kind of spy?"

"Snitch, more likely. He's ICP and pretty high up. They all snitch."

"We have to tell Mom."

"We can't. It's too dangerous . . . for her and for us."

"But we're in danger anyway," she said. "I was just chased down the street by a stranger, and Mom's got a snitch living with us. I think things are dangerous already."

His face dropped. Casey thought about what she had just said and realized her mistake.

"Living with you?" he asked.

"No . . . not living." She sighed. "But she did give him the code."

He was about to say something when Dan appeared in the doorway.

"Sorry to interrupt," Dan said. "But she's here." He brushed the hair from his eyes.

Her father stood and put his hand on her shoulder. "Case, I'm going to need a minute."

7

Casey followed Dan back into the main workroom.

"Can I get you anything?" he asked.

Casey shook him off. "No, I'm all right."

She didn't have a desire for much of anything—except going home. It had been a long day, maybe the longest, and she wanted to be done with it. Dan offered her a seat at the table at the center of the room. She again declined. She was too antsy to sit. Dan politely excused himself and sat at his desk behind her.

Beth came in with a stranger in tow. The stranger, a woman maybe thirty-five or forty years old, looked overdressed and out of place in her fancy black dress, high heels, and updo. Upon seeing Casey, the woman smiled at her, but it was not the same warm smile she had received from the rest of the team. Casey smiled in return but instantly disliked her. Leaning back, she nudged Dan. "Who's that?" she whispered.

Without looking up, Dan answered, "That's Simone. She pays for things."

Judging by her diamond-studded accessories, it looked like she could pay for things with ease. If having Jennifer as a friend had taught Casey anything, it was how to spot expensive—and this lady was full of expensive. "Look at her. Was she pulled like the rest of you?"

Dan turned. He glanced at Simone and then up at her. He smirked. "Hardly," he said. "She's our contact . . . well, really, your dad's contact."

"Contact with whom?"

"We like to call them our benefactors. They set all this up. Like I said, they pay for stuff."

"But she's clearly ICP. Regular people don't look like that."

"I don't ask. I just take her toys. She's your dad's business."

Her father strode into the room. Simone saw him, abruptly ended her conversation with Beth, and then followed him down the hall. Casey turned to Dan. She noticed the list was on his screen. Her name was still flashing red.

"Is the list ever wrong?" she asked.

"Not wrong. Incomplete, maybe. But not wrong. For example, your friend Martin . . . he never showed up on the list."

"But they did take him, right? We aren't crazy?"

"Crazy for questioning the ICP, yes—that's Civics 101. But not delusional crazy. They definitely took him."

Dan opened a tab on another screen. In it, Martin walked down the street, smiling, a skip in his step. She recognized the block and the bar. It was a scene from the night before, which seemed like a lifetime ago. She leaned forward, squinting and biting her upper lip. "No," she muttered. On the screen, the same fashionable couple that had come for her strolled into view. Casey reached for a chair, rolled it over, and sat.

"See . . . not crazy," Dan said. "We have them following your friend until the feed cuts out downtown."

"Who are they?"

"Contractors, maybe. We don't really know. Until tonight, we never had them on a feed where someone actually disappears."

"What do they do to them? The disappeared ones?"

"If they are young and healthy, Recruiting takes them. If not, who knows? Secret prisons, maybe. We're still trying to figure this stuff out."

"I doubt Martin would fight for them willingly."

"After Recruiting is done messing with his brain, all he'll want to do is fight for them."

"What are you saying? Recruits get brainwashed?"

"All I know is that when they resurface—if they resurface—they have no clue that fighting for the ICP wasn't their idea, and they're pretty damn good at it. I had a buddy. He was hacking away one day, then gone the next. They told his folks he joined up. Trust me, there's no way he would have. But a year later, after quarantine, he's all soldier, and he swears it was all his idea."

"That's why you're here, isn't it?" she asked.

Dan shrugged. "I guess I failed Civics 101 too."

"Do you miss your family?"

"A ton," he said. "It kills me that they don't know I'm all right."

Dan told her about his little brother and how he was pretty good with computers, too, and that there was so much he wanted to teach him. It was clear getting pulled was hard, but Dan was still optimistic. He insisted it didn't have to be forever. One day, when the threat was gone and the ICP exposed, they'd be reunited with their families—all of them would be. Casey liked his optimism.

From down the hall, she heard shouting. She edged her chair to the end of Dan's desk. Casey listened intently but couldn't make out what the heated exchange was about. She peered around the corner, but the door to the office was closed. She moved her chair back. "So," she whispered. "No one seems to want to tell me what's going on." She tilted her head toward the hall. "What's going on?"

Dan looked over his shoulder at Beth. "I don't think—"

"Please."

He glanced over at Beth one more time.

"Simone wants to chip you and send you back," he whispered.

She was confused. "Simone wants to what and what?"

"She wants us to put one of her high-tech tracking chips in you and send you on your way home. But we know you'll never make it that far. They'll grab you long before that."

"They'll take me to wherever they took Martin."

"That's the idea."

This was not what she had expected. She looked at her name flashing red on Dan's screen. She looked at her bandaged hand. She looked at the paused feed of the couple tracking Martin. The danger was everywhere, and Simone wanted to put her in even more of it. "That's nuts. You know that, right?"

"A bit." Dan looked over his shoulder at Beth one more time. "The thing is, you're the only person who's gone red that we've gotten to first. You're still in play."

"I thought you were all on the list."

"We were, but until I got us access to the list, your dad was flying blind. He knew us all from before, as well as the danger we were in."

"He knew you all?"

"He arrested me," Dan said, pushing his hair from his eyes. "That was fun. But with Beth on the D.A. side, they sabotaged the ICP's case against me. The two are quite the pair. Dan paused. He rolled his chair back and peeked into the next room, then rolled back. "Garrett had been helping your father procure stuff for the neighborhood for years. He only got shut down after a generator slated for the mayor showed up at the clinic on Houston Street. They both still deny it was them, but it made them rock stars down here."

Darcy and Bill had it right: Her dad was loved—he was a rock star. Until tonight, she'd had no idea. She knew her father was invested in the people downtown, but this kind of sacrifice took it to another level. She wished he had talked about it some more. Maybe if he had, it would have helped explain why he left.

"So, chipping me and sending me back could help more people than just Martin?"

Dan nodded. "We're hoping to close the whole operation down."

Casey tried to game things out. She thought about the sacrifice she'd have to make. She could be risking her life, which was not something she had planned on doing today—or any day, for that matter. But she'd be helping Jennifer, she'd be helping Martin, and she'd be helping people like Dan, and Dan's friend—people whose lives had been stolen without their consent. She thought about the poster outside of Recruiting. It wasn't that she was opposed to character growth or a reason for being; it was that she'd never felt the need. Her big picture had always been rather small. But if there was a way out of the mess this day had brought, then helping her father and helping his team was the way. And if it ended up getting her life unstuck, so much the better.

In the end, there wasn't much of a decision to be made.

8

Casey, her father, and the rest of the team were gathered around the table. Simone had gone, but not before leaving the chip and a bunch of worried team members behind. Coffee had been brewed, and it was all very serious. Even Bart seemed on edge as he circled the table looking for food. In Casey's hand was a small rubberized box. Embedded inside was a chip no bigger than the nail on her pinky toe. According to Dan, the chip was guaranteed to be undetectable. It would track her, and through it, she could talk with the team. It all sounded great, but none of it allayed her fear.

"Where does it go?" she asked.

"Temple," Dan said from the seat across from her.

She felt the side of her head. It was just fleshy enough. She had a follow-up question, but Dan had turned his attention to a screen at the center of the table. On the screen were the chip's schematics. It all seemed very technical, especially from her layman's point of view. She looked at her father, who was sitting alone at the head of the table. She thought about dinner at the apartment earlier that night and how she had desperately wanted him at the head of that table. Now here he was, in his somber, bearded glory, filling that role. It was a dream come true, except for the whole life-and-death part. In the end, her father had made it clear that he did not want her doing this but understood if she felt she had to. She even sus-pected that he was proud of her for it. With all she had learned tonight, she was certainly proud of him.

As the team talked about their plan, Casey had trouble keeping up. She noted street names, time estimates, and that a maintenance truck would be used as cover. When they got to the bottom line—that they'd track her until they reached their destination and rescue her in due time—she was relieved. The less time in captivity, the better.

Then, before she knew it, they were all standing up and ready to go. Not sure what she should do, Casey stayed seated. As Beth passed behind her father, she gave his shoulder a squeeze. Her father looked back at Beth. There was an intimacy there that surprised Casey, and she found herself getting defensive. Had he, like her mom, moved on? Was it really that easy? But then she realized it did not matter—the defensiveness she felt was her problem. Her parents were living their lives. If having a Beth in his life, or a fuckhead like Bruce in her mom's, made them happy, then who was she to judge?

Dan walked around the table toward her. He held his hand out, and she handed him the chip. "Are you ready?" he asked.

Before she could answer, her father was behind her. He squeezed her shoulder as Beth had his. "You can back out at any time," he said.

"Not going to happen." She put a hand over his. "Just remember your promise."

He nodded and gave her shoulder another squeeze before let-ting go.

The promise she had extracted from him would be a hard one to keep—she was aware of that but did not care. Her father had agreed that if all went well, if they were able to expose Recruiting and the ICP, then he'd consider resurfacing. He and his entire team would come out of hiding and bring their fight out into the open.

It was a long shot, but a shot Casey needed.

She didn't want a life lived in the shadows, and neither, she thought, should he.

9

Beth was driving. Casey was in the back seat with her father next to her. Except for the clean bandage on her hand and the chip in her head, it was all eerily familiar. While she was determined to see this through, the reality that they were driving her back into danger was a bit overwhelming. Beth pulled over and double-parked at the corner of Second Avenue and Seventy-Eighth Street. Home was a block away, just past First Avenue. "Right here?" Casey asked, turning to her father. "Right now?"

"Right here, whenever you're ready. And if you're never ready, that's fine too."

She leaned in and hugged him tightly. She felt ready to forgive him or at least to let go of some of her anger towards him. "You and me," she said. "We're okay."

They let go, and he kissed her on the forehead. She turned to Beth. "Take care of him."

"I always do."

She opened the car door, letting the night's heat pour in. She took a deep breath and got out. Her father followed, closing the noisy door behind him, its rusty cry much less noticeable on the busy avenue. They hugged one more time before he got into the front seat. Casey turned and walked toward the curb. She could feel his worried eyes watching her go, but she refused to turn around. She wanted to get this whole abduction thing over with. Being strong and stoic was her goal. If all went according to plan, she'd be back with the team in no time.

She pulled the legs of her shorts down and stepped onto the sidewalk. She saw Beth turn left from the avenue onto Seventy-Eighth Street. The car went about halfway down the block, then stopped, its hazard lights blinking. On either side of her, people passed by, trying to cross the street. Casey tensed, fully expecting to be taken right there and then. But, no, she was just in the way. Stepping from the pedestrian flow, she looked up at the traffic light. She was worried about the surveillance camera embedded inside. "You sure the camera's out?"

"Fried like chicken," Dan answered in her head.

She grinned. She liked having Dan with her. She touched the right side of her head where the chip had been placed. It was still sore, but the skin was smooth thanks to the tiny incision and the synthetic healer. As she began walking toward First Avenue and home, she reached into her back pocket and slipped her screen from her shorts. She turned the lifeless glass over in her hands. Dan had warned that once it had been turned back on, the ICP would quickly get a lock on her. "Should I turn my screen on?" she asked.

"Only if you're ready."

She wasn't, but there was no turning back. She tapped the screen twice for power. For the first time in over two hours, it sprang to life. She had a bunch of new messages. The first few were from Jennifer—first touching base, then, later, wondering about her silence. The last one was from her mom. She was just checking in and worried that it was getting late. Instinctively Casey swiped at the screen to reply, but then she stopped. *No, you can't*, she thought, pulling her hand away, *not now, maybe not ever.* She did not like this new reality: She was a block from home, and yet she couldn't see or talk to her mother. Determined, Casey picked up her pace. She passed the double-parked getaway car containing Beth and her father. She didn't turn to acknowledge them. Strong and stoic, she told herself. Strong and stoic.

"Casey!" A guy called to her from across the street. It sounded like Greg.

Shit. Now was not the time. She tried not to look his way.

"Case!" he called again.

This time she looked. It was Greg, and he was waving his arms to get her attention. *Oh, man*, she hemmed and hawed in her head. He was standing between two parked cars, waiting to cross. Stan, Martin's friend, was with him, which was strange because the two usually didn't hang out.

She waved back.

"Casey?" Dan interrupted. "What's going on?"

She glanced over her shoulder at the double-parked car. Her father leaned forward in the passenger seat. She tilted her head toward Greg. Her father knew Greg, and he would understand the complication. He looked across the street and then grimaced. He got it. Greg was one of her chattier friends; he'd been caught by Greg more than a few times himself over the years.

"Casey?" Dan tried again. "Meeting strangers on the street is not part of the plan."

"Right. Getting drugged and thrown into the back of a van is. I get it, but he's not a stranger. Give me a sec."

She started toward the parked cars on her side of the street.

Greg looked both ways and, with Stan in tow, made his way across.

"I thought you went home," he said after reaching her.

She waved to Stan behind him. "Errand," she said. "My mom wanted ice cream."

"At one in the morning?"

"At whatever in the morning. Mind your own business." Casey pointed to the two of them. "What's with this?" She looked more closely at Stan. His cheeks were flushed. "Are you drunk?"

"A bit," Stan said, raising his thumb and index finger.

"We were over at Coastal," Greg said. "Stan here messaged about Martin, and I convinced him to come for a drink."

"We're best buds now," Stan said, pushing his glasses up his nose and smiling.

She smiled back, letting her guard down. Drunk Stan was a fun Stan.

Then, behind the new best buds, a car cruised past. It was a black sedan, going a little too slowly for Casey's liking. As it went by, the driver turned to look at her. He had pale skin and wore his hair slicked back. They made eye contact; a chill trembled through her. After what seemed like an eternity, the driver turned his attention back to the road. She was convinced she had just been made. Casey moved away from her friends. As she did so, she watched the suspicious car continue down the block. It stopped at the corner for a red light. She tried to shake her paranoia. *It's nothing*, she told herself. *It's just a car and a creepy-ass driver.* But she was having trouble buying it.

"Casey," Dan said, "the car that just passed—your father made it as ICP. It's starting."

She fought the urge to answer Dan or react at all with Greg and Stan right there.

"You okay?" Greg asked.

No. I'm not okay. I'm about to be abducted and who knows what else. "I'm fine," she said. "Listen . . ." she pointed towards home. "I gotta go."

"What's with the bandage?" Stan asked.

She looked at her hand. She'd forgotten she was wearing one. "I fell. No biggie."

Greg eyed her suspiciously. "Are you sure you're okay?"

Casey glanced to her left, towards home and potential doom.

"Casey," Dan implored. "You got to keep moving, or your friends there will be in danger too."

She tried again, more firmly this time. "Listen—I'm fine, but I really have to go." She started to move away. "I'll see you tomorrow, okay?"

Greg nodded, still looking wary. "But what about the ice cream?"

"Business, Greg. Mind it."

Casey turned and continued down the street. Looking over her shoulder, she saw the pair were crossing back again. Beth inched the car forward. Turning, Casey stopped short. Her knees went weak. Just past the corner, double-parked, was the black sedan. Maybe she was not ready to be abducted after all. She turned again to see where her father was. The car was closer, but not close enough for comfort. Why that mattered, she was not sure. The result would be the same: They weren't going to save her. Despite all the people watching her, no one was going to save her—not yet, anyway.

"Casey, what is it?"

"The car—the car you said was ICP. It's double-parked on the corner."

"I see it," Dan said. "Casey, we knew this would happen. We'll be with you."

"Yeah, then why do I feel so alone?" She started walking toward the corner. Her legs were far from steady. "Dan, I'm scared."

"I think we all are. You'll be okay."

As she reached First Avenue, she could see the awning of her building across the way. Derek was out front. She fought the urge to yell to him. Also, across the street, she spotted Garrett's undercover maintenance truck. Over her shoulder, her father and Beth were driving parallel to her but a few feet behind. She had the light and was free to cross, but what she desperately wanted to do was sprint the rest of the way to her apartment, lock the door, punch Bruce in the face, and make believe this freak show of a night was over. Instead, she stepped off the curb to cross. The double-parked sedan waited as the driver watched her from his side-view mirror. Her chills returned. She held her breath. The car's hazard lights tick, tick, ticked as they blinked. But then, before she could clear the back of the car, a black van screeched to a stop in front of her. She froze. On instinct, she turned to run. Behind her, the van's side door whooshed open and thumped into place. Before she could manage a step, hands—four in all—grabbed her arms and shoulders, jerking her inside. Casey screamed, she grabbed at the air, and her head hit the door frame. She screamed again, squirming and kicking with all her might.

"Do it," a man's voice said.

She smelled coffee on his breath. There was a prick against her neck, then her mind began to swirl. She tried to stay focused as her arms and legs lost all control. The van's door began to slide shut, bringing darkness with it. But before the door closed completely, she glimpsed Beth holding her father by the arm and shoulder as he tried to get out of the car. He looked as terrified as she felt.

After that, there was nothing.

CHAPTER THREE | BEST LAID PLANS

CASEY GROANED AS SHE STARTED to come around. For a brief moment, she was home in her bed, cozy, maybe hung over. Then she remembered. Bolting upright, she was in a bed, but not her own, and she was anything but cozy. She had been stripped down to her tank top and underwear. The mattress she lay on was bare and rough against her exposed skin. The right side of her head hurt. She remembered being pulled into the van. She remembered hitting her head. She touched the spot; it was sore, and the hair around it was matted to her scalp. She looked at her fingers. There was dried blood on the tips. Casey took a deep breath, trying to settle herself. It was obvious that her abduction had not been a gentle one and that her rescue had gone horribly wrong.

She looked around the well-lit room. It appeared she was in some kind of small prison cell. It was maybe five feet by ten, with cinderblock walls. Just past the end of the bed was a sink-and-toilet combination. There was a roll of toilet paper on the floor. The door to the cell had a window near the top and a hatch at its center.

Casey swung her legs over the side of the bed. The mattress

seam pressed against the backs of her thighs. She noticed the bandage her father had put on her palm was gone. The scrapes from her fall looked worse in the room's bright light. Then she remembered the chip and felt buoyed. "Dan?" she whispered.

She waited, but Dan didn't answer.

"Dan," she tried again, a little louder this time.

But there was nothing.

Deflated, she pressed her fingers to her temple; the area where they had implanted the chip was sore. Casey pressed harder, trying to feel for it. She thought maybe she felt a ridge or a bump, but she couldn't be sure. "Dan?" she tried one more time. But again there was nothing. If they weren't hearing her or weren't able to talk to her, she hoped they at least could still track her. That would be something, she reassured herself, trying to limit her panic.

She stood up, but, feeling dizzy, sat right back down. She waited a moment and then tried again. The concrete floor was cold against her bare feet. Stepping to the door, Casey tried pressing on the hatch to see if it would open. It didn't. Getting up on her toes, she peered through the small window. It looked out into a hallway. Across from her was another door like her own. To the left and right were more doors. Coming down off her toes, she wondered, *how long have I been here? How long was I out?* She felt the side of her head again. It must have been a while, because the blood was dry. Hungry and needing to pee, she guessed it must be morning.

She turned and walked to the sink–toilet combo. She pressed a button at the top of the faucet, and a burst of water sprayed out. Putting her hand under the spout, she pressed the button again. The water was cold, freezing cold. Of course it was. Self-conscious, she looked around the tiny room. They had to be watching her, but the walls were bare. She studied the caged light fixture on the ceiling. At the far end, she spotted a small, dark dome about the size of a dime. She climbed onto the bed to get a better look. Standing on the mattress, she leaned out over the edge of the bed. Her tank top rose, exposing her belly. She pulled it back down. Whatever it was, she could not reach it or do anything about it. She climbed down from the bed, one cautious foot at a time, then plodded back to the toilet. "Enjoy the show," she said to the ceiling as she pulled down her underwear and sat, covering what she could with her hands. The metal seat was cold.

"Dan . . ." She tried again. "I'm here."

Her shoulders slumped, and she bowed her head. It was no use; they couldn't hear her. She was alone. She moved her hands from her lap to her head. She felt completely overwhelmed and on the verge of tears. *So much for being stoic and strong.*

2

Casey woke with a start, feeling for the bed underneath her. She had not meant to fall asleep. Feeling groggy and sad, she sat up, then swung her legs off the edge of the bed. Again she wondered about the time. Her stomach told her it was right about lunchtime, but she was hungry enough that dinnertime was in the mix. She assumed they would feed her. They had to feed her, right? There was a rustling at the door, and the service hatch swung open. Finally, some food, she thought. Maybe they were reading her mind. Someone outside was moving about. As Casey sprang to her feet, a pair of boots and a pile of clothes—army fatigues, by the look of them—appeared on a shelf attached to the opening.

"Hello?" she called.

But there was no answer.

Via the chip in her head or in person, it seemed nobody wanted to talk.

She pulled the pile of clothes onto the floor, then bent and looked through the opening. She glimpsed a silver belt buckle before the hatch door closed. Frustrated, she banged the door with the side of her fist. Standing on her tiptoes, Casey looked out the small window. A broad-shouldered man dressed in military garb lumbered to the cell across the hall. He held another set of clothes just like the ones he had left for her.

"Hey!" she yelled, banging on the window. "Look at me!"

Still she got no response.

Across the way, the guard swung open a hatch like hers and placed the clothes on its tray. Immediately the clothes disappeared inside. Casey thought she saw someone trying to peer out, but before she could get a good look the guard closed the hatch again. He turned, glanced at her, and walked away. She banged on the glass again. Fuming, she watched him go. Turning her attention back to her neighbor's cell, she saw a face—Martin's face—staring at her through the window.

"Holy shit," she muttered.

Martin looked as confused and as scared as she felt.

He pointed to her. "Are you okay?" he mouthed.

She nodded and smiled; she put her hand up against the glass. She was so relieved to see him. "You?" she mouthed back.

He nodded.

She wanted to tell him help was on the way, though she could not be sure that it was. The plan hatched with her father had her home by breakfast. Clearly things were not going according to plan.

3

Casey sat on the floor with her back pressed up against the cell door. She rubbed her eyes, upset that she had fallen asleep again. Casey began to suspect all was not well with her head; she thought maybe she had a concussion. A shiver passed through her. She was freezing, and the cold floor was not helping matters. She looked at the clothes strewn around her. There were pants, a T-shirt, socks, a pair of boxer briefs, and a sports bra, all in the same army green. She gathered the clothes on her lap. Using a hand for leverage, she managed to stand. Everything felt stiff. Her hunger became an afterthought. She turned and got on her toes to check the window. She couldn't see Martin.

Shoulders slumped, she stepped to the bed, the change of clothes pressed against her chest. She dropped the clothes on the mattress and sat on the edge of the bed. She really did not feel well.

She rubbed the side of her head. She was ready to be rescued, but since she hadn't been as of yet, it was likely not to happen. She began to realize she'd have to figure a way out herself.

Resigned, Casey decided to dress. Army green was better than half-naked and cold. She pulled the white tank she'd been wearing since who-knows-when over her head, then off. Her bra underneath had seemingly glued itself in place. She glanced up at the light fixture and shrugged. If they were watching, there was not much she could do about it. She unhooked her bra and set herself free. She rubbed under her breasts where the wire had begun to dig. She regarded the sink. It was time for a proper cleaning—well, as proper a cleaning as a sink with only cold water and no soap would allow.

At the sink–toilet combo, she splashed herself clean with one cold handful of water at a time, shivering all the while. When she was done, she patted herself kind-of dry with her dirty tank top. Holding the top over her chest, she moved to the bed and picked through the clothes. She pulled the sports bra over her shoulders. Surprisingly, it fit okay. She put the T-shirt on next, and that was way too big. She stepped out of her old underwear, tossing them and her tank top onto the floor. She grabbed her new boxers and stepped into them. As she did so, she heard a thump from out in the hall. She rushed to the window, holding the ill-fitting boxers up by the waistband.

In the hall, Martin was on a stretcher in front of his open cell door. He was dressed in the same army drab. There were two guards, one at each end of the stretcher. She recognized one of the guards as the guy who'd ignored her when dropping off the clothes. They were both broad and brutish. One grabbed Martin under his arms, and the other grabbed him by his booted feet. Together, they lifted him off the stretcher. He was clearly unconscious, with his head lolling around as they carried him to his cell. As he passed, she noticed a small white bandage at the base of his skull. His hair was shaved around it. Aghast, she covered her mouth. She dropped from the window, leaning her back against the door. She rested her hands on her knees. What the fuck they had done to him?

Whatever it was, she assumed she was next.

4

Casey paced the narrow length of the cell. She stepped past the toilet, the bed, and the door. She checked for Martin at the window, then did the same in reverse and back again. She was hungry, she was tired, and she wanted to sleep. With each pass, the bed called to her; with each pass, she ignored the impulse. She had slept enough already and wanted to be sharp when they came for her. At the door, she got on her now-booted tiptoes and checked for Martin again. She hadn't seen him since he'd been carried into his cell. She guessed that was a few hours ago, but she couldn't be sure—everything blurred together.

After one more pass, she stopped short of the door as she heard the lock snap open. She moved backward, deeper into the cell. *Shit*, she thought, *this is it*. The door swung wide, and Casey took another step back. Her legs felt wobbly; her heart rate ticked up. It was the same two broad-shouldered, broad-faced brutes that had dropped Martin off. One guard marched into the cell while the other stayed by the door.

"Recruit 742," the lead guard barked. "Front and center."

Huh? She now had a number . . . one she was supposed to answer to, no less. This was news to her.

"Recruit 742," he repeated. "Front and center."

Casey stayed back and to the side. She noticed they weren't armed—at least that was something. "What did you do to him?" she asked, pointing across the hall.

The lead guard stepped closer. She slinked back, but before she could get farther away, he was on her. He grabbed her arm, twisted it and her around, then slammed her, chin first, against the back wall of the cell. The pain sent flashes of white through her peripheral vision. She groaned and tasted blood. The guard held her there, her arm twisted behind her, pressing into her back. He put a hand on her head, planting the side of her face flush with the wall. He leaned his full weight into her. She could smell his cologne. It was a woodsy scent, with a hint of lavender behind it. In any other situation, it might not have been offensive. But, here and now, she was very much offended.

"You will respect our authority, Recruit," he said, leaning closer. His chin brushed against her ear. "Also, thanks for the show."

"Prick," she muttered, disgusted. She squirmed against his grip but couldn't budge.

Laughing, the creep twisted her around and tossed her to the floor. He followed her down, planting his knee in her back, knocking the air from her lungs. She gasped. He corralled and cuffed her wrists together as she fought to catch her breath.

"What did you call me?" he questioned.

As he pressed his knee harder into her, she said nothing. She was so done with this part of her day. She stared straight ahead, her chin touching the floor. The guard at the door smirked. She ignored him and focused on Martin's cell across the way.

"Good," the guard on her back said, standing.

He lifted Casey by the shoulders, then shoved her towards the door. The second guard grabbed her by the arm. Once she was outside the cell, the guard who had roughed her up took her other arm. Leading her down the hall, they passed more cells. A girl around Casey's age watched as they went past. Her pale face was gaunt. Her head had been shaved, and she had bruises around her lifeless eyes. Casey made and held eye contact, hoping to let her know that she'd been seen.

Noticing her engagement, asshole guard shoved her forward. "Eyes in front," he ordered.

"Fuck off," she said, more dismissive than angry while struggling against his grip.

"Keep it up, Recruit, and I promise you, you'll end up just like her."

Casey struggled some more, but it was mostly for show. They were too strong, and she was too tired. She hoped whatever came next at least included a nap.

5

"You could at least tell me what I'm waiting for!" Casey yelled. But it was no use. The guards were gone, and a closed door stood between them and her.

After an elevator ride, the guards had left Casey in a large conference room. There was a long table at the center and a set of high-backed chairs perfectly spaced around it. Across the room, floor-to-ceiling windows ran along its length. Stepping to the windows, she saw the conference room was about two stories up and overlooked a large gymnasium. The gym's floor was sprinkled with workout mats, and a track ran around the perimeter. There were pockets of men and women, dressed like her, doing various exercises and drills. They were recruits, she assumed, none of whom looked as if they were here against their will.

Turning from the window, she paced the length of the conference table. Its glass top was polished to a slick shine. She counted twenty-two chairs around it. Circling the room, she tugged at her bindings, the smooth plastic digging into her skin. She eyed the door, assuming the guards were still on the other side. Crossing the room, she put her ear against it. She heard nothing. She decided to try the handle to see if it was locked. She turned her back to the door and maneuvered her bound hands up to it. She pressed down until she felt the latch click. It was unlocked. *Huh*, she thought, surprised and unsure what to do next. She continued to hold the handle down. If the guards were on the other side, what then? Run? She was too weak. Besides, as her gym teachers could attest, running was not her thing. She could run and scream and make a fuss, which was more her thing. But before her debate could continue, she heard footsteps and voices outside.

"At ease, soldiers," one of the voices said.

It was a familiar voice, deep and gruff, but she couldn't place it. She inched the handle up until the latch set back in and scrambled away from the door. She took a deep breath, readying herself for whatever came next. The door opened. *Of course*, Casey thought, placing the voice with the face. In the doorway stood her best friend's father, Michael Hargrove, ICP leader and probable mayor. Much to her surprise, she felt relieved, overwhelmed even. His familiar face was somehow comforting. She thought maybe her weakened state had her feeling sentimental. Who knew? Maybe Jennifer had even asked him to help.

"Mr. H," she said, taking a step toward him. She was on the verge of tears.

Hargrove stepped into the room. The two guards, Prick and his friend, stuck close behind. Size-wise, he matched up well to them, except with more belly. His suit was impeccable, as always, and his bald head gleamed. He turned to the guards. "Why is she restrained?"

The guards looked at each other. "She was insubordinate, sir," said the guard who had roughed her up.

"Sergeant, we don't treat recruits that way."

"I'm not a re—" Casey began to say, but she stopped, savoring the guard's comeuppance instead.

The guard marched up to Casey, glaring. She glared right back and may have even snarled. He stepped behind her, there was a snip, and her hands fell free. Bringing them forward, Casey massaged her wrists and then her shoulders as the guard moved back behind Hargrove.

"I'm sorry for that, Casey," Hargrove said, then turned his attention to the men behind him. "You can go."

The pair saluted, turned, and left.

"Mr. H, what's going on? I'm not a recruit. I was abducted."

"Recruited, abducted, it's such a fine line."

She sighed. She let go of her last straw. He wasn't here to help.

Michael Hargrove stepped to the table, motioning for her to sit. Casey turned and walked to the window instead.

"Suit yourself," he said. "This doesn't have to be hard."

She turned back to the room, rubbing her sore wrists. She thought about Martin, who was locked away somewhere below them. "Did you promise Martin that it wouldn't be hard before you fucked with his brain?"

"You mean Recruit Santos? Oh, he'll be fine . . . standard procedure."

Casey rolled her eyes. "Jen liked him, you know?"

"My daughter likes a lot of people."

She edged closer. "Martin's different—but you already know that."

"I don't know much when it comes to Jennifer."

"And whose fault is that?"

He raised a finger, began to say something, then stopped. "Either way," he said. "The boy will make a fine recruit."

"Against his will."

"No, voluntarily."

"That's a lie."

Hargrove frowned. He tapped on the conference table, and a screen appeared embedded underneath its high-gloss finish. "Here are his papers." He flicked at the screen, sending it across the table. "Everything's above board, I assure you."

Casey stepped to the table. She grabbed the high back of the chair opposite him and pushed it out of the way. She touched the corner of the screen and dragged the document closer to the table's edge. Its heading read "Agreement to Serve" in a fancy font. Casey scrolled to the bottom. Martin's picture, signature, and fingerprints were there. "More lies," she said, flicking it back to him.

"I have a package just like that ready to send to your mother."

"She'd never believe it."

"I beg to differ." He waved for her to sit again.

"What do you want?" she asked, taking a seat opposite him.

Hargrove smiled. "I want to know where your father is."

She clasped her fingers together in front of her. Her wrists were red from the cuffs. She had no intention of telling him anything. "I don't know where my father is. You know that."

He looked disappointed. The slight head shake, the glare—it was a look she knew well, but with Jennifer on the receiving end.

"I told you, Casey—this doesn't have to be hard."

"And I told you that I haven't seen him. I haven't seen him in over a year, but again, you know that."

He reached into his suit jacket and pulled something out. "How about this, then?"

Gripped between his fingers was a small glass vial with a black rubber stopper at the top. Inside the vial was what appeared to be the chip, now bloodied, that Dan had implanted. She fought the urge to touch the side of her head. "I have no idea what that is."

"Please, Casey . . . I'm not stupid. I know he rescued you. I know he chipped you."

"I know I was on my way home. I know you threw me into the back of a fuckin' van. I know I woke up here. What I don't know is where my father is."

"That's a shame," he said, standing. He turned, walked to the door, then turned back. "Cooperate, and you can leave, no harm done."

Casey said nothing.

"Okay," he said. "Have it your way." Hargrove knocked on the door. It opened, and the two guards marched in.

She sat still, her clasped fingers turning red. She was determined to give him nothing.

"Take her to Dr. Marshall," he said to them.

"Can I use this?" the guard who had roughed her up asked, holding up a shiny, lipstick-like tube. Casey recognized it as the tranquilizer from her first abduction attempt.

"No," Hargrove said. "I want her awake for what's next. I have questions."

6

Kicking and screaming, Casey was dragged from the conference room. Whoever this fucking Marshall quack was, she wanted nothing to do with him. But, unfortunately, she had little choice, as moments later she found herself in what appeared to be an operating room—disinfectant smell and all. A man in scrubs, sitting at a control panel with his back to the room, turned.

"You couldn't sedate her?" the man questioned. "I could hear her yelling from down the hall."

"Boss wants her awake," said the guard who hadn't roughed her up.

Control Panel Guy rolled his eyes. "Strap her in." He waved toward a chair in front of him at the center of the room. It was padded, with a pair of straps on the armrests and another pair on the footrests. A crown, metal and with long screws, was attached to its back.

Casey continued to struggle as they led her to the chair.

"No! No! No!" she yelled, terrified.

Casey tugged at the plastic cuffs. She squirmed, shifting and twisting. She lifted and kicked her feet, forcing them to carry her weight, but it was no use. They spun her around and tossed her into the chair anyway. Thankfully, its padding helped cushion the blow. The guard who had roughed her up held her down by the shoulders. He grinned at her as the other guard strapped her ankles down.

"You can't do this!" she yelled, her adrenaline raging.

"Please . . . Shut her up," Control Panel Guy said. He was scruffy, with dark circles under his eyes. "I need to get this right."

The guard at her feet stood and grabbed something rubbery-looking from a table next to her. He came from behind, held her chin, pried her mouth open, and shoved it in. It felt like a retainer or something a dentist would use to make a mold of your teeth. She tossed her head about, trying to disrupt him. He tightened the mouthpiece against her lips as he strapped it around the back of her head. She tried to yell but couldn't. Her voice was trapped like the rest of her.

"Much better," the guard holding her shoulders said, still smiling.

Behind her, the other guard pushed her forward, then cut the cuffs from her wrists. Together, the two guards took hold of her arms and strapped them to the armrests. The guard who had roughed her up patted her leg and leaned in. "I'll see you later," he said.

"Fuck off!" she yelled, muffled but getting the point across.

He smiled wider before turning. "She's all yours," he said to the guy at the panel as the pair swaggered from the room.

The guy ignored the guards' departure, his attention focused on the panel instead. Casey thought he seemed stressed. She looked up at the crown hanging ominously above her head. Next to her was some kind of machine on wheels. It was black, about the size of a dorm-room refrigerator, with dials and flashing lights along the front and cooling vents along the back. Resting in a plastic sleeve at its side was what looked like a long needle. It had finger grips at its base and glowed white at its tip. Fuck. It was happening. They were going to mess with her brain. She tried to struggle against her restraints, but her arms and legs were tied tight. She yelled a muffled "Help!" to the frazzled guy, over and over again. After the third time, he stood and walked to her, looking at a screen in his hand.

"Recruit 742," he said. "I'm Nurse Kristof. I'll be assisting Dr. Marshall today." He sized her up. "All this—the struggling, the fighting—will do you no good. If anything, it could make things worse. So, please, just relax. It will be over before you know it."

She grunted and struggled some more.

Shaking his head, Nurse Kristof knelt next to the machine. Looking at his screen and then back at the machine, he fiddled with its controls. From across the room, a man in a white coat entered. He was short, with straight, thinning hair and glasses. He looked strangely familiar. And then it all came together: Dr. Marshall was Stan's father. No wonder he had been so freaked out when she'd asked about Martin's recruitment.

Nurse Kristof stood and hurried back to his station. "Standard loyalty and combat program?" Kristof asked, sitting again.

Dr. Marshall nodded. "Let's get her vitals checked too. She looks a little beat up."

"You think it may not stick?"

"It shouldn't be a problem. Use the T-2 chip, just to be sure."

Nurse Kristof got to his feet, rushing to a cabinet against the wall. He typed something into a screen on the cabinet door, and a small case emerged from a slot below the screen. He carried it carefully back to the desk and handed it to the doctor. After a moment, the nurse got up again and shuffled to Casey's side. She tried to plead her case with her eyes. She didn't want to lose herself; she didn't want to be a soldier. Kristof ignored her, attaching a patch to her forearm. A screen, one of two hanging in front of her from the ceiling, came to life. Her heartbeat, blood pressure, and other vital signs were displayed.

"She's good, Doctor," Kristof said.

"Okay. Prep her, and we'll start."

Standing behind her, Kristof lowered the crown. She whipped her head back and forth, trying to scream all the while. Dr. Marshall looked over but seemed unconcerned. The nurse grabbed her chin and forced the metal ring lower until she couldn't toss her head about anymore. He tightened the screws. Two pressed against her temples; two more pressed against the back of her head. Thankfully, their ends were capped with rubber. When he was done, he stepped to the stainless-steel table and grabbed a hair clipper. He turned it on and buzzed a patch of hair just above the nape of her neck. It was the same spot they'd shaved on Martin. He followed the buzzer with a razor and then wiped her clean. Fuck. She tried to struggle some more, but there was no point. She was as confined as she had ever been, and it was terrifying.

"You're going to feel a pinch," Nurse Kristof said, still behind her. "It's a local anesthetic. It should help."

The pinch wasn't too bad.

"She's ready, Doctor."

Dr. Marshall acknowledged the nurse, then strode past her without making eye contact. She heard a chair roll behind her, then felt pressure on the shaved part of her head.

Silently, she started to weep.

"Drill," Dr. Marshall said.

Fuck no, she thought, and her weeping turned to bawling. The drill whirred behind her ear. Her heart was pounding so hard she expected it to burst from her chest. She tried again to move, but the best she could do was clench her hands into fists and her toes into claws. She dug her nails into her palms. They broke skin where the pavement had scraped her palm, however many days ago that had been. Then the pressure came—pinpointed, like getting a filling in the back of your head. Her skull vibrated at a pitch she thought only dogs could hear. But then it was over, the pressure released, and the whirring stopped. She relaxed slightly, her toes and fingers cramped regardless. Her tears slowed to a trickle.

Dr. Marshall rolled his chair behind her, appearing at the boxy machine to her right. He slipped his gloved fingers through the grips of the needle holstered at its side. Nurse Kristof moved next to him, holding open the case with the chip she assumed would be going into her brain. Dr. Marshall, drawing the long needle free of its protective sleeve, turned to Nurse Kristof and placed its tip into the case. As he did, the other screen—the one not showing her vitals—switched on. After lifting the needle out, its tip went from white to red. Casey, disoriented for a moment, then realized the screen was broadcasting the view from the end of the needle. She could see her shoulders, then the back of her head as the doctor, who was about to alter her life in unknowable ways, rolled behind her again. The shaved patch at the base of her skull had a tiny, dark hole bored into it. She watched on the screen as the needle got closer and slid into her head. She balled her hands into fists again. She heaved a dry heave, thankful that they hadn't fed her yet. She felt pressure as the needle passed through gobs of bloody, folded white tissue. She heaved some more, her stomach muscles cramping from the effort. She closed her eyes, opening them again when she felt the movement in her head stop. On the screen, in a green font, flashed the words: Hippocampus Detected. The needle pushed on, stopping only when the screen flashed, now in red: Implantation Successful. After a moment, the needle started back, replaying its journey in reverse. And then, the pressure subsided completely.

"We're good," Dr. Marshall said as the screen that had chronicled the chip's journey went black.

Casey inhaled deeply. Her stomach settled. *We're good? That's it?* She gauged her mental state; hole in her head aside, she felt no different.

She heard Dr. Marshall's chair rolling back. "Patch her up, then call the guards," he said. "She may need an extra day or two before we turn it on."

Her restrained body seized again. *Turn it on? Fuck no. No one is turning anything on.* She struggled some more, despite its uselessness.

The doctor walked past her, snapping the gloves off his hands. He glanced down at her. "And for God's sake, tell them to feed her."

Across the room, the double doors swung open, and Jennifer's father barreled in. The doctor rushed to meet him.

"Turn it on," Hargrove demanded.

At the table next to her, the nurse grumbled his disagreement.

"It's too soon," Dr. Marshall said. "You know that."

"Will it work?"

"Yes, but—"

"No buts. I need some information before she forgets."

"Michael, give her a break."

That they were on a first-name basis surprised her. But then she remembered that their kids went to the same school, and they traveled in the same ICP circles. They could be friends—evil friends, but friends nonetheless.

"Not this one," Hargrove said.

The doctor sighed. "Two minutes, then I turn it off." He waved Nurse Kristof back. "She has to heal."

Hargrove turned to face her. "I'll only need one."

Kristof looked to the doctor. The doctor nodded his consent.

Casey closed her eyes. She was not prepared for whatever was next. She was not prepared for any of this. "Remember who you are," she repeated again and again. She opened her eyes, glaring. *You know me!* she wanted to yell. *You had me for dinner just last fucking week!* She closed her eyes again. Fuck Michael Hargrove. Fuck the ICP. Fuck being a soldier.

Remember that this is not the end.

Then, everything flashed white as if a flare had gone off in her head. She screamed again in muffled agony. It felt like her brain was being torn apart, although being rewritten was more likely. Seconds later, the flash slowly subsided, like a receding tide. She felt calm, overwhelmingly so. Her body relaxed. She kind of remembered fighting something . . . maybe nausea, perhaps the flu, but she couldn't remember what.

A doctor—Dr. Marshall, she remembered; Stan's dad, good guy—stepped up to her. He shined a light into her eyes and then checked a screen in his hands. "She looks good," he said. Reaching around, he loosened the straps from her head and gently pulled the bite guard from her mouth. "How are you feeling, Recruit?"

"I feel good, Doctor," she said, appreciating his kind bedside manner. "Is everything okay?"

"Sure," he said, giving her shoulder a light squeeze. "You took a little tumble, but you'll be fine."

From over the doctor's shoulder, she saw Jennifer's father standing a few feet away. Her heart swelled with feelings for him: pride, loyalty, love even. She knew, at that moment, she'd do anything for him. It was so great to see him. The doctor moved away as Jennifer's father came forward.

"We're good?" he asked Dr. Marshall.

"Two minutes," the doctor answered.

Hargrove rolled a stool next to her and sat. "Casey, I'd like to talk about your father. Is that okay?"

She felt a wave of anger. She had no problem talking about her father. He was a traitor, and she had no issue telling that to anyone who would listen. "Sure," she said. "No problem."

Hargrove leaned closer. He stared into her eyes. "Can you tell me where he is?"

7

Casey sat, shoulders slumped, on the edge of her prison cell bed. She was groggy, having just woken up caged again. She assumed she'd been sedated for the trip downstairs. The bleak room felt smaller and even more claustrophobic than before she'd been brought upstairs. She flicked at the mattress seam running under her thighs. She wanted to be home, on her bed, in her room. She needed her mother. She needed to be doted on. She needed a hug. Casey wondered what her mom must be thinking. Had she gotten documents saying her daughter was recruited? Had she reacted with disbelief or with relief? Was Bruce there? Was he all smug after having played a role? Fucking Bruce. Casey clenched the bed's seam in her hands. And Jennifer, how was she dealing with everything? Not only had she lost Martin, but now her best friend too. Casey sighed, relaxing her grip on the mattress.

She felt helpless, hopeless, and in desperate need of a nap.

On the floor of her cell, a sandwich wrapped in cellophane sat ignored. She was hungry but could not fathom eating. Her throat was choked with dread. She felt as if she'd done something wrong, horribly wrong, but she didn't remember what. She touched the bandage on the back of her head. She remembered everything from before the chip was powered on. It was the afterward that was fuzzy, like a dream lost at dawn or a word on the tip of your tongue—something that's there, but not quite. She remembered the drilling, she remembered the needle, she remembered Michael Hargrove's insincere smile. But then what? Had she given him what he wanted? Had she given up her dad? Fuck. Her stomach churned; she feared she had. What about Beth, and Dan, and Garrett? Oh, fuck, what had she done? Her faced flushed. Casey slid from the bed, careful not to trample the sandwich, and went up to the door. On her booted toes, she peered out, but Martin wasn't at his window. She hoped he was all right. Casey turned and paced, back wall to door and around again. She chewed at her upper lip, tapping her hand against her thigh. What had she done? What had she said? How could it be that she didn't know? She cursed the unknown and her utter lack of control.

There was a rustling at the cell door. Casey stopped mid-pace and shuffled back until she was flush against the wall. The lock clicked open with the door following. The two guards were there, and Nurse Kristof was behind them. She put her hands up, and the guards separated to let him through. While they were all tall, the skinny nurse looked tiny in comparison. He had a tablet-sized screen in his hand.

"Promise me you won't fight, and I'll have them leave." He gestured at the guards with the screen.

She nodded, raising her hands higher. She didn't have much fight left in her anyway.

"Good," he said, waving the guards away. He spotted the sandwich on the floor. He knelt, then placed it on the bed. "You really should eat."

Lowering her hands, she shrugged. "Why are you here?"

"I need to check your vitals. You were pretty messed up when they took you away."

"Oh, c'mon. Like it matters."

"Of course, it matters, Recruit." He waved her to the bed. "Sit," he said.

"Why?" she questioned. "So you can fuck me up more the next time?" She stepped to the bed and sat.

"No one is fucking you up . . . it's all standard ICP procedure." He placed a patch on her forearm and checked his screen. Nodding, he removed the patch again.

"Drilling holes in kids' heads is standard procedure?"

"Recruits aren't usually awake for that." He pulled a flashlight from the chest pocket of his scrubs and flashed it at her eyes.

"Being asleep makes it better?"

"The chip is standard stuff." He moved on from her eyes to check the back of her head. "It helps speed up your training." He peeled the bandage down.

"What if we don't want training?"

He pressed the bandage back into place, then stepped back. "You're here. You were recruited. Why wouldn't you want training?"

"Are you fucking kidding me? Do I look like I want to be here?"

He was staring at her now. "Your documents came through just like everyone else."

"I'm in a fucking cell!" She raised her arms, exasperated. "Don't let them do this to me."

The nurse flinched, taking another step back. "Guards," he called out the open cell door.

"No," she pleaded as the guards appeared.

"Recruit," he said, holding his hand up to keep the guards outside. "I don't know why you're in here. Maybe it has something to do with your attitude, but the sooner you realize we're all on the same side, with wars to fight and borders to protect, the better off you'll be."

He turned to leave. The guards made space for him to pass.

"I'm not a fucking recruit!" she yelled as the door to her cell closed.

With desperation overwhelming her, she finally let herself cry.

8

It could have been a day, maybe two, since she'd been back in her cell. Casey really had no idea. It could have been daytime; it could have been nighttime. Judging by the number of sandwiches piling up at the base of the door—six or so—she guessed she'd been back for two. Casey lay in the bed, staring at the ceiling, the bright light inflaming her brain. She was too weak to do much more. She hadn't checked on Martin for hours, though it could have been a day. When she did have the strength to check, he hadn't been at his window when she was at hers. Casey had heard his cell door open at one point, but she thought that more of a dream. She hadn't bothered with a trip to the sink for water since the last time she'd checked the window. Depriving herself, Casey reasoned, was the only form of resistance she had. They wanted her body, and she was going to give it to them broken rather than whole.

When they came for her, she was barely aware. Locks clicked open, doors creaked, and voices hovered around her. There was talk about the sandwiches on the floor, about calling the nurse, about getting a stretcher. She felt a pinprick in her thigh. She was relieved, really, as she drifted farther away. She hoped the next time she awoke, she'd be able to remember something of herself and what they had done to her.

CHAPTER FOUR | LIVING A LIE

|

THE SCRAMBLED EGGS LOOKED DRY. Casey sighed. What little eggs were left had caked and cooled around the edges of the pan. She had been late getting to breakfast again. While her training was going great, her sleep had been a little off. She'd never been a deep sleeper—her overactive mind saw to that. But the tossing, the turning, the more chaotic-feeling sleep she'd been having since arriving at the Academy felt different. At first, she'd attributed it to barracks living, but it had been a few weeks, and it was getting worse, not better. As she settled into her life as a recruit, she had expected it would get better. Her expectations were wrong.

Unhappy with her breakfast choices, she looked past the serving table and into the kitchen. She hoped for a fresh batch of eggs. But no, the staff—in their white coats and checkered pants—had already begun breaking down. Resigned, she scraped and scooped what she could of the remaining eggs. She added an equally dry pile of home fries, a glass of juice, and an apple before stepping off the line.

With her tray in hand, Casey walked the perimeter of the

cafeteria, looking for her group. There were rows and rows of tables, each chock-full of recruits. There was some chatter, but not like their more boisterous evening meals. Six a.m. was too early for boisterous. After a moment, she picked Brian out from the sea of buzz cuts and green fatigues. He was their group leader. His familiar face and easy demeanor had been a welcome surprise when she'd arrived at orientation.

"Recruits," she said as she approached the picnic-like table.

Martin looked up and tilted his head toward the empty seat next to him. Brian, who was sitting opposite Martin, looked up as well. He scowled at her, but just a bit, as she stepped over the bench to sit. Casey didn't blame him. She deserved the scowl: Late is late. There were rules, after all. Next to Brian, Recruits Harrington and Murphy nodded good morning.

Harrington, his face round and his cheeks chubby, scrutinized her tray. "You're going to need a bigger breakfast than that to beat me, Parker," he said.

She smiled at him. They had hand-to-hand drills scheduled for right after breakfast, and they'd drawn each other as opponents. "Peter," she said. "I could take you with no breakfast and my stomach pumped."

And it was kind of true. While Peter had about fifty pounds on her, Casey had taken quickly to their balance drills. She easily found herself able to hold her own, even against her bigger opponents.

Next to her, Martin grinned. She'd taken him down yesterday, so he knew where she was coming from. As with Brian, seeing his familiar face at orientation was a relief. And, thanks to having Jennifer as their common bond, they had become fast friends. She considered herself lucky that they had signed up at the same time.

After a few bites of her dried eggs, she looked up to find Recruit Murphy—Lara—staring at her. Lara was the only other girl in their group; as such, they had taken to protecting each other. "You okay?" Lara asked quietly. "You look tired."

Casey shrugged. She had seen the bags under her eyes too. In a world without concealer, there wasn't much she could do. "Yeah," she said. "Still not sleeping great."

"Maybe you're homesick?"

"Nah," Casey said. "Just too many snorers around me." She glanced sideways at Martin.

"Don't look at me," he said, waving a forkful of potatoes at her. "I don't snore."

"You don't snore?" Peter chimed in. "You don't snore like I don't fart."

Casey nodded. "It could also be the farts."

Despite the snoring and the farts, Casey knew the homesick option wasn't out of the question. While she'd been gung-ho, relishing the chance to make something of her life, she had found herself thinking about her mom and Bruce quite a bit. She hoped they were doing okay and had reacted to her recruitment with the same pride she felt joining up. Really, though, how could they think otherwise? Joining the ICP was an honor, not just for the recruit but for the whole family.

Lara turned to Brian. "Group Leader," she said.

Brian looked up from his tray. "Brian is fine, Recruit."

"Group Leader Brian," she said, smiling, her green eyes and freckles accentuating her impishness. "Speaking of home . . . when can we get in touch again?"

He pointed to the recruits sitting at the next table. "When we level up to—"

A buzzer signaled the end of breakfast. On cue, everyone stood. Legs swung over benches, trays were lifted, conversations ended.

"Four," Brian said, finishing his sentence.

Casey looked at her tray. She choked down one more bite of eggs and stood with the rest of them. She grabbed her tray and stepped over the bench. Brian held back, letting Martin pass, then sidled up to her.

"What's up, Boss?" she asked as they joined a line to return their trays.

"You're still not sleeping?"

"Yeah," she said, looking up at him. "I'm okay, though."

His brow furrowed. His pale eyebrows joined together, forming a ridge. "Your lateness says otherwise."

Casey studied him, wanting to be defensive, but she couldn't be. Rules were rules. She looked down. "Of course. I understand."

"It's all right," he said. "But, after hand-to-hand, stop by the infirmary. Nurse Kristof can give you something."

Casey froze. Nurse Kristof. The name resonated through her; carried along on a wave of dread. What the fuck? Confused, she questioned the sudden emotional onslaught. Nurse Kristof. She repeated the name. She didn't know Nurse Kristof any more than she knew the guy who cooked her eggs. She'd never been to the infirmary; she'd never even walked by. Quickly she tried to compose herself. "You got it," she said, stepping to the garbage bin. She knocked the remaining food off her tray and noticed her hands were trembling.

"Thanks," Brian said, knocking his food off. He didn't seem to notice her sudden dismay. "I'll see you in class." He strode away, slapping Martin on the back as he passed by.

Catching up to Martin, Casey tried to shake the whole thing off. Maybe it was Brian ordering her around that she didn't like? But he'd been doing that since day one, and she'd never had a problem before. That he had mentioned the infirmary? Could that have scared her? But, again, she'd never had a problem with doctors, with needles, with the poking or the prodding. It had to be Nurse Kristof—but why? She was at a loss.

"You okay?" Martin asked.

"Yeah, I'll be fine," she said, spotting Recruit Harrington up ahead. Refocusing, she pushed the dread away and began to imagine ways to combat his stocky design. "Yeah," she said again, more for herself than Martin. "I'm fine. Let's go kick some ass."

2

Casey didn't kick ass. In fact, she had her worst outing since arriving at the Academy. That she couldn't shake her discomfort about Nurse Kristof had her unnerved.

"Thanks again for coming with," Casey said to Lara.

"Not a problem," Lara said. "It's good to venture out."

Together, they were on their way to the infirmary. She had asked Lara to come along for emotional support, making up a fear of doctors. They were in a section of the facility she'd never been in but which somehow seemed familiar. Floor-to-ceiling windows lined the hall, overlooking the busy gym below. While the hall might have been familiar because she'd seen it from the gym looking up, she was sure she'd been down this way before.

"One second," Casey said, stopping. She turned.

"What's up?"

"I feel like I've been here before." Casey studied a door on the gym side of the hall. She pointed, then started toward it.

"Infirmary's that way," Lara said, pointing in the opposite direction.

Casey ignored her.

"Your dime," Lara said, following her.

They stopped in front of the closed door. "It's a conference room," Casey said. She pressed her hand against the back of her head. Her buzzed hair had grown enough to feel soft beneath her fingers. "Twenty-two chairs around."

"Did Harrington hit you too hard or something?"

"No, no. It's just weird that I'd know that."

She opened the door; it was indeed a conference room. She counted chairs: Twenty-two was the number. Damn. She'd been in this room before. She had to have been.

"I don't think we should be in here," Lara said.

"It's okay. There's no rule against looking around."

Casey walked past the large table. Its high-gloss finish was as familiar as the number of chairs. There were windows overlooking the gym, like those in the hall. She stepped to them. Recruits were running through their drills. She was convinced she'd been at this window before. She was convinced she'd seen this view before.

But how? She didn't know.

She turned. Lara was at the doorway, shifting from foot to foot, looking up and down the hall. Maybe Lara was right—they shouldn't be in here. If a room could have a feeling, this one felt threatening.

Casey took one last look around, then joined Lara at the door. After closing it behind them, they started back the way they'd come. But with each step, Casey's legs grew heavy, and her sense of déjà vu heightened. Fuck. She'd been down this hall before—but, she realized, not willingly. She felt scared. It was a real, visceral fear but with no apparent basis. All she knew was that wherever this hallway led, she, at one point, had been determined not to go there. It was bizarre and more than a little disturbing. She felt something, something real, but it had no actual memory attached to it.

"You okay?" Lara asked.

Frustrated, Casey clenched her jaw. It was the third time she had been asked that this morning. Maybe she wasn't okay. "You know," she said. "I don't know what I am."

"You are looking a little flushed." Lara took Casey by the hands. "Deep breaths," she said, holding eye contact. "It's just the infirmary. You'll be okay."

But it felt like so much more than that.

"Yeah," Casey said, taking a deep breath. "Thanks." Despite the misdiagnosis, she was genuinely glad for the support.

Lara let go of her hands, wrapped her arm around Casey's, and led the way. They strolled; elbows intertwined. Then, as they reached the end of the hall, Casey pulled back. Across from them were a pair of swinging doors, INFIRMARY stenciled on the subway tiles above them. "I can't," she said.

"Sure you can . . . the Casey I know has been fearless to this point. Going in there is the easiest thing you've had to do yet. Think of it as an order. And we don't mess with those."

Casey stood taller. "You're right," she said. "Orders are orders."

And, somehow, this worked. Casey got her legs under her. If Brian thought this was best, then who was she to flake out? Slipping her arm from around Lara's, she pulled her T-shirt down, pulled herself together, and marched through the infirmary doors.

To their left, a scruffy man sitting at a nurse's station looked up. It was Nurse Kristof—Casey was sure of it, despite never having seen him before. Her legs went weak again. He glanced at both of them, but really, he focused on Casey. He was tall, skinny, and tired-looking, all traits she remembered, sort of. Nurse Kristof stood and meandered around to the front of the desk. He seemed wary of Casey's presence.

"Recruits," he greeted them. "How can I help you?"

Casey didn't answer. Her brain was too busy wrapping itself around the fact that she knew this guy but didn't know how. He was familiar and unfamiliar at the same time. That he couldn't take his eyes off of her wasn't helping matters.

"We're here because my friend has been having trouble sleeping," Lara answered for her.

Grunting, he waved Casey toward a bed along the far wall, past the nurse's station. There were two beds there and another two along the wall to her right. All were empty.

"You wait here," he said to Lara, pointing to a set of chairs lining the wall next to the doors.

Casey followed him to the bed. Looking over her shoulder, Lara nodded her encouragement. He motioned to the bed. "Sit," he said.

"You're the doctor?" Casey asked, knowing full well the answer was no.

"Nurse," he said, shining a light in her eyes. "Nurse Kristof."

Casey had a sudden and overwhelming desire to run. Then a memory flashed in her head, like a subliminal message cut into a movie reel. She was strapped to a chair, unable to move, and she was scared. No, not just scared . . . terrified.

"So, you're not sleeping?"

"Not well," she said, her voice cracking.

"Can't fall asleep, or waking up too much?" he asked. Then he stepped to the nurse's station.

"Waking up, bad dreams . . . just feeling kinda chaotic."

He grabbed a screen from the desk and returned. After placing a patch on her forearm, he studied the screen. "Your heart rate is up," he said. "But everything else looks okay."

Another memory flashed. The light in her eyes, the patch on her arm: She had done all this with him before. Except with this memory, there wasn't as much fear. But there was worry, resignation, and even some guilt. Absentmindedly, she raised her hand and rubbed the back of her head.

The nurse stared at her. "Are you having any other symptoms? False memories, maybe? Déjà vu?"

Shit. He fucking knew. But how? She wanted to admit to it all but thought better of it. "No," she lied. "Just the sleep."

"Okay, Recruit."

"Casey," she said. "Casey Parker." She looked for some sign of recognition, but he didn't flinch.

"Okay, Recruit Parker. I'm going to give you something to help you sleep." He walked to a glass cabinet behind the nurse's station and snapped open its door. He studied the shelves, grabbed a bottle, then poured pills from it into another smaller bottle. "Take one, once a day, and you should start sleeping fine." He handed her the bottle. It wasn't labeled.

"Are they sleeping pills?"

"Something like that."

"But it doesn't matter when I take them?"

"Take them on a full stomach. But otherwise, no."

She opened the bottle and knocked a pill into her hand. She was hoping the tablet was labeled in some way, but it wasn't. "Do they have a name?"

"It's not your concern, Recruit." He sounded a bit exasperated. "Just take them. That's an order."

An order—of course. Seriously, what was she thinking? "Thank you," she said, sliding off the bed. "I really hope they help."

And, for the moment, she meant it.

3

Casey's legs felt strong; her breaths were steady and deep. With one lap to go, she was only a pace behind Martin and ready to pass him. His legs may have been long, but hers had power. This afternoon's 10K was turning out to be her strongest one yet. She had never been much of a runner before training began but had quickly and easily taken to it. Thanks to Kristof's pills, she seemed to be taking to things quickly and easily quite often now that her sleep was back to normal. She could run, she could fight, she could even fire a gun as if she'd been born with one in her hand. It was exhilarating.

Coming up to the next curve, she saw her opportunity to pass Martin. His strides were still long, but his pace was slowing. She powered up, slipping from behind him to the next lane over and catching him with ease. She smiled, glancing his way as she matched his pace. Martin turned. "What are you smiling at?"

"You." She looked him up and down. "For someone with such long legs, you don't have much speed," she said, pulling away.

"Oh . . . That's how you play." He sped up, trying to catch her.

But Casey wasn't having it. With her legs still spry, she kicked it into high gear. Turning, she waved goodbye. He slowed a step or two. Satisfied, she steadied her stride and headed for the finish line. As she approached, she raised her arms in victory. Sergeant Cruz, their endurance trainer, smiled as she went past. She slowed and stopped. She shook out her legs, walking back toward him.

"Good work, Recruit," he said.

"Thank you, sir," she said. Bending, she rested her hands on her knees. She lifted her head to watch Martin as he finished.

"You're not the star anymore, Recruit Santos," Sergeant Cruz said as Martin crossed the line.

"I know, sir. Next time."

Casey got Martin's attention, then pointed to herself with both thumbs raised.

Martin walked circles around her, catching his breath, then rested his hand on her shoulder. "That was good," he said. "Who knew how much a good night's sleep mattered?"

"Four out of five doctors recommend it."

Together they made their way off the track and crossed the gymnasium toward the lockers. Above the entrance to the locker room, about two stories up, was the conference room. Since Casey's trip to the infirmary, she had generally managed to ignore it. Today, however, was different. There were people inside it watching them train. The facility was hosting Jennifer's father today. He was taking a mayoral-elect victory lap, and the Academy was one of his stops.

They had been told to be on their best behavior.

Casey nodded to the conference room. "They're early," she said.

Martin looked up. "Crazy that her father is coming here. You'd figure the next mayor would have better things to do."

"He appreciates what we do. That's not a bad thing."

"Did you see the dress uniforms they left for us?"

"I did," she said. "Now, *that's* a bad thing. I'll be glad when tonight's over."

"But you know they're serving steak, right?"

She had not known. "After the steak," she said, "I'll be glad it's over."

As they neared the window, she glanced up at the conference room again. Jennifer's father was at the window. Hargrove's bald head and large build were unmistakable. She did not recognize the other guests. They seemed like a mix of military and civilian. Casey began to raise her hand to wave hello, but she realized that the closer she got to the window, the more uneasy she became. She felt her face flush and her knees weaken—it was like her reaction to Nurse Kristof all over again. But why? Jennifer's father never had this effect on her before. Sure, Jennifer had her issues with him. He could be controlling, but he'd been nothing but good to her, to the ICP, and to the soon-to-be soldiers around her. He was a man to be admired, not feared.

Slowing, she dropped back from Martin's side. He turned, following her eyes to the conference room window. She was about to say something when, from his perch, Michael Hargrove looked directly at her. As their eyes met, a flash of his sneering face snapped into her head. In the image, he was sitting across from her. They were alone in the conference room, the shiny table between them and twenty-two chairs around. Fuck. She knew she'd been in there before. And, somehow, it was with Hargrove. He wanted something from her—he wanted something very badly, but she couldn't remember what. She needed some context, but she couldn't place the memory at all. Frustration gripped her. The gym began to spin. Feeling queasy, she looked away from Hargrove, focusing on Martin instead. Whatever this reaction was, she knew now her lack of sleep had nothing to do with it. Something was really wrong. Pills or no pills, her brain seemed jacked.

"You okay?" Martin asked. "You're pale as hell."

"Not okay," she answered, holding her hand on her belly.

She glanced up again. Hargrove was watching her, but now another man was watching as well. He was a little man with straight hair and glasses. Shit. She had never seen the man before but knew him immediately as Dr. Marshall, Stan's father. Then she had another flash. This time it was of a needle being threaded through the back of her head. Her stomach churned. She wanted to throw up. No . . . she *needed* to throw up. Panicked, she ran a few feet to a used-towel bin just outside the lockers. Bending, she dry-heaved. That the container smelled like armpit wasn't helping. Martin stood behind her with a hand on her back. She heaved again, dry as before.

She heard Brian asking about her.

"I don't know," Martin said.

Fuck. She did not want Brian seeing her like this. She did not want him sending her to the infirmary again. Casey stood straight, inhaled deeply, and turned. Brian, Martin, and Lara formed a semicircle around her. Sergeant Cruz and the rest of Group One passed behind them. She hoped they hadn't noticed.

"Winning too much for you, Recruit Parker?" Henderson called.

So much for not being noticed. "At least I *win*," she said, rubbing the back of her head.

Henderson tossed his towel at her. She caught it. She feigned throwing it back at him, tossing it into the bin instead. As she did, a bunch more towels flew in her direction. She blocked some, while others floated past her into the bin.

Lara picked a towel off her shoulder. "You okay?"

"Yeah," Casey lied. "The run must have been too much."

"Are you sure?" Brian asked.

"Yes," she said, stepping toward the locker room. "Some water, and I'll be fine."

Seemingly satisfied, Brian continued on. She was glad he hadn't pushed it, but she noticed that Martin still looked concerned.

"It was nothing," she insisted. "Once I get that steak dinner, I'll be fine."

4

Casey leaned forward—studying her face and questioning her sanity—in the bathroom mirror. Around her, recruits, male and female, washed, dried, and prepped for tonight's big dinner. She turned her head way to the right, looking for where a needle, or whatever it was she'd seen, could have been placed. But she couldn't see anything. Her hair had grown back to the point of covering the spot. She ran her index finger over where she thought the hole would be. She kind of felt something, maybe a divot, maybe a rough patch, but maybe it was just her imagination.

Lara—who had been getting ready in the attached dorm—sidled up next to her. "What if I don't want the steak?" she asked.

"I'm sure they'll have other options."

Lara watched her in the mirror. "You feeling better?"

"I think so," Casey said. She rubbed her hand across the back of her head. "You still have those clippers you got from Supply?"

"I thought you were going to let it grow out."

Casey tilted her head left, then right. "Maybe just a trim in the back . . . Get a bi-level thing going."

"Sure, why not?" Lara said. "Give me a sec. I'll do it for you."

"Thanks," Casey said as Lara sprinted away. She looked at the guy one sink over. Casey recognized him as a Level One, but he wasn't part of their group. He had his head down. His hair, dark and thick, was buzzed to the scalp around the sides and back. She studied his head. Above the nape, he had a small, round scar where she thought hers should be. *That's weird*, she thought. Maybe the needle she'd imagined was some kind of vaccine all the recruits got—but she would have remembered something like that. Or would she? Maybe all those nights of not sleeping well had taken a toll on her head. The guy looked up from the sink and caught her staring. He stood straight, water dripping from his face, and turned the faucet off. He was taller than expected.

"You know how you got that?" she asked, pointing to the spot.

"Got what?" he replied, drying his clean-cut face with a towel.

"That scar." She pointed again, this time closer.

He tossed the towel over his shoulder and turned his head to see the spot in the mirror. "Huh. I haven't thought about that in years," he said, talking to her through his reflection. He traced his index finger over it. "I was little—maybe three or four." He turned from the mirror to face her. "And, as my sister tells it, we were jumping on the bed, and I fell." He scoffed. "I think she pushed me."

"You don't remember it yourself, though?"

"No, not really. Like I said, I was little."

Lara arrived back with the hair clippers in hand. "Ready," she said. Then she looked to the recruit Casey was talking to. "Hey," she said. "Lara." She held out her hand.

After wiping his hands on the towel, he took hers. "Sydney," he said, nodding to Casey at the same time. He grabbed his toiletry bag, tipped it toward her, then toward the back of his head. He smiled. "I have more if you want to trade stories." He turned from the sink, rubbing his hand across the nape of his neck as he left.

"Cute," Lara said. "What stories?"

"Nothing," she said. "He had a cool scar. I wondered where he got it." Casey pointed to the clippers. "All the way down, like a zero or something." She turned her head and put her hand under the ridge at the base of her skull. "Right up to here."

Lara grabbed a stool and brought it to the sink. "Sit," she said, patting the seat.

Casey sat. Lara snapped the power on, tilted Casey's head forward, and went to work. The clippers felt cold against her skin. She closed her eyes. She wanted there to be a scar but didn't at the same time. A scar would mean she wasn't crazy, that maybe things had happened to her that she had suppressed. But the consequences of that were even more frightening. Was the ICP messing with people's brains? Just thinking this treasonous thought made her head ache.

Opening her eyes again, she saw a pair of shoes, black and shiny, step into view. She glanced up to see Brian, dressed formally for the evening, looking down. Lara palmed her head to force her still.

"Little last-minute for a haircut, isn't it, Recruit?" Brian asked.

"It's never too late for fashion, Boss," Casey said, talking to his knees.

But Brian didn't answer. Instead, he moved past her to Lara. "I checked with the kitchen. There'll be fish, too."

Lara stopped trimming for a moment. "Thanks," she said. "You didn't have to."

"These stripes have got to be worth something." Brian stepped away, then stopped. He bent to make eye contact with Casey. "Don't be late, Recruit," he said, a small grin on his face.

"I will not be," she said.

The buzzer snapped off. Lara released her hold on Casey's head and brushed the loose hairs from her neck. Standing, Casey flicked at the back of her T-shirt, then rubbed her neck and nape. "Feels good," she said. "You have a future."

"Good to know," Lara said, swinging the clippers.

Casey leaned toward the mirror.

"I'll see you inside," Lara said, brushing more hair from Casey's back.

"Sure," she said, already distracted. Casey turned her head way to the right again. Fuck. Right where she thought it would be was a pea-sized scar. She touched the raised patch of skin. It was rough. Its existence was not her imagination. She turned and leaned against the sink. The bathroom had emptied of recruits. She took a deep breath and raised her hands to her face, rubbing them across her eyes. At least she knew she wasn't going crazy.

Where she was going, though, was still an open question.

5

With the formal dinner over, the cafeteria tables had been folded and rolled off to the side. The room buzzed with excitement as recruits and officers alike waited for Michael Hargrove to join them. After being segregated for the dinner hour, this would be the soon-to-be mayor's official meet-and-greet. Casey tugged at her shirt collar and fidgeted from foot to foot. She was nervous as-all-hell and far from ready for either the meet or the greet. Next to her, Brian, Martin, and Lara argued, but Casey was too distracted to care. She wiped her forehead with the sleeve of her shirt and tried to focus.

"He won by twenty percent," Brian said, with Lara nodding in agreement next to him. "That's pretty damn impressive."

"But he couldn't carry downtown," Martin said. "He's got to be mayor for everyone."

Lara leaned in. "Who says he won't be?"

It was Brian's turn to nod.

"I didn't mean it like that," Martin said. "I was just—" He rubbed the back of his head. "He will be mayor for everyone. I never meant to imply otherwise."

"You bet he will," Lara said as cheers erupted in the dining hall.

Heads and bodies turned toward the cafeteria's entrance.

Jennifer's father had walked in, flanked by two burly guards.

Casey recognized the guards, and her knees went weak. *Here we go again*, she thought, trying to keep it together.

But she couldn't.

A memory flashed. She was on the floor with someone's knee in her back. One of Hargrove's guards was in front of her—smiling like a creep—and, Casey assumed, the other was the one on her back.

Confused and reeling, she slipped behind her friends and tried to avoid eye contact. Then, just when Casey thought she was safe, Brian broke off, walking toward Hargrove—who was working the crowd like the seasoned politician he was. Martin and Lara eagerly followed after Brian. Left alone and exposed, Casey followed too. The guard who had her pinned, in a life she didn't recall, smiled at her. She remembered the smell of his cologne—lavender and woodsy—and her stomach turned.

What in the ever-loving fuck was going on?

As she made eye contact with Jennifer's father, her face flushed and her chest tightened. She looked away, eyes darting, hoping for a way out. But all roads led through him. Lara stepped forward. Hargrove took her hand, then Brian's, then Martin's. Casey wiped her hand on her uniform pants, then held it out too. Before taking it, he looked from her back to Martin, then Brian. Hargrove beamed. "The Roosevelt Prep recruits," he said. "How great it is to see you."

Brian beamed back. "It's our pleasure, sir," he said.

She wanted to beam—she knew she should feel proud—but it wasn't going to happen. She inched forward; her legs trembled. "Mayor Hargrove," she said with a forced smile and a slight bow.

"Oh, please, Recruit Parker, don't rush it. Mayor-Elect is fine." He laughed, big and broad, while taking her hand between his. He leaned forward. "It's excellent to see you again, Casey."

She looked at his hands on hers. More images flashed in her head. She was strapped to a chair, terrified, her arms and legs unable to move. A metal cage held her head in place. She recognized this memory; it was the same one with Dr. Marshall and the needle through her head. But, this time, Hargrove was there. He seemed to be arguing with the doctor. He wanted to turn something on. She remembered fighting, and screaming, and struggling to move. She remembered hating Jennifer's father more than she'd ever hated anything or anyone. Then there was the pain, searing and real. When it subsided, he was asking her about her father. And, holy hell, she was answering. She was snitching. She told him about the headquarters. And, fuck, she told him about Beth, about Garret, and about Dan.

How could she? What had she done?

Casey closed her eyes tight. She questioned reality—not the one imposing its will in her mind, but the one in the dining hall around her. Casey no longer doubted. She knew they had majorly fucked with her head. She remembered Dan telling her about his brainwashed friend.

That was Casey now: somebody's brainwashed friend.

She opened her eyes. Jennifer's father still had a grip on her hand. She felt both loyalty and hate tearing at her. She pulled her hand from his and closed her eyes again. She was back, strapped in the chair; he was sitting next to her, looking calm and collected—self-assured in his power. "Casey, I'd like to talk about your father," he'd said. "Is that okay?"

"No, it's not fucking okay!" she yelled. Her inside voice was now out.

She opened her eyes. Lara had come over and put her arm around her shoulder.

"Sorry, sir," Lara said. "Recruit Parker hasn't been feeling well."

Casey squirmed away. "I'm nobody's fucking recruit!" she yelled, falling to her knees.

Martin rushed forward, extending his hand. Casey grabbed at it but missed, landing flat on the floor.

People crowded around her.

Someone rolled her over.

Worried faces stared down.

"Give her air," a man yelled.

Then, Nurse Kristof—cleaned of his scruff and in his formal garb—appeared at her side. She instinctively squirmed away.

Kristof waved at Martin and Brian. "Help me hold her still."

Dropping to their knees, they did as they were told.

Casey struggled in vain. In Kristof's hand was a shiny, lipstick-like tube. She thought of Beth explaining to her what it was. Had she really given them up? A needle pricked her thigh. Arms, shoulders, faces blurred. No. This could not be happening. She whipped her head from side to side. She tried to hold on, but her muscles betrayed her. She went limp.

As her eyes closed, she made a promise to remember.

As she drifted away, she promised to make things right.

CHAPTER FIVE | ALIVE AND KICKING

I

CASEY OPENED HER EYES. She was in bed, under the covers, lights dimmed to a soft amber above her. For a brief moment, everything was all right. She was a loyal ICP recruit waking for another day of training. Then, she remembered . . . she remembered everything. She had been abducted, imprisoned, brainwashed, and more. But she also remembered signing up, the abundance of paperwork, and the pride she had felt through it all. She sighed. She tried to get a grip, but she had so little to hold on to.

She attempted to sit up, but her body was dead weight around her. She willed herself up on one elbow, then two. She was in the infirmary. Her uniform, dress shoes included, was folded and stacked neatly at the end of the bed. Lara was across the room, sitting cross-legged on the middle chair in a row of five, reading from a tablet-sized screen resting on her knee. The other three beds around the room were empty. Thankfully, Nurse Kristof was nowhere to be seen. "Hey," Casey said, her voice weak.

Lara looked up. She grabbed the screen and slipped her legs off the chair. "Hey," Lara said as she put the screen down and rushed over. She put her hand on Casey's forearm. "How you feeling?"

It was a good question. She felt horrible, really. "I'm okay . . . How long have I been out?"

"A couple of hours," Lara moved to the head of the bed. "Here," she said, propping and adjusting the pillows. "Lie back."

Casey dropped from her elbows. "You're missing the party."

"It's okay. Didn't feel much like it after you—well . . ."

Casey grimaced. "Yeah, sorry."

"Nurse said they want you to stay overnight and have the doctor check you out in the morning."

Under normal circumstances, that was not the worst thing. But there was nothing normal about what was happening. She may have been let out of her cell, but Casey was still a prisoner. That needed to end. "I don't think that's a good idea."

Lara tilted her head.

Shit, Casey realized, she didn't know if she could trust Lara. On a gung-ho scale of one to ten, Lara was a Brian-level ten. But, then again, Casey had considered herself a solid eight on that scale up until a few short hours ago. Was Lara a ten because she'd been brainwashed too? Was that the case for everyone? If so, Lara, and the rest of the recruits, had a right to know. Feeling stronger, she pushed herself into a seated position. "Can I tell you something?"

"Of course," Lara said.

Casey tapped the bed for Lara to have a seat. She did, facing Casey with her knee on the bed. Casey wasn't sure exactly how to broach the subject. She decided a build-up was better than a blurt-out. "Remember how I wasn't sleeping?"

Lara nodded.

"And then how I was freaking out about going to the infirmary?"

"Yeah . . . You hate doctors."

"Well, not really," she said, fidgeting with her hands in her lap. "Here's the thing . . ."

And she told Lara everything, well, almost everything. Casey left out the part about her father, the Resistance, and her abduction being planned. There was no need to test Lara's loyalty. When she was done, she had Lara feel the back of her head.

"That could be from anything," Lara said, pulling away.

"But I'm telling you, it's not. They took me—those two goons with Hargrove—kicking and screaming into some kind of operating room, drilled a hole in my head, and stuck a fuckin' chip in me."

"I don't know," Lara said. "You're probably just mixing things up."

Casey took a deep breath, frustrated that this wasn't working. "Remember the cute guy from the bathroom?"

"Sydney? Yeah."

"He had one, too . . . in the exact same spot."

"You saw it? You're sure?"

"Clear as day."

"What about me? You're saying I'm here against my will? Sorry, but that's not possible. I've dreamt about joining the ICP since I was a little girl."

"Feel the back of your head."

Lara scoffed. "Oh, c'mon."

"You don't want to know?"

"I know I'm here voluntarily and that maybe you need to rest."

"Please—just check."

"Fine," Lara said. She reached back and began feeling around. After a moment, she stopped. "Nothing. Smooth as a baby's bottom."

"May I?" Casey asked, leaning forward.

Lara turned, switching knees, forward to back. Her hair was thicker than Casey's and had grown out some from their orientation-day cuts. She maneuvered Lara's head forward, ran her fingers through, feeling, splitting, and searching. But there was no scar. Her heart skipped a beat. It was one thing to trust Lara as a fellow abductee, but quite another as a volunteer to the cause.

"Huh," she said, sitting back.

"See?" Lara turned to face her again. "I think you just need some rest. Making up stories is not going to help you or our group as we level up."

Casey twitched with anger. Making up stories? Making up fucking stories? What she needed was for her friend to believe her, but instead, she got this. Closing her eyes, she took a moment to compose herself. If she pushed harder, who knew what Lara might do?

She could turn her in before she had the chance to plan an escape. Casey opened her eyes. "You're right," she said. "Maybe some rest. Let them check me out in the morning."

"Good," Lara said, getting off the bed. "You want me to stick around?"

"No. I'm going to close my eyes for a bit. Who knows, maybe I'll sleep."

"Okay. Nurse Kristof said he'd be back to check on you. I have a free period after Strategy. I'll come see you then."

"Thanks," she said.

Lara turned.

"Wait," Casey said, an idea brewing in her head. "Could you leave me your screen? Maybe I'll catch up on some homework if I can't sleep."

2

Casey turned Lara's screen over in her hands. During her time in training, it hadn't dawned on her before to see if she could get a message out. Casey assumed the urge to call home had been deprogrammed from her. She tapped the screen. A logo for the Academy popped up. It was a shield, an eagle, and a couple of swords. Emblazoned on banners above and below were the Academy's name, Todt Hill, and "Established 2032." An upwards swipe took her to the log-in screen. After erasing Lara's name and password, Casey entered her own. A custom screen with her reading assignments and links appeared. Tapping on the messaging icon, she debated whom to reach out to. She needed to talk to her dad, but she had no idea how to contact him. She decided to try her mom. The thought of speaking to her mom had her both excited and sad. She missed her mom, but she was also worried about her. With Bruce around, playing ICP snitch, who knew what kind of danger she was in? She typed in her mom's Web ID, not sure exactly what she would say. She tapped the screen to start writing, and a pop-up, accented in red, alerted her that her mom's number was an "invalid outside contact." Shit. Casey typed the ID again, hoping she had gotten it wrong, but no, she got the same invalid result. If not Dad, if not Mom, number three on her most-trusted list would be Jennifer. She tried Jennifer's ID. Surely the soon-to-be mayor's daughter was a valid outside contact. But that didn't work either. She needed another way.

Casey closed the messaging app and opened her browser. It dawned on her then that all her bookmarks were for military stuff. There were no band sites, no music review sites, no animals, no books, no culture. She didn't recognize the person who had saved these. Reluctantly, she gave the ICP credit for being thorough. She typed in the address for Roosevelt Prep. Success! Her school's website loaded. Its blue and white colors comforted her as she scanned the page. There was a call for volunteers to help with the year-end fashion show. The field hockey team was a stunning 3–0, and there was a Recruiting event scheduled for the new year. At that last one, she bristled. She scrolled farther down. There was a picture of Jennifer—she had her hair down and was wearing a leather jacket. It appeared as if she'd been written up after her father's win. The article's headline read: The Rebel First Daughter. Casey smiled; the light reading would have to wait. But, rest assured, whatever her best friend had to say, it was sure to get her in trouble.

Tapping on the log-in menu, Casey signed into the student portal without a problem. Although she had no assignments pending, generic school messages were still coming in. She opened a new message window and typed in her mom's ID. She lifted her hands, waiting to be thwarted. But this time, she wasn't.

"Mom," Casey typed. "Are you there?" She hit send, her heart racing.

Across the room, the swinging doors swung open. Fuck. Not now. She stuffed the screen under her pillow and dropped down, closing her eyes. She peeked. It was Nurse Kristof. He was talking on his screen and heading straight for her bed.

"No, it's fine," he said. "I shouldn't be here much longer. I just have to check up on the Parker girl real quick."

Casey kept her eyes closed and feigned sleep.

"Yeah, the one that came in all messed up. She lost it after dinner. She hasn't been sleeping."

He stuck a patch on her upper arm.

Then, from under the pillow, the screen vibrated. No. This couldn't be happening. Give me one second, Mom.

"They don't know what's wrong. Doc thinks the procedure could be slipping."

The screen vibrated again. One more second . . . just one more second.

"I know. I tried to tell him she was too messed up, but he wasn't having it."

He pulled the patch from her arm, and his voice began to fade. She unclenched.

"We'll see in the morning. He's coming in then. They're going to redo the procedure. She's looking better, so maybe this time it will stick."

Yeah. No. No sticking. Casey didn't know how, but being here in the morning was not going to happen. She cracked, then opened her eyes. Kristof was gone, the swinging doors settling closed behind him. Sitting up, she reached under the pillow and grabbed the screen. Fuck. She had missed a video-call from her mom. She tapped to return the call. It rang. Her nerves peaked. What would she say? Everything, she guessed.

The message connected, and Casey gasped. It was Bruce, not her mother, who answered.

"Casey!" he said, bright and cheery. His hair was perfect, his skin tan. "What a pleasant surprise."

Casey's pale skin, on the other hand, crawled. "Why are you answering my mother's call?"

"She's in bed. Is everything okay?"

Casey checked the time at the top of the screen. It was almost ten-thirty. Not unheard of for her mom to be in bed already—she was an early riser. But, still, why was fucking Bruce answering the call?

"Fine," she said, stone-faced. "Just had a chance to talk."

"I thought the rule was no contact for at least the first few months?"

He wasn't wrong. "Special dispensation tonight. They're lightening things up, thanks to a visit from Michael Hargrove."

"Oh, good. Are you enjoying yourself, Casey? We're both so proud."

She wanted to punch the screen. "Can you wake her?"

"No. She has a big—"

The screen froze. Bruce's square jaw was left open, and his eyes were half closed.

Fuck. "Bruce, get my mom on the fucking call!"

But no. After another second, the browser crashed. No. Just no. Then the screen itself crashed, with a spinning pinwheel to let her know. Casey lowered the screen, thinking the worst. Had someone cut her connection? Had someone powered down the screen? "Shit," she muttered, kicking the sheets off her legs and her clothes to the floor at the same time. She grunted her annoyance and slipped off the bed. However, her legs weren't having it. She collapsed to the floor, rag-doll style. She moaned, she groaned, she shifted to her knees and used the bed to lift herself up. There were cuff restraints attached to the corners of the bed's frame and half-tucked under the mattress. She was pleased not to be in them. Once on her feet, Casey stood tall, testing her bearings. She was steady but took careful steps around the foot of the bed to her clothes. The pile had stayed together but in reverse, with her shoes blunting the fall for her shirt and pants. She bent, holding onto the bed's frame, and gathered her stuff. She got dressed as quickly as her partially sedated body would allow.

It was time to go, but not without Martin. There was no question he was here against his will, and he was a good enough friend to believe her. As she headed for the exit, Casey examined the cabinets and drawers behind the nurse's station. If this was to be their big escape, some kind of weapon would be nice. She hurried behind the desk and began rummaging through the cabinets. She pulled open a drawer, and, sure enough, a range of gleaming tools greeted her, each one protected in a cushion of foam. She searched for one she could possibly use as a weapon.

Spotting what looked like a scalpel, she picked it from its bedding. A light at the bottom of the thin handle flashed green. She held the instrument between her thumb and forefinger. There was a raised section just above her thumb. She pressed it, and a blue, pulsing blade formed at the tip. She debated testing it against her own skin but thought better of it. Instead, she pulled the front of her shirt from her pants. She ran the blade across the fabric. It cut through easily, leaving a wisp of smoke behind. She wondered if she could really cut someone if it came to it. She turned the blade off and slipped the scalpel into her back pocket. She knew it wouldn't do much good against an army of recruits, trainers, and at least a few guards, but it was something . . . a very sharp something.

Stepping to the doors, she peeked out. The windows overlooking the gym were across the way. Voices carried from around the corner—VIPs, she assumed, from the conference room down the hall. She ducked back inside, afraid of being seen. But she didn't have much choice about that: The only way to the barracks, and to Martin, was past the conference room. "Fuck it," she said, pushing open the doors. So long as she could avoid Jennifer's father, his goons, and Nurse Kristof, she should be okay.

Stepping into the hall, Casey saw that the brainwashing room was next door. She remembered more, and her stomach dropped. She had gone in kicking and screaming; what part of her had come out, she still wasn't sure. She thought about the pain when they turned the chip on—the searing, excruciating, and total pain. Never again, she vowed, not only for herself but for others, too. After she was out of here and back with her father and his Resistance team, she was going to take this whole damn place down.

Determined, she continued forward. Her legs were feeling stronger by the minute. She stopped before the turn to the conference room. Looking around the corner, she saw people mingling, some in uniform, some civilian, most with drinks in their hands. The only person she recognized was Sergeant Cruz. He was talking to a woman, his arm around her shoulder, pointing to something down in the gym below. His stocky frame looked sharp in the dress uniform. She didn't think she needed to worry about him, but who knew?

She turned the corner, walking down the hall as if she belonged, but steered clear of her trainer by hugging the opposite wall.

"Recruit Parker," Sergeant Cruz called.

Shit. She slowed and half-waved.

"Come . . . meet my wife," he said.

She crossed the hall, trying to play it cool, covering the I'm-no-longer-brainwashed sign on her forehead with a loyal swagger. She tried to remember if he had been in the cafeteria when she'd had her breakdown. She didn't think so, but he had been in the gym for breakdown number one. Still, he wasn't looking at her with concern. If anything, he seemed smiley, maybe a bit tipsy.

"Recruit Parker, this is my wife, Justina."

"Hello," Casey said, holding out her hand.

They shook hands. "Nice to meet you, Recruit Parker."

"Call me Casey," she said. "Nice to meet you, too."

"Recruit Parker is one of our best," Sergeant Cruz said.

"Oh, I don't know about that." Casey fidgeted with the cuffs of her shirt. She eyed the entrance to the conference room. There was a flow of people in and out, but so far, no other familiar faces.

"Don't be modest. The ICP is lucky to have you."

Like I had much of a choice, she thought, wondering how much Sergeant Cruz, or any of these people, knew about what was going on. "It's my honor, really. I wanted to join for as long as I can remember." She tugged at the collar of her shirt, then wiped a bead of sweat from her forehead.

The Sergeant's wife studied her. "Are you feeling all right? You look a little pale."

"I'm fine, thank you," Casey said, pointing down the hall. "It's been a long day. I should get going."

They exchanged a few more pleasantries, and then Casey was on her way. Stepping back to the opposite wall, she kept her head down and her eyes on the open door to the conference room. As she went past, Casey saw Jennifer's father a few feet inside. He had a crowd around him, Nurse Kristof included, holding court. She put her hand up near her face for cover, noticing only then that it was trembling. Glancing over again, Casey glimpsed a familiar-looking woman talking to Jennifer's father. She took a few more steps so as not to be seen, then stopped, carefully staring over her shoulder. In a room full of expensive-looking people, this woman, with her flowing blonde hair and shiny jewels, looked the most expensive. Then it hit her. It was Simone from her father's headquarters—their benefactor, as Dan had called her. The one who got them stuff. What the hell was she doing here, and why was she talking to Jennifer's father? Part of her wanted to run to Simone and be saved; another part was repulsed. Either way, if she could speak to Simone, then maybe Simone could help her get a message out.

"Casey," a voice called from behind.

Startled, she jumped and turned to see it was Brian. "Hey," she said as he walked up.

"Should you be out of the infirmary?"

"Yeah. The nurse said I was good. Wanted me to sleep it off." Using Brian's broad body as cover, Casey subtly peeked around him. If Simone looked her way, she wanted to get her attention.

"You don't look good."

"It's been a long day," she said, distracted by Simone's potential to help her escape.

Brian followed her gaze. "What are you looking at?"

"Nothing," she said, snapping back, then nodding toward the conference room. "I thought maybe I should apologize."

"C'mon," he said, turning. "I'll bring you in."

She grabbed his arm. "No, no. It was just a thought. I don't think I'm up to it."

"Okay, that's understandable." He pointed down the hall in the opposite direction. "I'll walk with you."

"Sure," she said, glancing at the conference room one more time as she turned. But Simone was gone, swallowed into the crowd. Together they headed off, the chorus of VIP voices dying down behind them.

"So, what was that all about tonight?" he asked.

"I don't know. Maybe I'm not cut out for all this."

"Parker, c'mon . . . you've been doing great."

She thought about Brian's presence here. Clearly he hadn't

needed to be brainwashed, but how could he not know she was? He knew her. He's known her since fucking junior high. "Thanks, but I don't know. It's been kind of hard."

Side by side, they arrived at the elevators. She placed her hand on a screen that was jutting out at an angle between the two banks. It lit green, and an arrow, pointing up, appeared above the doors on their right.

"Hang in there," he said, looking at her. "I wouldn't want to lose you. You are an asset to the team."

An asset, yes. But an unwilling one. The elevator arrived, dinging to make its presence known. After stepping inside, Casey turned to him. "You know me, right?"

"Sure. We go way back."

"Weren't you surprised when I showed up here?"

He squinted and rolled his head. "I guess not—not really. We all find our way here for different reasons." He smiled. "I was just glad to see you'd finally come around."

She smiled back. Brian wasn't to blame for her circumstance, and she wished she could tell him the truth. A small part of her thought he, as her friend, would understand, but she couldn't risk it.

She turned, noting the panel next to the door. They had been on B-1. The barracks and gym were on B-2. She remembered being brought up from her cell. That elevator had had a G level: the ground floor, she assumed. However, this one, the recruit elevator, did not. No *escape*, she thought. How could she have not noticed that before? Again Casey marveled at how complete the ICP's mind-fuck had been.

3

She found Martin.

He was where he was every night: in the library, ensconced in a study cube, goggles on. He was there despite study hall being waived for the night. Standing in the doorway of his cube, she passed her hand in front of his face.

Pulling the goggles from his head, he frowned at the interruption. "Casey?" he questioned, seemingly surprised to see her. He started to get up. "Shouldn't you be in the infirmary?"

"Long story." She waved him down. "Shove over."

"Well, you look like crap," he said, sliding down the bench.

"I've felt better, too." She grabbed a pair of goggles from the desk in front of her. The study cubes were made for groups of four, two on each side. "Put yours back on," she said, holding hers up. "Mute it, though. We need to talk."

"What's up? Should I worry?"

They put their goggles on and were immersed in tomorrow's assignment, a virtual desert battlefield. A drone flew overhead. A battalion of soldiers in formation marched toward a city, and a grid settled over the entire image. Text across the top read: Luther's Formation. A deep-voiced narrator intoned the same. Casey tapped the side of the goggles to turn off the sound. Bombs exploded silently in the city as the mass of armaments moved forward.

"This is going to be on the test," Martin said.

"No. I'm not taking any more tests, and neither are you."

She sensed him looking at her.

"All right, what's going on?"

She told him everything. She did the best she could, piecing more of it together for herself as she went along. She told him about the couple who had followed him. She told him he had been abducted and that she had followed right after to help get him out. She explained that a chip had been put in his head, that his warm feelings for the ICP were not real, and that they had programmed him to be a soldier. She told him that Jennifer's father was behind it all. He stopped her a few times to tell her she was nuts, but Casey persisted. Again, she explained that none of what he was feeling was genuine—that they had done something to his brain, that his girlfriend's father was not what he seemed.

But Martin remained incredulous.

Casey stopped talking and took off her goggles. Then she turned to Martin and lifted his from his head.

"I signed up willingly, Casey, not at gunpoint."

"Trust me . . . I thought I did, too." She took his hand. "But those memories aren't real." She lowered her head and guided his index finger to the scar at the base of her skull. "They did some kind of surgery on us." His brow furrowed further as she ran his finger over it. "You should have one right there, too. It has something to do with the hippocampus."

Martin felt the back of his own head. "Huh," he muttered.

"Yeah." She nodded. "Huh."

"No," he said. "I got that as a kid. I was jumping on the bed—"

"And you fell."

"Yeah."

She shook her head.

"My grandmother took me to the hospital where my mom worked. I remember it like it was yesterday," Martin insisted.

She sighed. "It was more like a month ago." This was going to be more challenging than she thought.

"Come on . . . If I had been abducted, my mom would be raising holy hell about it."

"The ICP makes it all very official-looking. I saw your papers."

"No way. My mom would see through it."

"You don't question the ICP—your mom knows that. Besides, how would you even know? It's not like we can call home or anything." She tapped the table, and the Todt Hill Academy logo appeared. She flicked the screen in front of him. "Log in. Try to call her."

"No. It's against the rules."

"Fuck the rules."

Martin's shoulders dropped. "Casey, no one is forcing me to be here. I love this place and what we are doing. For the first time, I feel like I belong."

Tapping the table again, she checked the time. It was almost eleven. She needed Martin to help her, not necessarily to believe her. They could work on the believing part. If she wanted to contact Simone, she couldn't waste any more time. "Okay," she said. "I get that. I really do. I guess I'm going through something."

"Just get some rest. You scared us tonight."

"I will," she said. "But could I ask you a favor?"

"Of course. Anything."

She told him about Simone. She left out the part about her being a benefactor for the Resistance. Simone was a family friend, she was in the conference room, and Casey wanted to say hello, but couldn't after the scene she'd made. Maybe talking with a family friend would help with her head.

"Will you just let her know I'm here . . . see if she has a minute to talk?"

"Not a problem," he said.

Casey slid off the bench and out of the cube. "She's wearing a black dress. Blonde hair. Very fancy."

Martin followed. "But after, you get back to the barracks and rest."

"After is what I am looking forward to."

4

Martin was taking way too long.

Casey, sitting in the study cube, fidgeted with the goggles. She passed them between her hands. She turned them over and back again. She checked the library entrance. Two recruits, dressed down from their dress uniforms in T-shirts and fatigues, chatted by the arched doorway. She tapped on the table to check the time: ten minutes past eleven. He'd been gone almost fifteen minutes. She thought that more than enough time to get to the conference room and back.

Then Martin appeared at the library's entrance.

Relieved, she set the goggles down.

But her relief didn't last. Nurse Kristof, still decked out in his formal whites, appeared next to him in the doorway. Shit. Martin was a snitch. On the bright side, at least he wasn't with Hargrove and his goons.

As the pair walked in, she slid from the cube. She looked for a way out. With more study cubes on either side, the only way out was past them. She reached into her back pocket, pulled the scalpel out, and palmed it. She still didn't know if she had the guts to use it, but she was a lot closer to finding out.

Martin came up to her, leaving some space between himself and Kristof. "I didn't tell him what you said," he whispered, touching her shoulder. "Just that you didn't seem well."

Fine, maybe he wasn't a full-on snitch, but still.

Kristof waved her forward. "You should be back in the infirmary, Recruit."

She stepped to him. "I woke up, sir. No one said I couldn't leave."

"Are you feeling okay?"

"Tip-top," she said. "Can't I just sleep it off in my bunk?"

He studied her warily. "No, Recruit, you can't. I have my orders."

"Orders are orders, sir. I understand."

"Good." He turned. She followed. "You could have gotten me in a lot of trouble if you had been seen," he said over his shoulder.

Fuck that and fuck you.

She was willing to play brainwashed recruit, but not for a second more than she had to. "I wouldn't want that," she said, then looked back at Martin. His concern seemed genuine. She wanted to be mad at him, but how could she be?

He wasn't himself.

5

Casey suspected Nurse Kristof was drunk.

As the pair walked the halls back toward the infirmary, he babbled on about higher-ups this, Dr. Marshall that, and something about school loans. Clearly, he was worried that her leaving the infirmary had put his job at risk. As he droned on, Casey ran her thumb across the scalpel in her palm and plotted a way out. There was no way she was staying another night. Foremost in her mind was the elevator by the infirmary. That was her way to the ground floor. She would deal with Kristof—however that might be—and then get the hell out of Dodge.

At the infirmary, Kristof led her through the doors, gesturing toward the unmade bed she had fled.

"Can I pee?" she asked.

"Sure," he said, pointing to a door just beyond the nurse's station.

Stepping past the nurse, Casey debated stabbing him right there and then. But she continued on her way instead. Pulling open the bathroom door, she looked over her shoulder. Kristof had gone behind the nurse's station. His head was buried in a cabinet. She thought about making a run at him, slamming the cabinet door, maybe knocking him senseless. It would be less bloody than using the scalpel—which was a good thing—but there would be more of a chance of him fighting back. Instead, Casey moved on, closing the door behind her. Sitting to pee, she knew she wasn't ready to act. She needed a plan. She turned the scalpel over in her hands. She wished it were a gun; at least then she could threaten him with some space between them. But she had to work with what she had. She slipped the scalpel into her front pocket and finished up.

At the sink, Casey washed her hands and splashed water on her face. She held her wet palms against her eyes. The cool water felt good. She wet her hands again and ran her fingers through her cropped hair. She leaned closer to the mirror, staring into her eyes. She ignored the dark bags beneath them. "You can do this," she said, determined.

At the bathroom door, she slipped the scalpel from her pocket. She powered it on and opened the bathroom door a crack. Kristof was still at the nurse's station with his back to her. He was holding something up to the light. Small and lipstick-like, it was another tranquilizer. No fucking way was she letting herself be shot up again. She left the bathroom, even more resolute than before. With measured steps, she came up behind him. He didn't notice her. He didn't move. The tranquilizer had his full attention. She gripped the scalpel tight, then sprung toward him, wrapping her arm around his neck.

"Wha—" he grunted, struggling and trying to turn.

She pulled him back, his neck sandwiched between her forearm and bicep. The tranquilizer fell from his hands, clinked, and rolled away. His hands landed on her arm. His fingers coiled around it and pulled. But she held on tight. His Adam's apple bobbed against her skin. It was an excellent chokehold. It seemed they had trained her well.

Kristof gasped for air.

Casey flashed the scalpel in front of his eyes. "Call out, move, and you die," she said, lowering the blade to his neck. His grip on her arm loosened. She lifted her arm up under his jaw and forced his head to the side. His veins bulged just beyond the pulsing blade. She picked a spot that seemed safe, then nicked him.

That did it. Kristof held his hands out in surrender, a spot of blood on his neck. "Don't do anything stupid, Recruit," he wheezed.

"No," she said. "Stupid's what you won't do."

She loosened her grip slightly. So far, so good. She looked over her shoulder at the bed. Lara's screen was on top. The sheets lay crumpled at the bottom. Then she remembered the restraints. Perfect. She could tie him down and go.

"You're going to walk with me," she said, moving backward.

"Recruit," he said, trying to look behind him.

Casey tightened her grip again. "Don't call me that. I'm nobody's recruit."

He nodded in her bent arm. "It didn't stick. Did it? You remember."

She stopped their awkward dance. "I remember," she said. "I remember everything."

"Oh," he said, his body deflating. "It must be very disorienting."

To say the least, yes. She had false memories piled on top of real ones, each vying for recognition and stuffed in her brain. "It's fine. I'm fine."

Casey jerked him backward, looking behind her at the bed again. She needed him restrained, but she didn't want to let go. She decided to improvise. Kicking his legs out from under him, she twisted him around. He grunted and landed on his knees facing the bed, his nose inches from the bed frame. He struggled. She pressed a knee into his back. "Stop," she said, flashing the blade. She turned his head toward the leather restraint at the top of the bed. "Buckle yourself in," Casey ordered, digging her knee deeper into his back. She pressed his cheek against the metal frame.

"Okay," he said, holding his hands out to surrender again.

Casey let up on her grip, keeping the blade close to his neck.

He put his left hand into the restraint. He buckled it with his right.

"Tug on it," she said.

He did. After a few pulls, Casey was satisfied. She let go of his neck and took hold of his free arm. Using her body as leverage, Casey pinned his arm against the frame.

"Please," he said. "What's the point here?"

She turned off the scalpel and slipped it into her back pocket. "The point is I'm leaving." She grabbed his wrist and forced it into the restraint at the foot of the bed. She slid its strap into the buckle and tightened it. "There is no way I'm letting you fuck with my head again." She tugged on his arm. He felt secure. She felt the same, for the moment, anyway.

"The only way this ends, Recruit, is with you back in that chair or dead."

Using the back of his head for leverage, she pushed herself up and his face down into the bed's frame. "I said . . . don't call me that."

She stepped back. She took a few deep breaths to steady herself. Kristof looked like some kind of Jesus, kneeling with his arms spread, the weight of an invisible cross on his back.

"It's not too late," he said, turning to face her as best he could.

She needed for him to shut up. Grabbing the sheet from the bed, she rolled it, swung it over his head, and forced it into his mouth. She tied the ends tight behind his head. She stepped back again, looking over her shoulder at the door. That's it. It's time to go. She found herself a bit excited. She would track down her dad, and, fuck it, she'd go see her mom—ICP list or not. Maybe even go see a band. But, to do anything, she realized, she needed money. Having been cashless for weeks, she'd forgotten the basics. Moving forward, she leaned in. "Your screen," she said to him.

Kristof made mouth noises and lowered his chin toward his front pants pockets. Not thrilled with the level of intimacy but determined nonetheless, she reached down and patted his right pocket. It was empty. Then she patted left and scored. Wedging it out, she held it to his face, unlocking it. His wallet app was docked at the bottom of the home page. She tapped on it. He had fifty bucks in cash. Hopefully, that was plenty to get her home. She checked the screen's settings and, after another pass in front of his face, she set the defaults to keep it unlocked. She backed away, sliding the screen into her back pocket. She smiled.

Yeah. Excited was what she was.

Casey turned and bolted for the doors. Pushing them open, she checked right, then left. She was good to go. Out and to the left, she stayed close to the wall and away from the overlook windows. She fought the urge to flat-out run. The elevator was only a few hundred feet away. The hallway beyond was a dead end. She got to it, then checked over her shoulder, across the gym's airy expanse, to the conference room. There were a few stragglers inside, none of whom were Jennifer's father. She turned to the screen angled next to the door. Closing her eyes, she put her right hand on it.

A rude tone snapped her straight.

A red glow surrounded her hand.

ACCESS DENIED flashed above her fingers.

Shit. She tried her left hand but got the same results.

She turned, shoulders slumped, profanities running through her head. She hadn't counted on segregated elevators. But she should have. She wasn't sure what to do next. *Kristof*, she thought, *he would have access.* She started back the way she came, but faster this time. She reached into her back pocket for the scalpel. Casey was going to need his help, but she doubted he'd give it willingly. What she really needed was his hand. She turned the blade on, holding it low and close to her leg. It was do-or-die time.

And she was fully prepared for do.

6

Back in the infirmary, Casey stood over the nurse. She'd just gone over his choices, and Kristof was debating her limited-time-only offer to not slice off his hand in exchange for his help. She assumed it was an offer he couldn't refuse, but his hesitation revealed otherwise.

"No," he said. The sheet she'd stuffed in his mouth was now more ascot than muzzle. "I don't think you'd do it."

"Are you kidding me?" she questioned, waving the scalpel at his face. "You don't think your programming covered that?"

"Your values are your values . . . the procedure doesn't change that."

Casey shook her head. She didn't have time for talk. Turning off the scalpel, Casey slipped it into her front pocket. She grabbed the sheet and forced it back into his resistant mouth. She unbuckled her belt, sliding it from its loops. "My morals may stop me from killing you," she said into his ear, "but maiming you, they have no problem with."

But they kind of did. The tremble in her hands served as proof.

Ignoring her shakes, she slid the belt around his outstretched bicep, pulling the strap through its buckle. She tightened it as tight as it would go. He'll be fine, she told herself. The loss of a hand was nothing compared to what he was complicit in. He watched her as she adjusted and tightened. He seemed more incredulous than scared. How was he so sure she wouldn't follow through? She wasn't. Did he know something she didn't? Had the procedure revealed something about her? It was true that she wasn't a fan of blood. It was also true that she took no pleasure in hurting people. Had these facts been accounted for when writing the new code for her brain?

Fuck. It was all too much.

Satisfied that her makeshift tourniquet was sufficient, Casey pulled the scalpel from her pocket. She turned it on, studying the sizzling blade for a moment. Then, she remembered the tranquilizer. That's it. She could put him under. That would help. She looked back to the nurse's station. She remembered the canister had rolled, but she didn't know where. She walked toward the desk and saw the shiny tube peeking out from under it.

Kristof must have remembered the tranquilizer, too, as he began to struggle. She could make out a muffled, repeated "no" coming from his stuffed mouth. Casey ignored him, bending to pick up the injector. Straightening, she inspected it. It looked okay, no worse for wear. With her thumb, she pressed at a ridge on one end. A tiny needle emerged from the other. The idea of cutting off a man's hand was getting more palatable by the moment.

With the tranquilizer in her left hand and the scalpel in her right, she stepped to him. Casey aimed the needle at one side of his neck and the scalpel at the other. "Not so sure now, are you?"

"Okay," he yelled through the balled sheet, the veins in his neck and forehead bulging.

Leaning forward, she studied his face. His eyes were wide, along with his pupils, and his forehead sweaty. *Better*, she thought, her confidence growing. She pressed at the bottom of the tranquilizer. Its needle descended, and she slipped it into her pocket. She jerked the sheet from his mouth. "You will help me? No games?"

"I will help you. No games."

"It's not just a hand you'll lose after this."

He raised an eyebrow. "I'm not giving my hand or my life for this place . . . I don't care that much."

Casey appreciated his ambivalence. It was a stance she could believe in. "Fine," she said, loosening the belt and slipping it from his arm. "But if you try anything . . ." She threatened him again with the scalpel.

"I will try nothing," he said. "Let's just end this. I need to get home."

"Yeah, me too."

Promises of help or not, Casey still wanted to keep Kristof restrained in some way. She looked at the cuff holding his left arm down. Lifting the mattress, she found that the leather strap that was attached to the cuff continued to about the middle of the bed's frame—it would have to do. With the scalpel, Casey cut the leather strap at its source. She had about a foot to work with. Keeping his wrist in the cuff, she strung the strap around his belt and into the belt loops of his pants once and then again, until his left hand was pulled flush against his waist. She tied it all up in a nice knot.

"This isn't necessary," he said as she tugged on his wrist. "I'm not going to fight you."

"I don't trust you," she said. Satisfied that her handiwork would hold, Casey switched to Kristof's right wrist. This time she left a bit of slack so he could reach the elevator's scanner.

She moved behind him. "Okay, stand up, and keep your back to me."

He did as he was told.

She grabbed hold of the back of his shirt and pushed him towards the door.

"It's not going to work like this," he said over his shoulder. "We need to be natural. The more you look like my guest for the night, the better off we'll be."

She stopped, pulling back on his shirt. "I don't need to look like anything. We're not going far."

"The sub-elevator?" He tilted his head to the left.

"Yeah, I guess." It was the only way out she knew.

"I don't have access to that one. I use the staff elevators." He tilted his head in the other direction.

"You're stalling. You were in my cell."

"No, I'm helping. I was always with security . . . they're the ones with access."

Shit. "You have got to be kidding me." She stepped in front of him, keeping the scalpel pointed at his abdomen. She pressed a finger above her eye. Her head was starting to hurt.

"Are you taking your pills?"

She lowered her hand. "This morning, yeah."

"You need to keep taking them."

"So I can forget again? No way."

"You're not going to forget. Once the procedure fails, it's done."

She waved him off, not appreciating the distraction. "So, how would you get us out?"

"Like I said, we need to be natural." He nodded toward a door behind the nurse's station. "My locker is just through there. I have a coat you could wear—a hat, too. For me, my uniform jacket is in there. If you're not going to untie me," he said, lifting his bound hands as far up as they would go, "you could at least drape it over my shoulders."

Casey glanced at the locker room door. "Go," she said, waving the scalpel.

He led the way but stopped when he reached the drug cabinet. "You should take pills with you," he said. "It's the methylphenidate, second shelf, all the way on the left. They'll help balance you."

"I don't need to be balanced."

"You're going to need something, trust me."

"Trust you? You let them drill a hole in my skull, stick a needle through it, and implant a fucking chip in my brain—and you want me to trust you?"

"You do have a point."

"I have lots of points." She pushed him forward. "Now, get your stuff, and let's get me the hell out of here."

7

The not-so-happy couple strolled down the hall.

Casey and Nurse Kristof were in a section of the facility she did not know. Signs attached to cinderblock walls directed them to the kitchen, the laundry, and the staff lounges. It was all very behind-the-scenes. As they walked, she kept a firm grip on his bound right hand. The jacket he wore over his shoulders had him looking very European and a little out of place, but it did the job of concealing his restraints. On the other hand, Casey felt very much at home in his black pea coat with its collar up and his black knit hat, its brim low. In her right hand was the scalpel. She kept it powered on and ready to go. Only if someone chose to pay close attention would they see the blue glow of its blade peeking out from beneath her upturned sleeve.

"This way," he said, taking her in the direction of the kitchen.

The lingering smell of steak had Casey's stomach grumbling. Kitchen staff and waitstaff passed around them; no one paid them any mind. She realized Kristof could have acted out at any point, but he did not. The pull of going home for the night was seemingly greater than that of being a hero. While she didn't want to let her defenses down, she reluctantly admitted he was being helpful.

"It's right past there," he said, jutting his chin forward.

As her escape became more likely, she worried about leaving Martin behind. He knew the truth now, and whether he believed her not, it was going to mess with his head. She promised herself that she would come back for him. She thought about Lara and their brief but budding friendship. She sighed, sad that loyalty to the ICP had come first, but also acknowledging that brainwashing came in many forms. She hoped to explain herself better one day, maybe with proof in hand.

Past the scurrying staff, a uniformed man exited the elevators at the end of the hall. Kristof tugged at her hand, stopping in his tracks.

"Shoot," he said.

"What?"

"Shoot," he repeated and began nudging her toward the wall. "That's my C.O. I need my hand. I have to salute."

"You better not be—"

"No time." With his left shoulder, he pinned her against the wall. He nuzzled his face into hers. "Let me out, now," he whispered, holding out his bound right hand.

Kristof smelled fresher than she imagined, and his skin was baby-bottom soft. She fought to keep her focus. Was he trying to pull something? Could she trust him? But there was no time for a debate. Casey grabbed his wrist, slipped her thumb under the cuff to allow some space between the leather and his skin, then sliced the cuff clean through. The smell of burnt leather wafted up. He shook his hand free, and the cuff, still looped to his pants, swung between them. She tried to catch it but was too slow. It dangled dangerously from his belt.

Together they turned toward his approaching C.O. Her heart raced. If he was going to turn her in, now was his chance. She kept her hip plastered against his to hide the swinging cuff behind them. Through a forced grin, Casey whispered, "You mess with me here,

I'll cut you, I'll cut him, and I'll drag your dying body over to the elevator and leave you to bleed out."

"I know you will," Kristof said through his own forced smile.

Casey didn't recognize the approaching officer. He had on a dress uniform, just like the rest of them, except his was adorned with a few rows of medals across his large chest.

Kristof saluted.

The man saluted back and stopped.

No chitchat. Please. No chitchat.

"Sir," Kristof said. "Enjoying the evening?"

There was chitchat.

"I am," his C.O. answered, grinning and leaning forward. "So much so, I'm looking for seconds."

He seemed drunk. It seemed everyone was drunk tonight except her.

"You're in the right place, sir," Kristof said. "Kitchen's right back there." He pointed behind them.

"Excellent," the man said, looking past them.

Together, Casey and Kristof began to step away.

"Not so fast," his C.O. said. "This must be the Alex you speak so highly of?"

Kristof nodded enthusiastically. He looked at her, smiling. "Yes, this is," he said. "Couldn't keep her from meeting the new mayor."

"Good to meet you." The man held out his hand.

Casey began reaching for it, then stopped. She almost forgot about the scalpel. Instead of going through with the handshake, she brought her hand down, tapped off the blade, and wiped her hand on her hip. "Sweaty," she said as she repeated the motion. On this second wipe, Casey slipped the scalpel into her pocket.

"Sorry," she said, raising her empty hand to meet his. "Nerves." At the same time, she saw Kristof looking at her hand. Fuck. She'd given him an opening.

"Sir!" he yelled, jumping from her side and throwing the jacket from his shoulders. His bound arm was now fully exposed.

She sprang at him.

There was no fucking way this was going to fall apart now.

Casey grabbed him around the neck with her left arm and grabbed the scalpel with her right. She whipped her leg around, knocking him off his. She lit the blade, dragging him backward toward the elevator. "Don't move!" she yelled at his C.O.

The decorated officer appeared baffled, then slowly raised his hands, beginning to catch on. A startled chef behind him ran into the kitchen. A waiter froze, a tray of coffee cups and saucers rattling on his raised and flattened hand.

"Sir!" Kristof yelled again, clutching at her arm with his free hand.

"You," she grunted, choking him hard, maybe too hard. "Stop it, or die."

Casey looked behind her. The elevator was only a few feet away. There were two sets of doors with the panel in between. Turning back, she saw the C.O. had moved closer. "I will kill this man!" she yelled, meaning it more than she'd ever meant anything before.

The C.O. stayed put.

As they reached the doors, she spun Kristof to get his free hand near the panel. "Touch it!" she ordered. He did. It lit green—it lit a glorious, glorious green. The doors on her left slipped open; the elevator car was empty. Casey tossed Kristof aside and hurried inside. She turned, keeping the scalpel front and center. Kristof was on one knee, starting to stand. A screen next to the door gave her three choices: B2, B1, G. She tapped on G, and the doors began to close. Just beyond the doors, the C.O. popped into view, baffled again. Then, inch by inch, as the doors closed, his window of opportunity to stop her closed along with them.

Casey stepped back as the elevator started up. *Holy shit,* she thought, trying to make sense of it all. She hadn't thought that Kristof was going to turn on her. Her chest heaved. They had been doing so well. She continued back until she was up against the wall. In her trembling hand, the scalpel was still up and ready for a fight. Letting her guard down, she leaned against the wall and lowered the blade. She rested her free hand on her knee.

That's it. She was on her way out.

What she would find up top was anybody's guess.

8

The siren should have been expected, but she jumped just the same. The sound was piercing, especially in the elevator's confined space. Casey pulled Kristof's cap down over her ears, hoping to muffle it. She was somewhere between level B-1 and G, with no idea how long it took to get to G. She hoped it would be soon, really soon. With the scalpel lit, she positioned herself at the doors, ready for when they opened. The air grew crisper by the second. She was glad for the coat and hat.

The elevator stopped. She made a plan to run and be wily. Casey was confident, glad to use their training against them. The doors opened. There was a sidewalk, then a crosswalk, then parked cars— lots of them—but no ambush. She was in a garage, not underground but covered. She ran, checking both ways. To her left, a line of lim- ousines and town cars waited for their VIPs. To her right, there was more garage. Ahead, past the rows of cars and beyond the low-slung roof, floodlights illuminated a well-manicured, snow-topped hedge.

That was her goal.

Buoyed, she sprinted. There were shouts from behind her. She turned to see two security guards giving chase. The ambush had arrived a few seconds late; however, the bullets didn't. With a spray of concrete, one ricocheted off the ground next to her, on her left. The gunshot sound itself followed, echoing through the garage. She dove the opposite way behind a row of cars. Righting herself, she serpentined between the parked cars. More gunshots, the crash of shattering glass, and the dull thump of fiberglass absorbing metal met her ears. Casey slid across the hood of a red sports car, letting herself drop between it and the car next to it. She stopped with the outer boundary of the parking garage a row away.

Yellow arrows, painted on the floor, pointed in both direc- tions. One set of arrows led to a quaint, red-brick booth outside. Its windows were trimmed tastefully in white, and a pair of red- and-white striped traffic arms projected from each side. An armed guard emerged from it and ran towards her. If she crossed here, he'd have a clear shot at her. Instead, she backed out, stayed low, and ran parallel to him in the opposite direction. The original two guards had stopped shooting. She could hear them a row away. She stopped, resting her hand on a rear bumper, waiting for the guard from the booth to pass. When he did, she bolted from between the cars and out behind him.

He turned, shouting, "Stop!" But he was too late.

She slipped between the last row of cars, hopped a low-slung wall, and ran into the floodlights with the snow crunching beneath her feet. Letting her momentum take her, she dove over the hedges just as a bullet whizzed past. With her arms extended, she cleared the hedges, the front of her coat just brushing the snow. Casey landed hands first, then shoulders, rolling in the snow and random brush. She came to a stop at a tree line that revealed a steep, woodsy incline behind it. Fuck. Going down was her only choice as more shots and shouts followed her.

So, down she went, slipping and sliding—first on her feet, then on her ass, then back on her feet. There was just enough light, moon or otherwise, to see her frenetic way. She tried to protect her face with one hand while attempting to slow her momentum with the other. Tree limbs, rocks, and who-knew-what-else pelted her on the way down. The snow helped soften the blows, but not by much. Then something ripped and cut at the back of her thigh. She grunted and growled from the pain. *Blood*, she thought, warmed the spot. After a few more yards, she hit bottom . . . bottom being a paved road cutting through more trees and more hill on the other side. A faded broken-yellow line separated one way from the other. Casey sat. The road was wet with melting snow. Her exhaled breath, expelled in rapid bursts, hung in the chilled air. The quiet around her was noticeable after the excitement above. Thankfully, no one had followed her down, though that didn't mean they'd given up the chase.

She grabbed at the back of her thigh. She was definitely cut, but she couldn't tell how badly. She pressed the flap of her torn pants against the wound and got to her feet. Through the trees, Casey saw the glimmer of lights below. She was high up but not in the middle of nowhere. She decided to take the road for a bit, although she was quite sure it wouldn't be safe for long. She walked downhill, testing her leg and the rest of her. She felt okay—beat up, but okay. She jogged, still testing, still feeling okay. There was a clearing ahead on the left side of the road. Casey crossed to it, and immediately the where-am-I part of tonight's equation was solved.

"Fuck," she muttered, stepping off the pavement and onto a patch of snow-covered gravel. She hadn't been too far from home after all, and she didn't need a map to know where she was. Glittering in the distance, over suburban rooftops and trees, was the majestic Verrazzano-Narrows Bridge. Its giant arches and swooping cables made it a favorite of hers. From the elevation and angle, Casey knew she was on the Staten Island side, up in the hills—Todt Hill, she assumed, based on the name of the academy behind her. She was so close to home, she could practically walk, though a bus or the ferry would be better. Casey thought of her mom. She thought of the hug she would give her. Overwhelmed, she wiped at her eyes as a light snow began to fall.

Then, from above, she heard a buzzing.

Fuck.

Having an idea what it was, she bolted behind the nearest tree. She stood still with her hands chest high and pressed against the rough bark. Carefully, she peeked out. As expected, a drone—black and menacing—hovered in the clearing. It had four blades attached to an angled, militaristic-looking body, and a spotlight beamed from the same. She turned, pressing her back against the tree, willing herself small. If the thing had a heat sensor, she was screwed. On her right was the road she'd just come off. On her left was another steep drop. She studied the road, contemplating a path through the trees to get to it. No, she thought, *just wait for one more second, and the drone will move on.*

But it didn't.

Instead, its white spotlight switched to green.

She was screwed.

A spray of bullets hit the tree. Casey flinched with each shot. Splintered wood flew past her on both sides. She eyed the steep drop; it appeared no worse than the last, but still, the road seemed smarter. Hoping to throw off the drone's heat sensors, she knelt while keeping her back pressed up against the tree—its bark grabbed and pulled at her coat. She scooped two handfuls of snow, then pressed the packed snow against her face and neck until the cold burned. She rubbed the remainder over her hands. When the gunfire stopped, she sprang from behind the tree, staying low as she raced to the road. She turned to glimpse the drone shooting skyward, its eerie green spotlight following her from above the trees. She skidded to a stop at the edge of the clearing as bullets pelted the road from above.

Shit.

She turned, then juked through the trees and up to the drop-off. Down was, once again, her only choice. She searched for a clear path, or the clearest she could find, then stepped off, digging her heels and leaning back to keep her balance. The drone was still overhead, seemingly following the road and not her. Her balance didn't last long as she began slipping from her feet to her ass and back again. The gash on the back of her thigh screamed for relief as more snow, more leaves, more branches, and twigs tortured it.

At the bottom of the drop was another road and another drop beyond it. Landing squarely on her feet, Casey sprinted across the road, her adrenaline negating the pain. The drone was still above, circling back, hopefully seeking but not finding. Off the road, she looked for a safe place to descend. She found a path and repeated her slide again. This time, her pace was controlled and more fully upright as the incline was not as bad. Nearing the bottom, the hill flattened out into a backyard. After that came a tarp-covered pool, a patio, and a large, fancy house.

At least someone was living their best life.

Glancing up, she spotted the drone. It was still one plateau above her. Also spotted: headlights, two pairs of them, speeding down the road. They were still closer to the Academy than to her, but that distance wouldn't last.

Landing in the backyard, Casey had an idea. She pulled the scalpel from her pocket and ran to the edge of the pool. Dropping to her knees, she turned the scalpel on, then cut a swath through the pool's tarp. She tapped the scalpel off, tugged at the sleeves of her coat and shirt, then dunked her bare arm through the flap in the tarp. The water was cold, freezing even, but not frozen. Her idea, as unpleasant as it would be, was to get in the fucking pool. If she wanted to lose the drone, the ice-cold water was the way to do it.

Looking over her shoulder and up the hill, she saw the drone and the headlights getting closer. Resigned, Casey turned on her knees and gathered the coat into a ball. Taking a deep breath, she shimmied her way backward under the sliced tarp. She held the coat out in front of her. Despite wearing shoes, her feet instantly cramped. But she kept going. The cold was biting, like pins and needles, or maybe more like nails and more nails. Casey closed her eyes tight, trying to will the pain away. On the bright side, the wound at the back of her thigh, now numbed, felt great. Then she dropped in the rest of the way . . . torso, shoulders, neck. Gasping, she couldn't catch her breath. Her body tensed and knotted. She floated, arms up to keep her coat dry. Her feet felt for the bottom, but there was no bottom.

Casey was in the deep end.

Her breaths came in short, erratic gasps. She fought the urge to panic. Instead, she concentrated on the drone as it buzzed closer and closer. It was overhead. She stayed still, perfectly still, listening in the darkness, her body getting accustomed to the cold.

Then the buzzing moved away, farther and farther. Except for the lapping of the pool's water, there was silence. Casey gave it a beat, then waded back to the hole in the tarp. She pushed through, coat first, then placed the garment next to the pool. Casey listened for one more moment, felt it was safe, then braced her hands at the edge of the pool. She lifted her popsicle body from it, flopped out, then rolled away from the edge.

She shivered uncontrollably. She imagined never feeling warm again.

Hands shaking, Casey unbuttoned her shirt. Sitting up, she took it off and threw the coat on. It was something—not warm, per se—but something. Shifting to her knees, she stuffed her sopping shirt into the coat's left pocket as she pulled Kristof's screen from the right. The screen looked dry and intact. Pleased, she scouted for danger. For the moment, at least, she seemed alone.

But she was sure it wouldn't stay that way for long.

Teeth chattering, Casey stood. She tugged at her wet pants, trying to separate them from her body. Her toes were still cramping inside her wet shoes. She stomped on them, soaked and sloshing, one foot, then the other, hoping to get them to relax. Casey scoped out the backyard. The grounds were fenced in on two sides. The fence on the left side stopped against the stately house, while the right side continued past it. She headed to the right, around the pool and onto a large patio with a fire pit at its center. As she stepped closer to the back of the house, a pair of floodlights lit the deck. "Shit," she grumbled, ducking, then sprinting out of the light. She kicked up fresh layers of snow as she ran.

Looking for cover, she fled toward the fence, traipsing through a dying flowerbed to get there. Despite the flood of light, the house itself stayed dark. She bent low, running between the fence and a row of skinny, bare trees. She watched the house. Nothing stirred. Casey stopped where the house did and knelt behind a bush. Shivering, she wrapped Kristof's coat around her as tight as it would go. An overexposed, snow-covered lawn stood between her and the street.

Then, down that street, maybe three or four houses away, a spotlight burst from the sky. It was the drone, and it had a man caught in its beam. The man—bundled from the cold but frozen in place—had his hands up, a snow shovel in one of them. The headlights came next. Two camouflaged Hummers sped past Casey, then screeched to a halt a few feet from the scene. Soldiers, four of them, poured from the vehicles and surrounded the surely confused man.

Putting her guilt aside, Casey recognized her opportunity. She slipped from behind the bushes and bolted—her shoes wet and heavy—across the lawn. She stopped, kneeling next to a parked car. The soldiers had lowered their weapons.

She didn't have much time.

Staying off the road and skimming next to the cars parked along it, Casey sprinted as fast as her thawing body and wounded leg would allow. Up ahead, a side street intersected with the street she was on. She bolted across the road. The drone's spotlight grew as it hovered higher. The soldiers were packing it in. Past the corner, Casey was out of sight again. She ran faster now, gaining some distance. She listened for the drone. Thankfully, the sky was quiet. What she needed was civilization. She needed to blend in.

She grabbed Kristof's screen, swiping and tapping until she got to his maps. She located herself and then what she was after: Richmond Road, a main thoroughfare with buses and businesses and people.

That was the cover she needed, and it wasn't too far away.

9

"You could take an anarchy ferry," Amir, the deli guy, said.

Amir was standing behind a counter, bagging Casey's stuff. It turned out civilization also included a twenty-four-hour deli with a helpful deli guy behind the counter.

"What's an anarchy ferry?" Casey asked, keeping an eye on the door. Cradled in her hands was a hot cup of coffee.

"Locals with boats. With the proper ferry gone, they take people across." He held out the plastic bag by the handles.

Switching the coffee to her right hand, she took the bag from him. She had bought a pre-made turkey hero, a bottle of water, and a bag of peanut M&Ms for her trek home.

"The new piers aren't far," he continued. "And twenty, twenty-five dollars should get you downtown." Amir gestured to a screen next to him on the counter. It had been flashing lottery numbers when she walked in. Now it had a WANTED poster with her face on it. "Plus, I doubt any of those guys would turn you in. It's not like what they're doing is legal."

Smiling, she nodded her approval. That Amir had scoffed when her photo popped up had been a good sign. That he considered any enemy of the ICP a friend of his was better—but it was the fact that he was actively helping her that really gave her hope. She'd been cut off from regular people for so long, she'd forgotten that not everyone believed in the ICP.

Casey placed her coffee on the counter just as a man, snow dusting his shoulders, entered the store. She turned to face away, adjusting the peacoat's collar higher to conceal her face. The man stamped the snow from his boots, then plodded past her and down one of the aisles. Casey angled herself toward the door. Reaching into her coat, she took out Kristof's screen and tapped it against the pay terminal.

"Would you like cash back?" Amir asked, keeping an eye on his new customer as he did so.

"Do the anarchy ferries have terminals?"

He smiled. "No terminals." He paused, studying his own terminal, then leaned forward. "And, unless you want more trouble, Mr. John D. Kristof," he whispered, "you should probably get rid of that screen, too."

She shook her head—rookie mistake. "Thanks," she whispered back. "This enemy-of-the-people stuff is new to me."

Still leaning forward, he pointed to a prayer rug next to the deli's entrance. "Trust me . . . you get used to it."

"I'm sorry that you have to," she said, pocketing the screen, then picking up her coffee.

Amir gave her directions to the makeshift piers. They didn't seem far, and with an abandoned hospital as her main landmark, the directions didn't seem complicated. From the back of the store, Amir's other customer emerged. He had a six-pack of something in one hand, a bag of chips and a carton of milk in the other. Casey whispered a rushed "Thanks" to Amir and left the store before the man reached the counter.

Outside, the snow was starting to accumulate. There was maybe an inch on the ground and on the parked cars at the curb. Casey hurried to the corner, gulping her cooling coffee, with the plastic bag swinging from her hand at her side. She was feeling warmer—partly from the coffee but mostly because of Amir. When she could, she'd write him a good review. At the corner, Casey tossed the cup in the trash. Slipping Kristof's screen from her pocket, she powered it down and threw it away as well. If she didn't kill the nurse the next time she saw him, she'd be sure to thank him.

Next to the trash can was a LinkICP kiosk. Her WANTED poster cycled through amongst the ads. In the photo, she still had hair, but Casey couldn't place the picture. She sighed, trying to grasp how different her life would be now. That she even thought she could visit her mom, let alone leave Amir a review, was so fucking naive it was beyond her. Forget about school, or seeing shows, or anything, really.

Her jaw clenched. She hadn't asked for any of this.

Checking for cars, she crossed against the light. Once across, she dug into the bag for the sandwich. She hoped eating something would help her insides warm even more. But then, from behind her, a siren wailed. Panicked, she flattened herself against a chain-link fence away from the curb. Her heart stuck in her throat as an NYPD patrol car, its lights flashing, drove by. The car slowed to a stop in front of Amir's deli. Two cops got out—their hands resting near their holstered guns—and went inside.

Fuck. She fought the urge to run toward the danger. Instead, she slunk away from it, along the fence, hating herself as she did. Amir hadn't asked for trouble, and neither had the snow-shoveling guy, but they'd gotten some because of her. And it just wasn't fair. Resigned, she started running, careful not to slip on the snow. She glanced over her shoulder to see if the cops had caught on. They hadn't, but she wished they had.

At least it would have taken the heat off Amir.

CHAPTER SIX | PICKING UP THE PIECES

|

THE ANARCHY FERRY WAS PRETTY MUCH as advertised. The pier itself looked to be part of a much longer structure with only the first few pilings still above water. There were three small boats tied up to it. When the operator of the third boat saw Casey, he waved her forward to the first boat in line. Once there, a bundled-up captain asked for her destination—downtown or midtown—then took her money accordingly. As Amir had said, the captain asked no questions. But, as he directed her to the cabin below, he did request she not bleed on his furniture. Casey agreed, self-consciously covering her wound with her hand as she walked.

Once below, she saw she was alone, and the space was anything but anarchic. There was a galley, a built-in sofa, and a large screen on the wall opposite those. Printed signs welcomed her to coffee, bottles of water, and use of the restroom. Content with her deli purchases and not needing to go, Casey chose none of the options. Instead, she grabbed a bundle of paper towels from a roll over the galley's sink, pressed the wad against the back of her leg, then took a seat on the steps she'd come down from. Closing her eyes,

148 | MARC DANIEL ACRICHE

she rested her head against the wall. She let her mind drift, and thought of her mom, hoping she was ignorant of her daughter's situation. Then she thought of her dad and hoped for the opposite. With Casey now a wanted fugitive, he had to already know the situation she was in, and she hoped he was expecting her.

A thumping on the cabin door above her startled her awake. Shit, she hadn't meant to fall asleep. The warmth and the boat's rocking must have put her under. Climbing the short staircase, she opened the cabin's door to find the night's snowfall had turned into a blizzard. Wind and snow whipped against her face as the captain explained that they were at the old South Street Seaport and that it would be best to walk west before heading north to avoid any flooded streets. She thanked him profusely as she disembarked. After orienting herself, she headed west. It had been the longest of nights, but she consoled herself with the fact that she was almost at her dad's headquarters and safety.

2

Casey had her hands buried deep in her coat pockets. Head down, leaning forward, thankful for Kristof's hat, she fought her way across Houston Street. The wind, gusting across the six-lane boulevard, pushed against her. At the median, a row of trees running along the divider swayed frantically. If she were the woo-woo type, she'd have suspected Mother Nature had something against her. She pressed her arms and elbows tight against her body, taking solace in the fact that her father's headquarters was not much farther.

At the median, she waited for the few cars on the road to pass before trying to cross. Through the whiteout, she spotted the hands of a large clock that was mounted on the roof of a building across the street. It was almost twelve-thirty and well past lights-out for the crew at Todt Hill. She wondered if her friends knew she was gone. She felt a twinge of regret, not only for leaving them behind but also because she wouldn't advance to the next level with them.

Frustrated, she clenched her fists inside her coat pockets. That was the brainwashing talking. She knew that, but it sucked just the same.

A yellow cab crawled past, taking extra care on the unplowed road. Casey stepped off the median, and fresh snow crunched underfoot as she walked in and over the cab's tire tracks to cross the street. Reaching the curb in the middle of the block, Casey landed in front of the building with the clock. Judging by the amount of graffiti and the sagging wooden planks around its doors and windows, it seemed the place had been shuttered awhile. She inched closer and peered through a crack in the boards; it was too dark to see anything inside. She turned and leaned against the boarded-up entrance to get a moment of cover from the wind and cold. The place was so deserted, Casey half expected zombie hands to come crashing through the cracks in the planks behind her. She debated which avenue to take north into the condemned zone. Avenue A would be safer, since it was not technically condemned yet; however, there would be less chance of being seen on Avenue B. Since stealth trumped safety, Casey chose B. She moved from the entrance, thankful no zombies were holding her back . . . regrets, maybe, but no zombies.

On Avenue B she picked up her pace. With only a few blocks left to go, her spirits were buoyed by the proximity to her father. Untouched snow carpeted the sidewalk; she felt like Neil Armstrong with each eager step. Cars stripped of their usefulness sat abandoned along the curb. Streetlights spotlighted the heavy falling snow. Casey checked over her shoulder. With no one around, it was quiet—wilderness quiet. She wondered if the group she'd met with Jennifer and Greg in Tompkins Square Park were still around. Darcy and Bill, she remembered. She thought them good people and promised herself to come back and say hi when things settled.

On the sidewalk up ahead, Casey glimpsed something moving. She stopped. She waited. She edged closer to the plywood-covered storefronts. Crouching, she pulled the scalpel from her coat pocket; cold air bit at her exposed fingers. Through the snow, she saw a pack of dogs roaming and sniffing their way toward her. She counted five dogs, with the largest of them in the lead. The fifth dog lagged way behind its peers. As the pack approached, she saw that they did not look well. They were bone-skinny and filthy; their fur was matted and in desperate need of grooming.

Not wanting to be mistaken for a midnight snack, Casey searched for a way to avoid them altogether. There was a doorway a few feet from her. It was an entrance to the abandoned residences above. Putting the scalpel away and keeping her back to the wall, she shuffled to it. She pushed on the door, and it opened easily. She ducked inside. Immediately, Casey was struck by an awful, rancid smell. It was like the smell of death at the Fourteenth Street subway station, but more immediate—as if whatever had died was hiding in the dark, merely feet away. She hoped it wasn't human. She stayed close to the door and kept it open a crack for air. With her hand over her nose and mouth, she spied on the dogs as they went by. Either they hadn't noticed her, or they didn't care. She relaxed a bit as the last one went past, counting the ribs encircling its gaunt body. Despite its poor condition, the dog seemed familiar. "Oh, no," Casey muttered, realizing this wasn't just any old, starving stray.

"Bart?" she questioned.

The dog stopped. Its ears perked up.

"Bart!" she called out, stepping from the threshold.

The dog turned its head. Its tail began to wag.

Casey stepped onto the sidewalk and knelt in the snow.

"Here, Bart," she called again, slapping at her thigh.

The dog limped toward her. She put her hand out, palm up. The dog pushed right past her hand and leaned into her knee. Up close, it was clear: this was Bart. Her heart sank. Why was he out here? Why was he in this condition? This was wrong . . . all kinds of wrong. She reached and pulled him closer. He leaned all of what little weight he had left against her. He was shivering.

"Bart," she said, tearing up. "What happened?"

Despite the snow, he dropped and gave her his belly. He was a mess of matted fur, lesioned skin, and protruding bones. He smelled terrible, too. She didn't care, gently rubbing his belly. Touching her coat pocket, she remembered she'd saved half of her turkey hero.

She took it out. "What happened?" she asked again, almost glad that the dog couldn't answer. Whatever it was, it wasn't good.

Beth would have never voluntarily left him behind.

3

The old tenement that had housed her father's headquarters was gone. With Bart at her side, Casey stood in front of the destroyed building, shaking her head. Her sense of relief at having made it this far had sunk to dread. It appeared as if fire—a raging one— had taken the building down. Its hollowed-out interior was framed by the charred remnants of its brick facade. Rubble littered the ground. Through the open front wall, more charred and pancaked planks jutted out of the snow. Her mind raced. Had anyone made it out alive? Was her father dead? She thought of Michael Hargrove, and she remembered—she remembered him talking about the minute he "needed with her" after the chip had been implanted. She put her hand to her mouth. "Oh, fuck," she muttered, her knees going weak. "Was this my fault?"

Her world spun.

Turning from the burnt-out building, Casey stepped to the curb. Hunched over, she dry-heaved, but only at first. The next contraction splattered her stomach's contents onto the snow. Steam rose from the freezing puddle. She rested her hands on her knees and closed her eyes tight; the ramifications calcified. The reason that the team hadn't come to rescue her was that she'd told Hargrove where they were. "Fuck!" She opened her eyes and rubbed her forehead. "Fuck me." She cursed herself for being weak.

Bart limped up next to her. Casey took her hand from her knee, noted that it was trembling, then gently rested it on his head. "I'm so sorry, boy," she said. His ears perked up, but not in acceptance of her apology. He looked up the street, barked once, then barked again. A car—no, a van—had pulled up to the traffic barrier. Its driver ignored the obstruction and drove up on the sidewalk, headed in her direction. Its headlights lit the snowy road. Its tires crunched the same. She assumed it was trouble—it had to be. If they knew enough to burn the headquarters down, they'd know she'd try to make her way back. Casey kicked at the fresh snow to cover the evidence of her weak belly. She stepped back from the curb, spotting a rusty mailbox on the corner. "C'mon," she said to Bart, and they rushed to it. Squatting behind the metal box, she directed Bart behind her and peered around it. The van, its side and rear windows tinted black, slowed to a stop across the street and killed its lights.

Behind the wheel, the driver's clean-shaven face was lit by a screen in his hand. Casey wanted to get back to the building, maybe see if there were any clues in the rubble, but that wasn't happening now. She turned, leaned her back against the cold mailbox, and gave Bart's head a scratch. Her hand was no longer trembling. The rush of adrenaline had focused her, but she was at a loss. She'd had no plan beyond getting back here. It was a foolish plan, in retrospect, but still necessary. She thought about trekking uptown, to her mom, maybe to Jennifer. But there were Jennifer's dad and Bruce—fucking Bruce—to consider. She decided to go to the park. Maybe she would find Darcy and Bill and see if they knew anything.

Casey scratched Bart's head. Would he be out here if any of them had survived? Probably not, she concluded. But that he had gotten out . . . there was hope in that. She scratched behind his ears. "You wanna make some new friends?" she whispered. His tail wagged, making a one-winged angel in the snow.

She peered out from around the mailbox one more time to see if it was safe to leave. The driver was still staring at his screen. She stood up, sprinting back the way she came. Bart followed. She checked over her shoulder: Neither the van nor the driver had moved. As she turned around again, she spotted a flyer attached to a streetlight near the curb. It had the word LOST in bold letters across the top. She creeped to it. LOST was a cat; its grainy picture was worn and weathered. Looking around, she noticed another flyer tacked to a telephone pole a few feet up. She studied the flyer, leaning in close. She put her hand up to her mouth.

Can't be, she thought.

But it was. It was a picture of her childhood cat, Timmy. Casey scrunched her forehead, rubbing her cold fingers across her brow. She was confused but slowly catching on. Her dread began to lift. The text below explained that the cat was indeed named Timmy and there was a reward for his safe return. At the bottom, there was a phone number. It was their old phone number from when she was a kid, from when her family lived downtown, just a few blocks south from here.

Not only was her father alive . . . he was also leaving her clues.

4

Flooded with emotions, Casey stood in front of the small, five-story tenement-style building she'd grown up in. Bart was at her side, practically glued to her leg. She pressed the upturned collar of Kristof's peacoat against her chin and neck as the wind and snow continued their relentless assault. It was cold, yes, but since freezing-swimming-pool cold was her new metric, she could deal. Still, they would need some kind of shelter soon. From the looks of the place—with its bricked-over windows and boarded-up entrance—it seemed just as abandoned as the rest of the neighborhood. Gazing up at the uneven, snow-covered stoop, she smiled. She had good memories from here: memories from before moving uptown; memories from before life had gotten complicated.

Scanning the dark husk of a building, she hoped to see some hint of light, or life, coming from inside. There was none, but these days that didn't mean much. It wasn't as if her father's former headquarters had looked any more vibrant on the outside. Casey went to the first step and cleared a swath of snow with her shoe. She tested the integrity of the stair tread; it was stable. She did the same with each step up as Bart followed behind her. Climbing the last step, she stopped on the landing and turned to take in the view. The street seemed smaller and more mundane than she remembered.

She turned back, inspecting the set of first-floor windows to the left of the entrance. The window guards were gone, and bricks had been laid over the openings. However, she could still picture her babysitter, Mrs. Sykes, standing there with her gray hair cut pixie-short, stirring a pot on the stove and keeping a watchful eye. More warm feelings enveloped her. She remembered when she turned seven, maybe eight, Mrs. Sykes would let her play on the stoop alone. There, relegated to the top steps only, she had waited for her parents to come home. Even at that young age, it was an exhilarating taste of freedom.

Brushing off her nostalgia, Casey studied the building's entrance. Worn and weathered plywood had replaced the glass and oak door she remembered. A wooden board—laid across the middle and nailed on each side—served as security. Wedging her fingers behind it, she tugged, testing it. It was far from secure. She pulled a bit harder, and the board came loose in her hands. Careful not to stick herself or Bart with the exposed nails on the board's under-side, she placed it next to the door.

Where the board had been was a smooth, round hole for the door's missing lock. Casey bent, peeking inside. It was pitch black. Putting her fingers in the hole, she pulled at the door. It creaked a bit but opened rather easily. She propped the door open with a nearby rock and peered inside. The streetlight helped illuminate the vestibule somewhat, but she could've really used a flashlight. For her next escape, she promised to plan better. After waiting a moment for her eyes to adjust, Casey stepped over the threshold. The vestibule smelled dank—clearly the East River had taken at least one turn through here. On her right was a bank of mailboxes. The bottom row was rusted through, but it looked like their old box, third across on the second row, had been spared. She ran her fingers across the cutout where their name used to be. As with the stoop outside, Casey remembered how important she felt when her folks started letting her get the mail on her own.

She took a step past the mailboxes, going deeper into the vestibule. Rubble crunched beneath her shoes. She peered into the darkness. On her right, she could just make out the first step of the staircase leading to the apartments above. Next to the stairs was a gaping hole in the tiled floor. The hole seemed to go back quite a way, so up was her only option. That her father wasn't already on his way down to greet her was worrisome.

She tiptoed to the staircase. She looked down, expecting Bart to be at her side, but he wasn't. Turning, he'd stayed back, by the mailboxes. He was standing, tail wagging and alert with his nose up, sniffing the air.

"What is it, Bart? You know something I don't?"

He ignored her. She shrugged and turned, stepping to the stairs. She kept her left hand out in front, and with her right she felt for the wall. "Hello?" she called up the stairs. She waited, but nothing. "Hello?" she tried again. Still nothing. She found the wall, and, keeping her back to it, she took the first step, then the next. "Hello? Is anybody there?" She was fast concluding that either her father had abandoned this place, or she'd misread his intentions with the flyer. Either way, she was starting to lose hope.

She inched her way back down the steps. Bart was still in the vestibule, but now, instead of just sniffing the air, he was clawing at the mailboxes with his overgrown nails. Afraid Bart would cut himself on the rusted metal, Casey hurried the last few steps. She reached him, placing her hand between him and the boxes. As she did, she saw he wasn't pawing at any old box: he was pawing at her old box.

Then it dawned on her: Her dad hadn't abandoned anything, and she hadn't misread. "Why didn't I think of that?" she questioned, nudging Bart aside and clawing at the box herself. A curl in the metal, at the top corner, let her fingertips in. She pulled. The door sprang open, clanging against the metal behind it. She reached inside; she felt something—leather, maybe. She pulled whatever it was from the box and held it up to the open door and the streetlight. It was a pouch. She unzipped it, her hands unsteady. Inside were four screens with a note stuck to the first. START HERE, it read. Despite the poor lighting, Casey recognized her father's handwriting. An overwhelming amount of relief grounded her. She closed her eyes, holding the pouch to her chest.

She believed he was okay. Maybe they all were.

They had to be.

5

They weren't all okay.

Still in the vestibule, Casey sat cross-legged on the floor, her back against the mailboxes. Bart was lying next to her, his bony back pressed up against her leg. On her lap were the pouch and three of the four screens. The fourth was in Casey's hands. On it was her father's face—a screenshot, frozen at the point she'd stopped watching. The light from the screen illuminated her chin and the tears dropping from it.

Her father didn't look well; his eyes were swollen and red. There was a dirty bandage on the left side of his face. Below the dressing, his beard was singed, his skin raw. Slowly shaking her head, she wiped tears from her cheeks with the back of her hand. Of course, Casey was glad her father was alive—and, according to the video, Dan was too—but Beth and Garrett were not. They hadn't made it out of the headquarters. Her father thought the building had been bombed.

She hit "play" again, ready to hear more.

"I'm sorry, Casey," her dad said. "We lost our track on you right off. Dan thinks the van was shielded . . . he's probably right." He looked away from the camera. "It all went so wrong."

She touched the side of her head where the chip had been. No, she thought, fighting through her false memories. Maybe the van did have some kind of shielding—who was she to question Dan? But she did remember hitting her head on the way in. That was also a possibility, and she couldn't blame them for that.

"Casey, use the screens. I left money on each of them. They'll stay active for a month after you turn them on. Dan and I will regroup, and I promise I will find you. If it's the last thing I do, I will find you. I love you." The screen froze again on his pain-filled, burned face.

"I love you, too, Dad," she said between sobs, wishing she had told him so the last time she saw him.

She sat for a moment longer, staring at the screen until it went dark. She looked at Bart, who was still sleeping. Outside, the snow was letting up. That was something. She closed her eyes and curled up next to him. She didn't care how bad he smelled. With the fight drained out of her, all she wanted to do was go to sleep. Maybe, when she woke up, her father would be there. Maybe, when she woke, she'd find out this whole fucking mess was a dream.

6

Someone called Casey's name.

It was a man's voice. It was a voice that sounded familiar, but at the same time it did not. Slowly, time and place came back to her. She was still in the vestibule; she must have dozed off. She opened her eyes and saw a man standing over her, looming in silhouette. She scuttled backward, kicking her feet and scratching her palms on the cracked tile. She dug into her coat pocket for the scalpel. She found it, turned it on, and thrusted the glowing blade toward the intruder.

"Casey," the man said, raising his hands. "Easy." He edged back. "It's Dan."

"Dan who?" she questioned.

"Your father's Dan." He raised his hands higher.

Fuck. Of course.

"Dan," she said again without question and with much relief.

She saw Bart was next to him, his tail wagging. Outside, the weather was still rough. She got to her feet, feeling stiff. She looked Dan over. It was hard to believe he was here—she kind of wanted to cry. Turning off the scalpel, she slipped it into her pocket. Stepping forward, Casey hugged him, his arms trapped beneath hers. Bart circled their legs, his tail slapping her with each pass.

"You don't know how good it is to see you," she said, letting go.

"I kind of have an idea."

They stood facing each other, just inside the doorway. Illuminated by the ambient light, Casey noticed a scar running from behind his left ear down to his neck. She assumed it was from the fire. It formed a thick, red ridge with areas of raised, pale skin throughout. It looked painful.

"Are you okay?" he asked.

"Are you?" She pointed to the scar.

"Yeah," he said, adjusting his scarf to better cover it. "That wasn't much fun."

Dan had dark circles and bags under his eyes, both unsuccessfully hidden under his plastic frames. His hair, once sort of long and floppy, was buzzed down to stubble. It appeared as if he'd been to war and back. She could relate.

"I watched the . . ." she started to say, and then she remembered the screens. Shit. She patted her pockets. She searched around and saw the pouch and the screens scattered about the floor. She knelt, snatching them up. "I'm so sorry," she said.

"Thanks. I'm sorry to you, too. We let you down. I let you down."

Casey winced. "You made no promises. I knew the risks."

"Still," he said. "It wasn't supposed to be like this." After a moment of awkward silence, he looked at Bart. "I can't believe you found him."

"We bumped into each other about a block from here."

"I've been searching, leaving food around. We knew he survived the blast, but we got separated during the fire." He lifted his messenger bag up over his shoulder and head. He knelt and, after a bit of rummaging and a few nudges from Bart, pulled out a plastic bag filled with bone-shaped treats. "I refused to believe he didn't make it out." He opened the bag and fed an eager Bart from his hand.

"Good thing."

He nodded. "We really should get going," he said. "I'm sure they're looking for you."

"Tell me about it. My face is everywhere."

They stepped from the vestibule. Dan swung his bag back over his head and onto his shoulder. While the wind had kept its frenetic pace, the snow had slowed to a flurry. Casey tugged her cap down as far as it would go. Despite all the bad news, she felt optimistic. It was only a matter of time now before they began to set things straight. Down the stairs they went, Bart at her side.

"So, where's the new headquarters?" she asked.

Dan stopped mid-step.

"There's no new headquarters, Casey. It's just me."

Casey was confused. "My dad didn't send you?"

"No. I saw the news and figured you'd end up here. I was going to wait for you . . . camp out." He pointed to the bag on his back. "But you beat me to it."

"What do you mean, it's just you?"

Dan didn't say anything, his silence telling.

"Casey," he said, finally. "I don't know where your father is."

7

"No note? No, nothing?" Casey asked.

They were headed to the St. Mark's Hotel. Dan said it was a cash-only, no-questions-asked establishment. It was where he and her now-absent father had taken refuge after the fire.

"Nothing. I woke up, and he was gone. I never heard from him again. It's not like him."

Casey thought it was exactly like him. He'd done pretty much the same thing to her and her mom. One morning he was gone: no note, no nothing. That he was under investigation for embezzlement made his disappearance understandable to most people, but not to her. For one, she never believed it to be true, despite the supposed evidence against him. And, two, leaving your family high and dry was anything but understandable. Casey bristled at the possibility that history was repeating itself.

Dan pointed ahead. They were coming up on the hotel, its name inlaid with contrasting brick and tile on the side of the building. The rust-colored awning was battered and torn.

"Any problem with Bart?" she asked.

"No. If anything, they'll be happy to see him." He grabbed the hotel's brass-handled door and held it open for her. A staircase covered in worn, flowered carpeting led upstairs. "They'll be happy to see you, too."

She scrunched her forehead. "You talk about me?"

"Some of the more Resistance-sympathetic staff know the broad outlines," he said from behind her as they entered. At the landing, they passed a clerk sitting behind a plexiglass partition. The clerk, a young, bearded, tattooed guy, did a double take when he saw Casey, then another when he saw Bart. He looked at Dan, who smiled and nodded. The clerk stood from his desk. A door next to the window opened. The clerk was there, smiling and offering his hand. On the underside of his wrist was the same circle-and-double-line tattoo Darcy and Bill sported.

Dan egged her forward. "Casey, Jarred. Jarred, Casey."

Confused, she took Jarred's hand. "Nice to meet you," she said, pumping twice, then letting go.

Jarred pointed at Dan. "He's been worried about you."

Though she didn't like being talked about, Casey appreciated the concern. "And I'm glad for it. He was a sight for sore eyes."

Dan blushed. "We should head up," he said, shooing her along.

"I hope you find your father," Jarred said after them. "He's one of the good ones."

Up they went another flight of stairs. "He knows my dad?"

"Everyone down here does."

Yeah, she thought, *I'm getting that.*

After another flight of stairs, they waited at the top for Bart to catch up. Down the hall, they arrived at the room. Dan unlocked it with a key card and moved aside to let Casey in. On her right, there was an open door to the tiniest bathroom she'd ever seen. A pedestal quarter-sink bumped up to a toilet, which itself partially blocked a shower stall. Like the hotel generally, the bathroom had seen better days. Its floor, tiled in black and white like a chessboard, was chipped, and its white walls were yellowed with age. A short hall led to the main room. There were two double beds—the closest one unmade, its flowered bedspread a mess at the bottom. Across from the beds was a beat-up dresser with an old flat-screen television on top. The edges of the TV screen were held together with duct tape.

"Does it work?" she asked.

"Yeah, but only ICP news and alerts."

"Fair and balanced, I'm sure."

Dan smiled, but he seemed sad. Casey imagined she seemed the same. Bart, on the other hand, appeared thrilled. He was exploring the room, sniffing at everything. When he stopped, it was at a duffle bag on the floor next to the unmade bed. Dan walked past him, tossing his messenger bag on the bed. He took off his parka and threw that on the bed as well. Grabbing a takeout container from the bedside table, he wiped it clean, then knelt on the floor next to Bart. He pulled a bag of dog food from the duffle bag and scooped a healthy portion from it into the container. Bart circled, his tail wagging, as Dan laid it on the floor for him.

Casey stepped past the beds, ignoring her reflection in the dresser mirror as she did so. There was a quarter table with two chairs tucked in the corner. Next to the table was a window with its curtains drawn; the outdated curtains matched the bedspreads. A heater below the window pumped out warmth that was more than welcome. Casey pushed the curtain aside, peeking out to see that their third-floor view was of St. Mark's Place. There was an open bodega across the street, its neon sign reflecting off the snow. She thought of Amir, once again thankful for his discretion and help. She let the curtain fall back and turned to face the room. "I assume I'll take this one." She gestured to the made bed.

"Unless your father suddenly reappears, it's all yours," Dan said, lifting the duffle bag from the floor. He began moving gear from his messenger bag into it. He looked up. "We have enough money if you want your own room. I don't want you to be uncomfortable."

She hadn't thought of her discomfort, but she appreciated that he had. "You know, that would be nice. I could use the space." She pulled off her cap and shed her coat, placing both on the made bed. She noticed him watching.

"That cut," he said, pointing at the back of her leg. "You should put something on it." He tossed a first aid kit onto the bed. "Let me go get you checked in. I think the room next door is free."

"Thanks," she said as he left.

Casey stepped to the mirror on the dresser. Turning, she held back the torn fabric of her pants and twisted around to get a look at the wound. Shit. It was longer and more jagged than she had realized. Also, the warmer she got, the more it throbbed. She turned to face the mirror full-on. Her face was dirty and scratched. Her formerly starched, pristine dress shirt was wrinkled and ragged. She ran her hand over her head, squeezing the stubble at its crown. She closed her eyes, sighing. She wanted the night to end. She opened her eyes. Looking at her grimy self, all she wanted was a shower, a warm bed, and to be done. But Dan needed to know the details of her stay at Todt Hill.

He needed to know his predicament was all her fault.

8

Casey came clean.

Sitting at the corner table, with their chairs facing each other, she told Dan her story. She began with her waking up in the cell and ended with her escape down the mountain. In between, she told him about the procedure—how they had drilled a hole in her head and implanted a chip in her brain; how she must have given up the location of their hideout while under its spell. She showed him the scar on her scalp. Dan was sympathetic throughout, insisting that the destruction of their headquarters and the deaths of Garrett and Beth were not her fault. Besides her not being in control of her faculties, he blamed a rushed and unreasoned plan that had put her in a bad situation to begin with.

He wasn't necessarily wrong, but she was not ready to forgive herself either.

"Todt Hill," he said, standing.

"Todt Hill Academy," she confirmed.

He left the table, returning a moment later with a tablet-sized screen. "Huh," he muttered, sitting down. "It's on the map." He laid the screen between them, tapping on a dropped pin.

On the screen was what appeared to be the main entrance to a stately Ivy League school. The school came complete with a well-manicured lawn, neatly trimmed bushes, and, of course, the ivy—climbing and wrapping around the walls and windows. She tapped through the posted images, but none of them seemed like where she'd been. "That's not the place. We were underground—never saw the sun once."

He looked up. "Man, I'd go crazy."

She nodded but realized it hadn't made her crazy. Until the procedure failed, it hadn't bothered her one bit. Sequestration was part of the training, and acceptance was built in. She twitched at the thought.

Dan zoomed in on the location, swiping past the entrance and to the main building.

"Stop," Casey said. Just past the building was the quaint guard booth she'd zipped by before her trip down the mountain. Behind it was the covered garage she'd escaped through. "That's where I came out." She pointed at the screen.

Dan flicked his fingers for a closer look, but the image behind the booth was blurry. "Someone doesn't want us to see."

"With good reason."

Dan took the screen and started typing. "Now that we know where you were, maybe I can access their network."

She sat back, dropping her shoulders and letting out her breath. With her abduction and internment now being given purpose, she felt a bit lighter. On the table next to her sat the key card to her room. A shower, a bed, sleep—it all sounded perfect. But it wasn't. She had one more thing to do. While she couldn't contact her mom because of Bruce, she could contact Jennifer. She needed her best friend to know she was okay.

Turning to the bed, she gathered Kristof's coat. Searching the pockets, she found the active burner screen left for her by her dad. "Can I send a message on this thing?"

Dan looked up; he shook his head. "Not unless the person you're messaging has the encryption key."

"How do they get that?"

"Only in person."

Then in person it would have to be. She checked the time on the screen. It was almost two a.m. Technically it was still Thursday night. If Jennifer had kept their old routine, she might still be out. "Can we do one more thing before calling it a night?"

Dan laid his screen on the table. "Sure," he said. "I'm not having much luck here anyway. It's like the place doesn't exist."

"You've heard of Jennifer Hargrove?"

"You can't," he said.

"She needs to know I'm okay."

"You want to contact the mayor's daughter?"

"No. I want to contact my best friend."

Dan let out a small sigh.

Casey stood, grabbing the screen as she did. "She may be able to help with your access problem."

"And why would she do that?"

"Dude, Jennifer Hargrove's been part of the Resistance since the first day she could talk."

9

Dan was driving. Casey sat in the passenger seat. They had left Bart behind, sleeping blissfully in the warmth and comfort of the room. They were on First Avenue heading uptown. Traffic was light. On her lap was Dan's screen. Casey worked it with one hand while holding onto the dashboard with the other. Dan was driving a bit too fast for her liking, especially in the snow.

Dan slowed as he approached the next green light.

"Almost," she said, swiping at the screen. She was scrambling the street cameras as they went. "Okay, you're good."

He picked up speed.

"The next two are broken," she said.

He nodded. "You're sure she'll still be there?"

"No, but it's worth a shot."

"And you're sure she'll talk to me? I'm not really the pick-up-girls-in-bars type."

Casey could tell he was sweating this. He could hack into a

government server with no problem, but ask him to talk to a girl, and he got all nervous. It was endearing.

"You're a guy, and you're cute. She'll talk to you. Just have a drink, then buy her a drink."

"I'm not a big drinker."

"You'll be fine."

Casey sat back. While sure that Dan would be fine, she wasn't so sure how fine she would be. Their covert attempt to make contact with Jennifer was all taking place too close to home. Coastal, the bar where they'd usually spent Thursday nights, was about half a block from her building, and with proximity came feelings. There were so many feelings. Casey missed her mom desperately. She wanted to hug her; she wanted to let her know she was okay, but she also wanted to yell at her for bringing Bruce into their lives. She knew, however, that her anger was not justified. After all, her mom hadn't been privy to all the covert stuff. She didn't know her husband was the leader of the Resistance, and she didn't know her boyfriend was an ICP snitch. Casey was convinced that with more information her mother would make better decisions, and that she deserved the benefit of the doubt.

A block from their destination, a car pulled from a parking spot on First Avenue. The bar was kitty-corner across the street. "There," Casey said, pointing and ignoring her nerves.

Dan pulled up in front of the empty spot. A three-foot-high hill of plowed snow ran alongside the cars parked at the curb. He tapped the console screen between them, and the car slipped through the gap in the snow left by the vehicle before. Snow crunched beneath the tires as the car rocked and rose, coming to a skidding stop. He turned the headlights off but left the engine running. "You going to be okay here?" he asked.

"I'll be fine."

"How's the leg?"

"I'm dealing."

"Okay. I guess I should go."

"Go."

Dan opened the door. It bumped up against the snow piled

alongside. He checked for traffic, squeezed out, then high-stepped his way through the mounds and across the street. After a slight hesitation at the bar's door, he went inside. Operation: "Hug Your Best Friend and Recruit Her to the Resistance" was officially underway.

Casey leaned forward, resting her elbow on the dashboard and her knee on the seat. A snowplow rumbled by, loudly scraping the pavement as it went. An undisciplined salt spreader at its rear pelted the car with hail-like stones. She watched the traffic coming uptown through the front seat's headrests and the rear window. The roads were quiet by Manhattan standards, with only a handful of cars—yellow cabs, mostly—on the way up. She turned back to the bar. The surrounding sidewalks, again by Manhattan standards, were quiet too. At the corner, the traffic light went from yellow to red. Stopping at it, in the lane next to hers, was a procession of black SUVs. There were three in total. Casey leaned back against the passenger door. They were ICP—she was sure of it. Without waiting for the light or signaling, they turned right, onto her block. "Shit," she said, sliding down the seat.

They had to be here because of her.

Casey grabbed Dan's screen from the dashboard. She needed to see what was going on. Having already scrambled the feed from the camera on the corner, she checked for another one. She cycled through every view she could find, but nothing showed her the outside of her building. She thought about unscrambling the feed on the corner, but that would put Dan and Jennifer at risk. If she wanted to see, she'd have to get out.

Sitting up, she slid the screen into a pocket along the passenger door. She reached to the driver's side and tapped the engine off. She pulled her hat down and checked the traffic, both car and pedestrian, in front and behind. There was a couple, arm-in-arm, on the sidewalk and some cabs in the road. Casey waited for the couple to pass, then opened the door as far as the piled snow would allow. Squeezing out, she used the top of the door for leverage, then found a path at the rear of the car to the sidewalk. Lifting her collar, she walked on the packed snow, careful not to slip.

At the corner, Casey saw them. Across the street, about fifty yards down, the motorcade had double-parked in front of her building. She checked the bar across the avenue; it was still quiet. Slowly, Casey moved down the block, then took cover, high-stepping into the knee-high snow behind a parked, snowbound car. Leaning past its snow-entombed windshield, she saw Bruce, fucking Bruce, talking to someone in the back seat of the middle SUV. Casey could see only the top of his head, but his stockbroker's hair was unmistakable. Then she saw her mom, and her heart sank. Her mom was in the lobby, at the front desk, talking to Derek. She looked haggard, her curly hair unruly. She wore her coat over a pair of sweats. Casey's hopes for her mother's ignorance dissolved. She watched, heartbroken, as Derek made his way around the desk and hugged her. Casey wanted to die. She wanted to do the hugging. She wanted to let her mom know she was okay. Turning, Casey leaned against the car; snow clung to her shoulders and back. She closed her eyes. Contrasting flashes of how things had been, and were now, piled onto her sadness. She fought back tears, recognizing that this was not the time or place.

Then someone grabbed her by the shoulders. Her eyes sprang open, remembering the danger. But it was Dan, not danger, staring her in the face.

"What the fuck, Casey?"

"I saw the ICP trucks," she said, tilting her head back.

"No shit. You can't be out here. Not now—it's too soon."

She'd never seen Dan get mad, and despite his generally gentle face, Mad Dan was effective. "I know," she said.

He looked past her, across the street. "Is that your mom?"

"Yeah."

He turned his attention back to her. "Sorry," he said. "Under better circumstances, I'd be honored to meet her . . . your father said only good things."

"Until he left, there were only good things to say." A tear ran down Casey's cheek. "It's just so hard not being able to talk to her."

"Trust me, I understand."

Casey nodded. Separated from his own family, he did understand; that helped.

Dan stepped back, holding out his hand. "Come on—I have a surprise."

She took his hand, letting him pull her from the car. Snow fell away from around her. "I told you she'd talk to you," she said, letting go of his hand and brushing more snow away.

"She thinks I'm a stalker." Checking over his shoulder, he kept himself between her and the activity across the street as they walked. When they reached the corner, he swept his hand out in front of him. "Surprise," he said.

Jennifer was there, pacing the sidewalk. She had her back to them, kicking up loose snow as she went. Jennifer wore a parka similar to Dan's, but hers was fur-lined and designer-made. She had the hood up, and her hair spilled out from around it.

Casey smiled wide. The relief she felt was instant. A weight lifted.

Jennifer turned. She looked worried, then relieved when she saw her. They rushed towards each other, hugging at first contact.

They separated, but only a bit.

"I can't believe it," Jennifer said, her eyes wet.

"Me either."

They hugged some more. And, in its own way, this made up for not being able to hug her mother. Jennifer was family, and the moment felt like home.

"Don't you ever leave me again," Jennifer said.

Casey felt her best friend's tears on her cheek. "Never," she said as they hugged even tighter. Jennifer's chest heaved against her shoulder. Unable to hold it together, she cried as well.

"I love you," Jennifer blubbered.

"I love you back," Casey returned, meaning it more than she could ever remember.

10

Things felt better—not right, not whole—but better.

"I missed you so much," Jennifer said from the back seat, settling into the space between the headrests.

Casey angled herself, putting her knee on the seat. "I missed—"

she started to say, but then she realized that until only a few hours ago she hadn't missed her best friend. Until a few hours ago, her training and the ICP were her only concerns. "I missed you too," she said—not willing to admit to, and still blaming herself for, what she couldn't control. "I'm glad I took a shot that you'd be out tonight."

"I actually hadn't been out since our last night together—I just couldn't. But with this . . ." Jennifer showed Casey her screen—on it was the same ICP alert she'd seen on the kiosks around town. "I knew if you made it back and wanted to get in touch, I had to be there." She rested her screen face down on the seat back, keeping her hand on it. She looked away, her chin trembling. "And I wasn't going to leave until they kicked me out."

Casey put her hand over Jennifer's. Her heart hurt for her friend more than it hurt for herself. She studied her through the dim lighting. Her skin was blotchy, and, like Dan and herself, she had dark circles under her eyes. But, unlike them, Jennifer had the option of makeup. That she chose not to bother covering up said a lot. They had all been put through the wringer, it seemed.

Jennifer put her other hand on top of Casey's. "You need to tell me everything."

Casey looked at Dan. "I have nowhere to be," he said.

And, for the second time in a matter of hours, Casey told her story. But it was more difficult this time. This time, her audience had more at stake.

||

The car's windows had steamed over. A spectral blue glow from Dan's screen lit the interior. Casey had just wrapped up her tale of abduction, brainwashing, and escape. Jennifer sat back into the shadows, letting it all sink in. Casey felt sorry for her best friend. It was one thing for your father to be a political hack with outdated ideas and a racist streak; it was quite another for him to be abducting kids and turning them into zombie soldiers.

"And Martin was going along with all this? Even after you told him?"

"He was unfazed."

"That's so hard to believe," Jennifer said.

"Not with that chip in him."

Jennifer leaned forward. She rested her arm on Casey's seat. "And you want me to what? Help you hack in there?"

Dan turned to face her. "I think I can get in from your father's computer. I just need access to it."

"I don't know," Jennifer said. "You're asking me to betray my father. I may hate him, but he's still my father."

"I know, it's a big ask," Casey said. "But this is bigger than us and bigger than you and your father. Who knows how many lives he's hijacked?"

Jennifer ran her hand down her face. "Okay," she said. "I'll let you in there. But what if he finds out?"

"I can't guarantee that he won't," Dan said.

"If he finds out," Casey said, "you can join me at the beautiful St. Mark's hotel. The amenities are to die for."

Jennifer smiled. "Fuck, Case—how is this our lives?"

"Between your father and mine, I think it's always been our lives. We just didn't know it."

12

They drove Jennifer home. Her family's brownstone wasn't far, a few avenues west, just off Central Park. They were parked at a hydrant with a view of the stately manor. Casey waved the passenger window down. A blast of cold air blew inside. The five-story brick building looked quiet. The bottom floor was lit, but the upper floors, where the family lived, were dark. "Anybody home?" she asked, waving the window back up.

"Mom's in Aruba, and my father must not be home yet." Jennifer, propped between the front seats, pointed at Dan's screen. On it was a close-up of the brownstone, its arched windows capped with snow. "My father's office is on the fourth floor."

"You have the whole building?"

"Yes," she said.

"And security?"

"Face ID to unlock the gate and the door. Cameras, outside only. There's a guy in the basement watching the feeds."

"Is he a problem?"

"No. They know not to get in my business."

"And the cameras—where are they?"

"Top of the gate and above the front door."

Dan tapped on his screen. "Got it. I can loop us out." He tapped some more, turning to Casey when he was done. "You okay waiting here?"

"Only if I can take a nap."

Dan smiled. "You can take all the naps you want." He reached behind the driver's seat for his bag. "If this works, Casey, it's the beginning of the end for the Mayor, for the Academy . . . hell, maybe even the entire ICP." Eyes wide, he tossed open the front flap of his bag and stuffed his screen inside. "This is big."

Judging by Jennifer's glare, it was clear that Dan was a little too enthused.

"I realize I don't know you," Jennifer said to him. "But this is my world you're talking about ending."

"Sorry," he said, composing himself to match the seriousness of the moment. "You're right, but it's been a rough go, and we don't get many breaks like this."

"We? As in the Resistance?" Jennifer questioned.

"Yeah—what's left of it." He looked at Casey, his brow heavy with loss.

Casey nodded slowly back to him, appreciating and feeling the same.

Jennifer squeezed her shoulder. "Shoot. I'm sorry, too. It's a lot to take in."

Casey grabbed her hand. "Are you sure about this?"

"No," Jennifer said. "But I'll worry about that later."

"Thank you," Casey said, letting go.

"No, Case. Thank you." She slid toward the passenger-side door. "After the shit you went through, I owe you this."

13

Casey dozed. She hadn't meant to but found herself relaxed enough to drift off. When she awoke, she saw that a black SUV had pulled up in front of Jennifer's brownstone. How long had it been there? She couldn't be sure, but she didn't think she had been out for more than a few minutes. Either way, what had previously been a quiet brownstone was now busy. At the front of the house on the second floor, the formal living room had its lights on. Gauzy curtains revealed two figures in silhouette, a large man and a petite woman, intimately spaced, face to face. The man was Jennifer's father—his large stature left no doubt. The woman was too small to be Jennifer's mom, whether she was in Aruba or not. That Michael Hargrove was unfaithful was no surprise. That he'd bring his mistress home, especially with his daughter upstairs, was.

Disgusted, Casey dug into her coat pocket for the burner screen. If Jennifer and Dan weren't already aware, they needed to know they were not alone. "Shit," she said, remembering that they hadn't set up Jennifer's screen so they could talk, and she had no Web ID for Dan yet. Casey checked the brownstone's upper floors: There were no lights on, but the fourth-floor office glowed. Dan was doing his thing, she assumed.

"Be careful," she whispered.

Two floors below, Hargrove and the woman sauntered away from the window, their arms wrapped around each other as they moved out of view. A moment later, from the top of the brownstone's front step, the door opened. An outdoor light above it switched on. The woman appeared first, with Hargrove following behind her. *Ew,* Casey thought, recognizing the woman immediately. It was Simone. She must have come back with him from the VIP reception. But why? Were they a thing? Was Simone literally sleeping with the enemy? Or did she not consider him an enemy at all?

Casey's head spun with implications.

Simone stepped past the threshold. She wore a fur coat down to her ankles. Hargrove, his tie loose and jacket off, stood in the doorway with one hand on its frame. He checked over his shoulder, then pulled Simone in for a kiss—full-on lips, and lingering. Needing to look away, Casey rechecked the fourth floor. Jennifer, highlighted by the computer's glow, was at the window, watching. Casey's heart sank . . . this was the last thing her best friend needed to see. Jennifer looked away and then towards Casey. Their eyes locked, confirming each other as witnesses; then Jennifer turned from the window. Her father's betrayal was complete.

Back at the stairs, with the kiss over, Simone started down. Her coat opened with each step to reveal her glittering gown and graceful legs. From the SUV, the driver, clad in a black suit and tie, jumped out. He circled to the passenger side and graciously helped Simone up and into the car.

Shit. Simone couldn't just leave. She was a link—maybe the only link—to her dad.

Casey scanned the fourth floor as the driver came back around. She needed Dan to be done, but he wasn't. And, even if he was, could he even leave with Jennifer's father around? She knew what she had to do. She had to follow the SUV. There was no way she could confront Simone here . . . that would be dumb. She also knew that to do this, she had to leave Dan behind. However, she was sure he'd be okay and that Jennifer would figure out what-was-what once she realized the car was gone. They were a resourceful bunch.

Casey shuffled over the center console and into the driver's seat. Keeping an eye on the SUV, she took a second to familiarize herself with the dashboard. The last time she'd driven was for her road test three months ago. She had passed, but learning to drive and actually driving when living in the city were two different things. Keeping her foot on the brake, Casey cautiously put the car into drive and waited. After the SUV's lights came on and pulled away, she did the same. She silently wished Dan luck as she pulled out. The road was slippery but not too bad. The first stoplight was green, and the SUV turned right, heading uptown. She followed, then remembered the stoplight cameras. With no way to scramble them, she continued on. It's not like she could be any more wanted, so what the hell.

Driving carefully on the plowed street, she kept a safe distance to avoid the driver's attention. The streets ran into avenues; the avenues turned into highways. They were headed north, eventually exiting in the town of New Rochelle. These roads were pretty well plowed, but the driving was still slick and slow going. Any clouds from the earlier storm had been blown away, and a full moon lit the night. The untouched snow around them amplified the light. Casey had been driving for a very long fifty minutes when the SUV pulled into a circular driveway. Driving past, she made a U-turn, then parked in front of the next house over.

For the aura of wealth Simone exuded, the house seemed relatively modest. There were two columns, tastefully lit from below, framing the entranceway. On either side of that, there were two large windows. The second floor had three windows jutting from its shingled roof. Simone stepped out of the SUV and hurried into the house.

Not sure if she was home alone, Casey debated her next step. But, before any pros or cons were addressed, the front door opened, and two large Boxer-type dogs burst from it. Simone emerged next, still in her fur, but she had replaced her high heels with boots. The dogs bounded and danced in the snow, stopping only to relieve themselves. Simone, leaning against one of the columns, watched them, smiling. If the dogs had been waiting to be let out, that was pretty good proof that Simone was alone. Emboldened and a bit nervous, Casey tapped off the engine and got out of the car.

As she came into view at the top of the driveway, the dogs noticed her first. Their barking had Simone stepping from her porch toward them. She cocked her head when she spotted Casey. She scolded the dogs until they quieted, then strode up the driveway. The pair protectively joined her on either side. Casey marched forward as well.

"Casey Parker?" Simone questioned when she got close enough. "What the hell are you doing here? How do you know where I live?" She looked past Casey, then over her shoulder. "It's not safe."

"Where's my father?" Casey asked, getting in her face.

"What are you talking about? I don't know where your father is." Simone edged back. Her eyes darted about. "You should know better. We can't be out here." She stepped aside, waving Casey toward the house.

Instead, Casey stood her ground. "I know about you and Michael Hargrove," she said.

Simone stopped trying to egg her forward. "Okay," she said, stepping in front of her again. She leaned in. "I get it. You followed me." Her eyes darted to the street. "But did anyone follow you?"

Casey glanced at the street behind her. She thought she'd been careful, but who knew. "I don't think so," she said, disarmed by her potential lapse in judgment.

"All right," Simone said, her posture relaxing. "Wait. What do you mean, where's your father? I messaged him your location. I'm the reason you're standing here."

"Excuse me?" she questioned, genuinely dumbfounded. She hadn't had help. Well, maybe the nurse, but that was short-lived. "I got myself out." She pointed at her general state of disrepair. "It wasn't fun."

"I don't understand. Once I confirmed you were there, and where 'there' was, I let him know."

"You messaged him?"

"Yes."

"And he replied?"

"Right away."

"I doubt that, highly. Dan hasn't seen or heard from him in weeks."

"What are you talking about? He answered me."

"Someone answered you—but I don't think it was my dad."

14

Simone was in a state of panic. They were inside her house, and Simone was on her knees digging through a hallway closet, her fur coat spilling out around her. Casey stood to one side, watching. On the way in, Simone had explained that if Casey's father was missing, then whoever texted her back was probably on to her and that she needed to leave.

"And what about the benefactors? Aren't you the connection?" Casey asked, unbuttoning her coat.

Simone popped her head out from inside the closet. Her hair came undone and unspooled around her face. "Benefactors? There are no benefactors." She dove back into the closet.

"Then who financed all that equipment at my dad's headquarters?"

Simone dragged a large duffle bag from the closet and along the hardwood floor. "The ICP did; Hargrove did. I've been siphoning money from their accounts for years." Still on her knees, she unzipped the bag and pulled out a gun. She ejected its clip, checked it, snapped it back in, and then put the gun in the pocket of her coat.

"So, you're undercover?"

"It's a little more complicated than that, but yes," she said without looking up.

"I saw you make out with the mayor."

Now Simone stopped what she was doing and looked up. "You saw that?"

Casey nodded. "And so did his daughter."

Simone shook her head, then went back to digging through the bag. "Listen, you're playing a dangerous game here. I don't know what to tell you. I met with your father three weeks ago. He looked like absolute crap. He told me about the headquarters; he told me about Beth and Garrett. They were my friends, too. It's all fucking tragic."

In the bag were a bunch of screens, a bunch of passports, and clothing. Simone stood up. She had two of the screens in her hand and was offering them to Casey. "There's money on these. Take them," she said.

Casey took the screens and pocketed them.

"Do you have a gun?"

"I don't need a gun."

Simone knelt and started rummaging again. "You need a gun."

She pulled another gun from the duffle bag and handed it, along with an extra clip, to Casey. "I suspect you know how to use it."

"I've been trained, yes."

"Good," Simone said, standing. "The safety is set to Public. Pair it when you can." She threw the duffle bag over her shoulder, then slapped at her leg. The dogs raced to her side, their claws scratching along the floor.

Casey followed her into the kitchen, through a side door, and into a garage. A red SUV sat idling, its rear hatch open. There were two dog crates secured side by side in the back. Simone snapped and pointed, prompting the dogs to jump into their crates. She locked them in, pulled the hatch down, and kept moving. Swinging open the passenger door on the driver's side, Simone threw the duffle bag onto the backseat. Next, she turned and searched the shelves along the wall. Struggling a bit, she pulled another duffle bag from the shelf and to the floor. She opened it and confirmed its contents: bags of dog food, colorful bowls, and quarts of water. Simone closed the bag, lifted it with two hands, and tossed it into the car as well.

"If you see your father," she said, waving the garage door open as a lip of unplowed snow tumbled in, "tell him I'm following the plan. If there's a chance I can find him, I will. But I need to lay low first and figure this shit out."

"You think he could still be all right?" Casey asked as Simone jumped into the front seat.

Simone paused. "No, not really," she said. "I'm sorry." She closed the door and waved her window down. "Just go back to wherever you guys are hiding, and stay put. Kill time. If we're lucky, maybe I'm overreacting, and I'll stay in Hargrove's good graces. If I hear anything, I'll contact you on one of those screens. But whatever you do, do not try to contact me. And, for heaven's sake, do not follow me. It's too dangerous . . . for all of us."

The SUV started out of the garage. "The door will close in thirty seconds," she called behind her. "I suggest you get moving."

Casey stood inside the garage for a moment, reeling in Simone's wake. That Simone's fear was palpable gave Casey pause. She stepped from the garage. The weight of her new handgun hung heavy in her coat pocket. In the distance, past the tree line, the first hint of a new day was dawning. As the garage door closed behind her, she knew there was no way she'd be laying low. Inaction was not an option. Fuck that. She had Jennifer; she had Dan. And, assuming Dan's hack went well, they had Hargrove over a barrel.

Their fight was only beginning.

CHAPTER SEVEN | RISING FROM THE ASHES

I

IT WAS ALMOST NOON when she woke.

Casey had slept well, really well. It was a deep and, thankfully, dreamless sleep. With the chip no longer in control, she hoped it was the start of a trend. Dressed in a tank top and sweats—the clothes were a donation from Jennifer—she was in her hotel room's tiny bathroom, washing up. Tiny or not, that she was even in a hotel room was kind of hard to believe. If she hadn't been cut, bruised, and stiff as all hell, her mad dash to freedom would've felt like a dream.

Splashing water on her face, huddled over what could have been the smallest sink ever, she did her best not to get the excess on the floor. She lifted her head, and water dripped down her cheeks and chin. From a shelf next to her, she grabbed a towel. She patted her face dry, then ran the towel over her head and down the back of her neck. Despite getting adequate sleep, the girl in the mirror looked tired. Her skin was pale, and the circles under her eyes were dark. She needed to get some sun.

Being careful not to bang her knee on the toilet, she made a tight turn and draped the towel over the shower curtain rod to dry.

Crumpled on the floor were her clothes from yesterday. Casey had shed them and showered before going to bed this morning. She gathered the soiled clothes, keeping them an arm's length away, and stepped from the bathroom. Walking down the short hall, she limped slightly thanks to the tightening cut—now cleaned and bandaged—on the back of her leg.

Casey's room was the mirror image of Dan's. In addition to the tiny bathroom, it had two beds and the same run-down decor. Like Dan, she had slept in the bed closest to the door; its comforter now sprawled off the end and onto the floor. On the other bed was the bag Jennifer had packed for her. From toiletries to clothes, the essentials were all there. She examined the getaway clothes in her hands. The tear in the pants was too ragged to mend, so she tossed them into the garbage pail next to the dresser. Stepping to the head of the bed, she tossed the rest of the clothing onto the floor between the bedside table and wall. She would wash those items later. On the bedside table sat a bottle of water, her burner screen, and the gun Simone had given her. As a concession to her soldier side, she had paired the gun with her grip before going to bed. *Better safe than sorry,* she'd told herself.

Grabbing the water, she moved around bed number one and over to bed number two. She sipped her drink, eyeing her wardrobe choices. After putting the bottle on the dresser behind her, she picked out the jeans Jennifer had packed. They were black and well worn, just to her liking. Holding them up, Casey could tell they would be too big: Jennifer's height and hips could account for that. Thankfully, Jennifer had also packed a belt—the two-holed, black-leather one Casey had always liked—and she could always cuff the legs. From the ragged jeans to the belt to the basic-black color palette, these choices were a measure of how well Casey's best friend knew her.

On the bedside table, her screen vibrated. With only two people having the number, it had to be either Jennifer or Dan. Lying and stretching across the unmade bed, Casey reached for the screen. Rolling onto her back, she held it above her face. It was a message from Jennifer, hoping the clothes were to her liking and letting her know she'd be coming by after school. Casey smiled, lost for a moment in a simpler time. She typed her thanks and her love.

Lowering the screen, she held it against her chest, letting herself relax before the day's complications set in.

2

"Hey," Dan said, opening his hotel room door.

"Hey," Casey said in return as she walked inside. After catching each other up on the latest developments—Casey rested, Bart rested, and Dan had been up all night—she followed him into the room. Bart, who was napping on the far bed, perked up and gingerly jumped down to greet her as well.

"You cleaned him up?" she asked, scratching Bart's head.

"Yeah," Dan said, sitting at the table by the window. "A quick once-over in the shower. He's still pretty matted, but the smell is mostly gone."

Bart dropped and offered her his belly. "Who's a good clean boy?" she asked rhetorically, kneeling to give him a generous rub. She could feel some knots in his fur. Hopefully, they didn't hurt too much. "Does he have a vet or a groomer we can take him to?"

"Beth used to take him to a vet on Avenue A, near the park," Dan said, turning to point out a McDonald's bag and a large coffee on the dresser. "That's for you. I hope you like eggs."

"I do. Thanks." She grabbed the bag and the coffee. "Maybe I should make an appointment for him," she said, putting the coffee on the heater and sitting on the bed.

"Yeah," Dan said absent-mindedly, his eyes glued to a pair of tablet-sized screens on the table.

Casey dug into her breakfast bag and pulled out an Egg McMuffin. It was the classic kind, with cheese and Canadian bacon; she hadn't had one in years. Its waxy wrapper felt familiar in her hands. She held it to her nose. Breathing in, she could smell the sweet glaze of the bacon through the wrapper. That she was nostalgic about a breakfast sandwich caught her off guard. Her dad was the McDonald's breakfast fan—the McMuffin was his favorite. With her mom opposed to McMuffins of any kind, it had become a secret thing between them, something she'd forgotten about . . . until now.

"Your father started me on those."

"I'm not surprised," she said, unwrapping it. With the wrapper on her lap, she took a bite. It was more rubbery than she remembered, possibly because it was cold. Still, the taste—buttery, salty, with a hint of sweet—was precisely the same. It wasn't good, per se, but it was comforting.

Putting the sandwich and the wrapper to one side, Casey dug into the McDonald's bag again. Littering the bottom were packets of sugar, containers of cream, and stirrers. She picked out two sugars, one cream, and a stirrer, placing them next to her coffee. "Are you finding anything?" she asked.

"Lots," he replied.

As she'd learned this morning before turning in, not only had Dan successfully hacked into Jennifer's father's computer, he had managed to put a tap on it as well. As long as the tap stayed undetected, they had access to the computer's archives and anything new that was coming in.

"Anything incriminating?" She peeled the lid off of the coffee cup. The coffee was cold, too, but she didn't mind. Luckily, cold coffee was her thing.

"Immoral is more like it," he said, reaching for his own cup of coffee that was sitting on the table. "Michael Hargrove's been feeding the ICP brainwashed soldiers for years now. His rise up the ranks, and his bid for mayor—it's all because of that." He swirled the cup, then drank.

"And you have proof?"

"Emails, reports, schematics . . . you name it." He put the cup down, grabbed a screen, and turned to her. On the screen was a map of the United States. "But here's the thing. For now, that machine they used on you is one of a kind." He tapped on the screen. "But they have plans to build more and plant them all over the country." On the map, a series of pins dropped. Dan pointed. "Chicago, L.A., Miami . . . Todt Hill was just the beginning."

"Shit," she said.

"Shit is right. If one source of recruits made him mayor, then all of this," he swiped at the screen, "all of this could make him president."

Casey ran her fingers over the scar from the procedure. Her anger grew. "We have to stop him. He can't keep stealing people's lives."

"I agree."

"Can't we just publish what you found? Put it on the internet, give it to the press? The outrage alone—"

Dan was shaking his head. "There's no outrage to be had, Casey. The people who decide whether this is important or not are too comfortable to care. You know that."

She grimaced; she did know that. But knowing and succumbing to that knowledge were two different things.

"Besides," he continued, "we've had damning stuff before. Remember when the ICP was implicated in the Mexico City bombings, and what a massive story that was?"

No. That wasn't right. Casey remembered a local water gang claiming responsibility. "No," she admitted.

"Exactly." He placed the screen on the table. "We had evidence that they were behind that. We went to the press. Beth had connections. The reporter was dead the next day."

"Fuck."

"Yeah. Lots of fucks. Beth barely, if ever, got over that. Your father took it pretty hard too."

Bart appeared between them.

"What about the internet? We could just put it out there."

"We've tried the internet." He scratched Bart's head. "The moment one of our packets hits one of their choke points, it's scanned and quashed. Gone," he snapped his fingers, "just like that."

"But we have to do something."

Bart circled their legs.

"Yeah," Dan said, standing. "That's what we still need to figure out. I assume we go after Todt Hill, take out his source of power. Cause some friction, rescue your friends."

Casey was nodding. Friction was good; rescuing friends was good. And not succumbing was very good.

Dan pushed his chair back, and it butted up against the dresser behind him. He ruffled Bart's fur. "In the meantime, this guy needs to go for a walk."

She waved him back down. "I'll do it," she said. "I could use the fresh air."

"What about your breakfast?"

"I'm suddenly not that hungry."

3

After receiving a safety briefing, Casey was off. Everything east of the hotel was good; everything south of Fourteenth Street was good, too. With the power out so often and the general state of disrepair downtown, the ICP's cameras were basically useless. The useful cameras could be avoided with an app Dan had installed on her screen. With Bart on a leash, Casey headed east on St. Mark's. Most of last night's snow was now a messy mix of slushy footfalls and packed ice, with all of it melting in the brisk, sunny afternoon.

Casey, bundled in Kristof's peacoat and a hoodie provided by Jennifer, carefully plodded through the slush. Bart, caring a bit less, led her to the curb. He sniffed out a spot next to an ICP kiosk and proceeded to piss all over its snow-covered base. "Good boy," she said, appreciating the gesture.

As Bart did his business, Casey closed her eyes and lifted her face toward the high-noon sun, basking in the vitamin D she'd been lacking. Letting her mind wander, she thought about her mom. What could be going through her mind? Her only child was wanted by the ICP. Did she buy it? Was she so turned around by Bruce that she couldn't see the truth? Sighing, Casey opened her eyes. These were questions for another time and for a reunion she was determined to make happen.

With Bart's business complete—at least the number one half—they kept on heading east. The plan was to check out the vet on

Avenue A and maybe stop by the old apartment again to see if her dad had tried to make contact. St. Mark's, a street she knew to be historically busy, was quiet for a Friday afternoon. There were only a handful of pedestrians navigating the slick pavement with her, and car traffic was nonexistent. Casey assumed it was because of the snow, but a closer look revealed that many storefronts had been boarded up. The open businesses consisted of a combination of head shops, tattoo parlors, and noodle shops. The lack of business and busyness only increased the farther east they went.

It wasn't until they got to Avenue A that some semblance of city life returned. As it had been when she'd been there with Jennifer and Greg, Tompkins Square Park was buzzing with activity. People milled about on both sides of its wrought-iron and chain-link fencing. Inside, below snow-covered tree limbs, rows of tents and makeshift shelters could be seen with people clearing and shoveling snow from around them. Open fires burned in barrels along the paths. Outside, a church van with a serving area set up next to it had a line of people waiting for a chance at a meal.

Casey and Bart crossed over. Casey noted the sidewalks had been shoveled on this side of the street, with the excess snow piled up along the fence and curb. Bart sniffed the air, pulling her towards the food. "You've eaten a ton," she said, tugging him back gently. A priest shadowed the line with a bullhorn, preaching on about accepting Jesus, being saved, and a whole bunch of other stuff Casey had no interest in.

Turning to go in the opposite direction—uptown and toward the vet—she spotted a group of people, maybe ten in all, bundled up and carrying shovels. She picked out Bill immediately, his size leaving her in no doubt. Darcy was there too, her hair now tamed by a floppy knit cap on her head. As they went past Casey, she made eye contact with Darcy and half-waved hello. She hadn't expected to be recognized, but she was wrong.

Darcy touched Bill's forearm, said something, then broke from the pack. She looked tiny in Bill's wake but was not short by any means. "Hey, Parker," she said through a bright, wide smile. "Long time."

"Darcy, right?" Casey held out her hand.

"Yeah," Darcy said, switching her shovel from right hand to left. She took Casey's hand but held onto it more than shook it. "I've seen you on the kiosk. You are one popular girl."

"I know . . . It's all hype."

"I'm sure," Darcy said, letting go of her hand. She gave Casey the once-over. "You've been through some shit."

"Is it that obvious?"

"It is—but you still look good. The buzz cut suits you."

"Thanks," she said, blushing, feeling an attraction, sensing it was mutual, and dismissing it all at the same time. Again, it was not the right time or place. She had enough shit going on in her head and didn't need the distraction.

Darcy looked at Bart. "Who's this?" she asked, kneeling and petting him. "Wait," she said, looking up. "Is this Bart?"

Casey nodded. "You know him?"

"Sure. He's skinnier than I remember, but he's Beth's dog." Darcy stood.

"You knew Beth?"

"Knew?"

"Yeah. She died."

Darcy's bright expression slipped to dark. "The fire?"

"You know about that too?"

"Bill and I went by after. It looked suspicious . . . more like a bomb than any kind of fire I've seen."

Casey agreed wholeheartedly.

"We didn't know," Darcy continued, "but we speculated that it had something to do with the Resistance." Darcy lifted the cuff of her coat sleeve and showed Casey the tattoo Greg had seen. On the inside of her wrist was a circle with two lines inside. "We're supporters."

"You knew that Beth was part of it?"

"Yeah. Beth and your father. It was all rumor and ghost-like shit, but we knew. They were generous to us, dropping off generators, clothes, you name it." She looked away, then back. "Fuck. Beth. Really?" Her large brown eyes were wet.

"Really."

"And your father?" She touched Casey's arm. "Please tell me he's okay."

"From the fire, yes. But he's gone missing since."

"Shit."

"Yeah." Casey looked at Bart, then back to Darcy. *Fuck it,* she thought. She had a lot to say, and when was the right time or place anyway? She pointed uptown. "You feel like going to the vet? I'm going to bring Bart by."

"Damn . . . I'd love to, seriously, but we're doing the neighborhood." She held the shovel up. "It's hard enough to live down here, so we help out."

"No, no . . . That's cool, and that *is* cool. You guys seem like a community."

"Adversity will do that."

"I'm learning."

Darcy touched her shoulder. "You should come by." She tilted her head. "We slip in at the entrance on Seventh. Just ask for me. Someone will find me." She knelt again to pet Bart. "Good luck with him, too." She stood up to go.

"Thanks," Casey said. "Entrance on Seventh. I'll come by."

"Cool."

Separating, they went off in opposite directions. Casey turned and caught Darcy looking back over her shoulder, too. They both smiled. Casey turned back and continued on, her step lighter than it had been before.

Maybe this was exactly the right time and exactly the right place after all.

4

It was just past seven p.m., and Casey was on her way to the park. She walked south on Avenue A, heading for the entrance at the corner of Seventh. With the electricity out, Dan had loaned her a flashlight. She'd left him at the hotel, as before, in his seat by the window. She'd asked him to come along, but he'd said no. He was on a roll formulating a plan, and didn't want to lose momentum.

His plan was all about the chip in her head: specifically, how it had been turned on, then off again after she'd been questioned by Jennifer's father. Dan thought he could fashion a way to turn the chips off en masse with his hacked schematics, thereby freeing Martin and the others all at once. It seemed like a worthwhile plan, nascent as it was.

From the back pocket of her jeans, Casey's screen vibrated. Slipping it out, she saw there was a message from Jennifer, who was apologizing, again, for not making it downtown after school. Her father had ordered security to accompany her, or, as Jennifer put it, "I have a fucking leech in a suit who won't leave my side." Casey replied that it was okay and very much expected. Thinking about it, she realized how fortunate she'd been to reach Jennifer before her father had.

It was a win . . . a small one, but still a win.

As she approached Seventh Street, there was a line around the corner to enter the park. She walked past the front of the line and around, counting herself about tenth. Getting in line at the back, she tapped off her flashlight. There were two girls in front of her, vaping and chatting as if they were waiting to enter a club. As the line moved forward, she could see ahead to the front: a big, burly guy was next to go in. After stuffing his backpack between the loosely padlocked fence poles, he knelt down and squeezed inside sideways.

Then, from around the corner, some kind of light, a spotlight, switched on and illuminated the street. Calls of "Cops!" echoed inside the park. Casey's nerves, pretty quiet since her escape, were suddenly jolted. The searchlight was moving south, towards Seventh . . . and her. She crept backward off the line, turned, and strode in the opposite direction. She looked over her shoulder and saw one of the club girls frozen in place, her silhouette captured in the spotlight as her friend moved out of it. Casey kept walking, only faster. After a moment she glanced back again. The girl in the spotlight was on her knees now, her hands over her head. Two cops were moving toward her with their guns drawn. They took her down with a shove to the sidewalk. *Fucking excessive*, Casey thought, rushing to hide behind the nearest tree. The girl, now cuffed, was being dragged to the corner. A van—not the black, unmarked ICP kind, but one with "NYPD" painted across its side—sat waiting. Its spotlight glared from on top. Then, it was over. Doors thumped closed, the spotlight switched off, and the van pulled away. Casey, left breathless, leaned her hand against the tree. The dark and quiet settled back in.

"Fuck," she said as her breathing steadied.

She felt bad for the stranger but relieved for herself.

After a moment, she stepped from behind the tree. She stomped snow from her shoes, then slapped at her cuffed jeans to rid herself of more. Everything below her shins felt cold and wet. She debated calling it a night; the risk of recapture felt all too real. But with the line gone and a life still to lead, she hurried back to the corner. At the not-so-secret entrance, she scooted through the loosely chained fence poles, ducked under the chain and padlock, and slipped inside.

The relief from one side of the fence to the other was palpable.

Walking a path, she turned her flashlight on. There were benches on her left and a darkened statue of a man pointing on her right. Each section of the park was defined by chest-high wrought-iron fencing. Tarps and tents filled the space. Even with the power down and the police on the prowl, there was an electricity to the place. People passed her, both coming and going. Almost all accepted her presence with a nod or a pleasant hello.

Up ahead was a plaza, or what looked like the park's central gathering area. There were maybe fifty people, solo and in groups, milling about. Here, she figured, is where she'd ask around for Darcy. She was nervous but eager to make a new friend. Stepping into the space, she realized there was a plan to the chaos. As before, there were tarps and tents around the circular perimeter, but these weren't for sleeping; they were organized for the park's needs. There was a first aid tent, a charging station, a commissary, and a library, all advertised by handmade plaques and placards. Walking through the plaza center, Casey saw a large tree stump with displaced cobblestones around it. Past the stump was a string of benches in a semicircle formation. Again she spotted Bill right off, sitting on the back of a bench at the end of the semicircle. She didn't see Darcy in the group around him, but Bill saw her and waved her over.

"Hey," Casey said. "Bill, right?"

"Yep," Bill said. "Darcy said you might stop by." He tapped the space on the bench seatback next to him. "Sit."

Turning off her flashlight, she climbed up on the bench, careful not to bump into an electric lantern sitting on its slats. From her perch, she had a better view of the space, and it appeared as if it was filling up. "Something going on?" she asked.

"Assembly time. We gather every night."

Of course they did. Then, next to her, Darcy seemed to appear out of nowhere. As she settled in, Darcy pressed her shoulder into Casey's. The contact, as innocuous as it was, launched a smattering of butterflies in her belly.

"You made it," Darcy said.

"Just barely. Cops showed up at Seventh Street. I backed out, but they took one girl away."

Darcy leaned forward, looking at Bill. "Who'd they get?"

Bill shrugged. "I haven't heard."

"Shit," Darcy said, leaning back. "Sorry about that."

"Not your fault." She waved Darcy off. "Do the cops always mess with you guys?"

"Yes and no. Maybe once a day they hassle people, then leave." Darcy nodded toward the plaza. "With all this in here, it could be worse."

"It's because they don't give a shit," Bill chimed in, keeping his eyes on the crowd. "There's no grift to be had, no way to line their pockets." He turned to them. "We're all too poor."

Near the center of the plaza, a woman jumped up on the tree stump, a lantern in her gloved hand. She wore a large down coat, and her long gray hair spilled from underneath a peaked hat. A set of deep wrinkles framed her mouth. "Good evening, Park people," she said loudly, but not yelling. The people around her repeated what she said. Then a layer of people behind them did the same, and again for another group behind them until it seemed the whole park was engulfed. "We'll make this quick since it's cold out here," she said, and again it was repeated, and repeated. "Section heads, please report."

Next to her, Bill put his arm up and got to his feet. "Security reporting," he said, and the crowd repeated.

They were so involved, Casey thought, just then noticing a sheriff-style badge pinned to Bill's coat.

Bill announced that an entrance was being added to the Avenue B and Tenth Street side of the park. He warned everyone to try and avoid lining up when coming inside. "If there's congestion, loiter; don't line up." He lowered his arm as his message spread.

As the last of his words died out, Darcy stood on the bench with her arm raised. "Sanitation reporting," she said, and the crowd repeated.

That both her and Bill were so engaged with this community had Casey feeling lacking. She studied Darcy, admiring her self-assuredness as she checked off the day's shoveling accomplishments and called for more volunteers.

When Darcy was finished, she sat down again. From across the plaza, standing in front of the commissary, the next section head's hand went up. As a request was made for instant coffee and dry goods in general, Darcy leaned into Casey's shoulder again. "How'd I do?" she asked, her voice low.

"From where I'm sitting, great," Casey whispered.

Bill leaned over and held out his fist for a bump. Darcy reciprocated, smiling.

"It's my first time as a section head," she said. "I was so fucking nervous."

"You'd never know it."

Darcy smiled widely and her shoulders shimmed.

Next, from somewhere behind them, a woman spoke up. She announced herself as the head of the Disobedience section. Gripping the seatback, Casey turned to see her. The woman, dressed in a hooded parka, stood at the top of a small hill and held her arm high. There were tents planted around her. She updated the crowd on a protest taking place tomorrow with their friends from City Hall Park and Washington Square Park. The protest's goal was to shut down First Avenue and send a message to the mayor that the planned highway on First Avenue would not be tolerated. Wrapping up, she implored the gathered crowd to "make good trouble," and the park community responded with a chant of the same.

And, with that, Casey's first park assembly wrapped up. People streamed from the plaza to the paths surrounding it. To her, it was all new and sort of eye-opening. She hadn't really thought of what went on in the park. From the outside it seemed very ragtag, but clearly it was anything but. "That was great," she said to Darcy.

"Right," Darcy said. "Blew me away the first time, too."

Casey nodded.

Darcy turned to face her. "Hey," she said, her face lighting up like she had some big idea. "You want to see something else great?"

"Sure," Casey said.

Darcy hopped down from the bench and looked to Bill. His attention was elsewhere, so she smacked his leg. He turned to face her.

"Is the garage open?" she asked.

"I think so—Paul's doing inventory."

"Great," she said, taking Casey's hand and practically pulling her from the bench. "C'mon. You're going to love this."

5

"A car repair shop?" Casey asked. "I'm not really a—"

Darcy looked up from her screen. "Just wait," she said, tapping out a message.

Casey stepped back from the single-story building, shining her flashlight across its brick facade as she did so. There was a garage door to her left protected by a rusty gate. Darcy was at the shop's entrance; its gate was down as well. Above the entrances, on the top half of the brick building, snow-capped, weather-worn signage read " UDLOW GAR GE" in blue and "AUTO REPA R" in a smaller, red font underneath. They were on Ludlow Street, hence the garage's name, about a ten-minute walk from the park—a walk during which Casey let Darcy dominate with talk of her time in the park and how she came to be there.

Darcy had been living in Brooklyn with her grandmother until Hurricane Betty flooded them out. She had managed to get her grandmother, whom she lovingly called Nan, into a home. But Darcy was a college freshman, working only part-time, and she couldn't afford college housing on top of the bill for her Nan's care. With no place to call home, she ended up in Tompkins Square Park because her school was nearby. "You get used to the bad," she'd said, citing the noise, the cold, and the lack of privacy. "But you stay for the good." Here she talked about the community, the democracy, and the friends she'd made.

Darcy held up her screen. "He's on his way," she said—the "he" being Paul, one of her aforementioned friends.

After another moment, the main gate rattled up, and light spilled out, interrupting the quiet and dark around them. Holding the door open, Paul waved them inside. He was tall and square-jawed. He wore a motorcycle jacket, jeans, and a few days' growth of stubble. If Jennifer hadn't found true love with Martin, Paul would have been right up her alley. As Casey passed, he smiled warmly, and she reciprocated. Once they were through, he rolled down the gate, then closed and locked the door. Its glass panels were blacked out with some kind of shiny film.

Darcy made the introductions, but Paul, like Darcy and Bill before him, seemed to know already who she was or knew of her heritage. She heard once again how her father was a hero and an inspiration. Paul's accolades were heartfelt, as those of the others had been. Casey appreciated the words but took them as more bitter than sweet, what with her father being MIA and all.

Darcy grabbed Casey playfully by the wrist and followed Paul inside. A pair of construction lights, set on tripods raised toward a high ceiling, lit the space. Stepping past them, Casey took care not to trip on the cables running from the lights to a generator in between. There were three spots for car repairs, complete with hydraulic lifts, some rusted-out tool cabinets, and dormant diagnostic equipment.

Darcy led Casey toward a truck—medium-sized and parked facing the wall—at the far end of the room. They stopped at the back; its cargo door was rolled up and open. Inside were a bunch of boxes stacked up high. The boxes, each about the size of a knapsack, were labeled "PowerLite" in a fancy font on the side. After grabbing a tablet-sized screen from the truck's deck, Paul jumped inside and began examining the boxes while tapping at the screen.

"This is what I wanted to show you," Darcy said, hopping up onto the truck. Lifting a box from the closest stack, she waved Casey closer, then handed it to her with a warning about its heft. Jumping down, Darcy then took the box from Casey and knelt with it on the grease-stained floor. She glanced at the shop's entrance, then peeled the top open, angling the lid so Casey could see inside.

"A portable generator?" Casey questioned.

"Yup . . . lots of them."

"I'm not sure I get it."

Darcy stood up. "It's not the generator itself. It's that we have them at all." She sauntered to the truck and patted its side panel. "You see this truck here? It was meant for some stuck-up, upstate country club, but the driver knew your father and had other ideas. When he couldn't find your dad, he came to us." She moved toward Casey, proud and smiling. "These will now go to the people who really need them."

Finally, Casey got it, and she did indeed love it.

"Detective Warren, up at the Ninth," Darcy continued, "says they're looking for them. But he promised us a heads up if they get too close."

"The Ninth? Warren was my dad's partner."

"Yeah—he's our mole. Nice guy."

Huh, Casey thought. This was all about carrying on her father's work: inside and out. Her heart swelled. "That's excellent," she said, gesturing at the open box, then covering her mouth and chin with her hand. "It would make him very happy," she said, fighting back tears.

"Shit," Darcy said, stepping closer. "I didn't mean—"

"No . . . it's great. It's just been a hard couple of months. All of this kinda brings that fact home." Casey inched back, turning her head, hoping for composure. She didn't like or want to be vulnerable.

Darcy took her hand and forced eye contact. "You've been through a lot, Parker. You're allowed to feel it."

"It's not the time."

"No," Darcy said, glancing back at the truck. "It is the time . . . it's always the time." Keeping hold of Casey's hand, she led her away.

Casey looked at their clasped hands. Even with her sadness, the act's intimacy was not lost on her; it was welcome. Shading her eyes, they walked past the lights and into a waiting room next to the shop's entrance. There was a small reception desk to their right sporting a faded "Ludlow Garage" logo on its front. A cracked plexiglass window behind the desk looked out into the garage, and plastic chairs lined two walls. The third, far wall was occupied by a half-full water cooler, the stagnant water tinged brown. Next to the cooler was a folding table. A coffee maker and some weathered and worn paper cups, arranged in short, uneven stacks, sat on the table.

"Sit," Darcy ordered, pointing to the chairs.

Together they sat, with Darcy resting a knee on her chair to face her. Through her jeans, the chair's plastic seat rubbed against the wound on the back of her thigh. She shifted, putting her knee up as well, letting it touch Darcy's ever so slightly. After a little more encouragement, she told Darcy her story. She started with the day they had met when looking for Martin and ended with Dan in the hotel room formulating a plan. In between, she showed her the video her dad had left for her. Darcy was appropriately outraged and sympathetic in all the right places. Casey let her feel the scar where they had implanted the chip. All the while, they continued to touch and hold hands. Casey hadn't let anyone get close since her father had left, if not longer. This contact—physical and emotional—was nice.

When Casey was finished, Darcy went silent. After a moment, she began to nod. "I'll help you, you know?"

"You are helping."

"No. I will help you shut down that place." She pointed at Paul. "We all will."

"I can't ask you—"

"You're not asking, Parker. I'm offering."

6

On their way back to the park, Jennifer messaged. She'd ditched her tail and was on her way downtown. She said she had a surprise; moreover, Dan was in on it, and Casey was to meet her at the hotel. Darcy was game, so together they headed back. With the heavy feelings behind them, the cold walk was full of laughter, shoulder brushes, and light, playful hand-holding. Neither of them acknowledged what exactly was happening, but Casey was falling, and she hoped Darcy was too.

At Dan's hotel room door, she started to knock but stopped. She looked at Darcy, who was smiling, infectiously so.

"What?" Darcy asked.

"Thanks for listening back there. I needed that."

"No problem, Parker. Maybe for our second date, you can counsel me."

"We're calling this a date?"

"Shit, yeah. I'm not like this with everyone."

Casey smiled. "Shit yeah," she repeated, knocking on the door.

Jennifer answered with Bart by her side. She hugged Casey before she could get out of the hall. After reintroducing Darcy, they headed inside, stopping to say hello to Bart along the way.

"How did you manage to ditch . . ." Casey started to ask, but she stopped when she saw who was waiting for her. Hovering over Dan at the back table were Greg and Stan. She was indeed surprised—not so much by Greg, because he was one of their crew, but by Stan for sure. Maybe the two had become best buds after all. They turned to face her.

"Ta-da!" Jennifer said, sweeping her hand in front of her.

Greg walked past the beds—the unused one was piled with their winter attire—and came in for a hug. This was new. Sure, they were friends, but they'd never been hugging friends. Just extraordinary circumstances, she assumed.

"It's so good to see you," he said as they separated.

She choked up at the sentiment. "You too," she said.

Stan came up next; he extended his hand awkwardly. She swiped it aside and hugged him as well. When Casey was done, he stepped back, gazing down as he did so. "I'm sorry I wasn't more helpful before your recruit . . ." He checked himself, looking up. "Abduction."

"You were as helpful as you could have been," she said, then looked at Jennifer. "I guess you told them."

"Half the school came up to me today."

"I didn't think I was that popular."

"Neither did I," Jennifer said, smiling. "Don't worry, though. I was selective with your story. No point in making everyone accomplices."

"Like we aren't all complicit in some way anyway," Greg added, brushing his bangs from his eyes. "We just went along with whatever Recruiting did, like it was a blessing and not the curse it really is."

"Damn straight," Darcy said, putting her fist out for Greg to bump.

Dan got up from his window seat and joined them. The dark circles under his eyes had darkened further since the morning. Casey introduced Darcy to him and the group. Darcy bounced between them, eager and happy to meet everyone, but she seemed reverent with Dan. "I've heard about you," she said, practically bowing. She looked at Casey. "Your father used to talk about this hacker guy." She turned back to Dan. "He called you 'the brains' of the crew."

Blushing a bit, Dan shook Darcy's hand.

"I'm sorry about Beth and Garrett," Darcy said before letting go.

"Thank you," Dan said, grimacing.

When all the introductions were over, Jennifer took the floor. She put her arm around Stan's shoulders; he sheepishly glanced at the floor. "Stan," she said, "has agreed to do some snooping around his father's lab."

"Hopefully, he can get his hands on some of his father's tech," Dan added.

"You sure you want to do that?" Casey asked.

Stan shrugged. "Yeah, I think so. Jennifer told me what he did to you . . . and Martin. It's not right. I feel horrible."

"What he did to me is not on you," Casey said.

"I know. But I can't sit by. I want to help."

"Me too," Greg said. "Anything." He looked at Darcy. "Just as long as I can get one of those kick-ass tattoos."

"Hell yeah," Darcy said. "We got a guy at the park. He's talented."

"Looks like you got a team again," Jennifer said to Dan.

Dan looked to Casey. "Your father would be proud."

"Yeah, but it would be better if he were here to lead us."

"I think you'll do just fine," Darcy said.

Casey scoffed. "I'm no leader."

"Sure you are," Dan said. "It's in your blood. People trust you."

She didn't think she had earned their trust, and she certainly didn't think she was a leader. All she had done was get herself abducted and brainwashed. As her friends paired off—Darcy and Greg talked tattoos and anarchy, while Dan and Stan talked business—Jennifer put her arm around her.

"You okay?" Jennifer asked.

"Yeah," Casey said. "I guess." They sat on the edge of Dan's unmade bed. Bart jumped up to join them. "This leader talk is weird." Bart circled, then dropped next to her. "I'm not much for rallying the troops." She rubbed Bart's exposed belly.

"We don't need you to rally us. We're rallied enough. We just need you to be strong, to set an example. It's not about rousing speeches. It's about action. And more than anyone here, you've done that. Shit, Case—you agreed to be abducted and taken right into the fucking lion's den, all to help someone else—that's a leader."

Casey nodded along. Maybe she was discounting herself. It wouldn't be the first time. But there was more. What they were doing was dangerous, serious stuff, and she had never thought of herself as a serious person, let alone a leader. Yet here she was, being serious, with people's lives at stake. "What if something happens, though?" she questioned.

"I think we all know what we're signing up for."

Casey looked around the charged hotel room. Except for Dan, she didn't think they did know. She thought she had known, and yet she still ended up with a chip in her head. "Do they, though? Do you? The guards at Todt Hill—they shot at me. People could die, Jen. Fuck . . . people have died." She gazed at the garish carpet. "I don't know if I can live with the consequences."

CHAPTER EIGHT | BURNING DOWN THE HOUSE

I

THE BLOW STUNNED HER.

Casey staggered back, away from Bill. The sparring mats on the repair shop's floor sighed underfoot. Bill huffed and puffed, looking bigger and more menacing with each puff. She wiped the corner of her mouth with the side of her gloved fist. He'd drawn blood. So much for playing around. Casey showed him the blood on her padded knuckle.

His posture deflated. "Shit, man," he said. "I'm sorry." He lumbered forward, almost tripping on the edge of a mat. He had his hands up, surrendering.

"No," she said, shaking him off. "I'm all right."

"Damn right, you are," Darcy said as she watched from the sidelines.

Casey pointed at Darcy, then to her heart. "I fight for you," she said, double-tapping her chest with her glove.

Bill stepped back. "And who am I fighting for?" He swept his arms around, talking to a mostly empty garage.

"You're fighting for your pride, son," Darcy said. "That my girl is still in this should embarrass you."

Bill stood tall, squaring his shoulders.

"She's not wrong," Casey said, waving him on.

Bill smiled, wide and toothy. "Fine," he said, stepping forward. "But if I hurt you, it's on her." Bill pointed at Darcy.

"I'm not going to give you that chance," Casey said, dancing on the balls of her feet.

Bill came at her. He led with a right, which she easily ducked under. Dancing away, she smacked her fists together. There was no way a punch, even a clean one, would take him down. She needed to get at his legs. She watched his torso, waiting for him to signal his next move. She grinned to egg him on. He swung again, this time from the left. Casey pushed his arm out of the way, then barreled her shoulder into his side. He staggered, off balance, but she didn't let him get far. Before he could get his feet under him, Casey swept her leg around the back of his and took his feet out. Bill landed on his back with a thump. Casey landed next, but with her knee on his chest and her forearm under his neck.

"Glad we put the mats down now, aren't you?" she said, grinning.

Off to the side, Darcy cheered.

"Lucky," he said as she pushed herself off his chest.

Darcy stomped over to Casey, then held Casey's arm up, prize-fighter style. Together they danced, cheered, and ribbed Bill as he lumbered to his feet.

From the waiting area beyond the floodlights, Dan leaned out of the doorway, his hands braced on the door's frame. He had made the space an office for all things Resistance, and he was working inside. "I hate to be that guy," he said, "but it's late, and I still have these packets to prepare. We all have a big day tomorrow."

Despite his sounding like one, Casey resisted the easy 'Dad' reference. He was right, after all: It was getting late, and tomorrow was a big day. After weeks of planning, tomorrow they were infiltrating Todt Hill, and those packets he was preparing were the key to exposing Hargrove's operation.

Bill held his arms up in appeasement. "Sorry, man," he said, still a bit out of breath.

"Yeah," Casey said. "We didn't mean—"

"It's okay." Dan rubbed under his eyes, then waved them off. "Just get some rest," he said before ducking back inside.

Darcy let Casey's victory arm drop. "He looks beat," she said.

"Yeah. I don't think I've seen him go outside in days."

Darcy sidled up to Casey, slipping her hand into Casey's back pocket as they stepped off the mats. "That was pretty hot, you know?"

"What? Dan scolding us?"

"Stop. You—kicking ass."

Casey checked the office, then reciprocated Darcy's back-pocket move. She was not too keen on going public with Darcy just yet. They had a mission to get through, and she didn't want to be perceived as playing favorites. Bill knew they were kind of a thing, and, of course, Jennifer was entirely on board. Beyond that, the extent of their relationship was anybody's guess. After tomorrow, though, when the mission was over, the general public could know. Hell, after tomorrow, she'd shout it from the rooftops. "You thought that was hot?" she asked.

Darcy raised an eyebrow.

"Then maybe we listen to Dan and get some rest." Casey nudged Darcy with her hip. "They restocked the minibar this morning."

"Your room does not have a minibar."

"True," Casey said. "But there may be a bottle of bourbon I bought for tomorrow." She dug her hand deeper into Darcy's pocket and pulled her closer. "And the place does have ice."

"Are you propositioning me on the night before the mission?"

Casey's cheeks flushed. "All I mentioned was the bourbon and the ice."

2

Even before she could open her eyes, Casey woke, smiling. Behind her, naked ass to naked ass, was Darcy. Turns out there had been more than bourbon on the menu after all. After two weeks of impromptu dates, sly glances, and stolen kisses, they had finally had sex. Casey opened her eyes. Sunlight clawed its way in from around her hotel-room curtains. She rubbed her lids, slowly remembering that today was a serious day. She ran her hand down across her face, forcing her smile inside. In the context of risking life and limb, the sex made sense. There was nothing like the threat of death to put the present into perspective.

Casey pressed her ass into Darcy's, increasing and relishing the naked contact. Darcy's skin was slightly chilled, as they had lowered the hotel room's heat to accommodate their own. Casey raised her head, looking to the foot of the bed for the sheets and blanket, but they were lost somewhere off the end, kicked and pushed away during their frenetic night. She rolled over, big spoon to little, and pressed herself tight, trying for as much skin to skin as possible. Darcy stirred and shifted closer, wordlessly helping with the pressing.

Casey closed her eyes, inching up and resting her head against Darcy's shoulder. She shushed her mind as it tried to skip forward in the day. *Not yet*, she told herself. *For once, just be.* Darcy stirred again, then slowly turned. Casey slipped from her shoulder and rested her head on her arm and pillow. Darcy did the same, adding a caress of Casey's shoulder to their touching.

"Hey," Darcy said, a sleepy, soft smile on her face.

Casey brushed her fingertips across Darcy's hip. "Good morning," she said back.

"It is, isn't it?" Darcy moved in for a kiss.

Casey hesitated, night breath and all, but relented as Darcy's soft lips contacted, then separated her own. Tips of tongues touched. Casey let her arm slip from Darcy's hip and rest between her legs, pubic hair brushing on her wrist and thumb. Darcy's knees parted slightly, giving Casey's hand deeper access.

Darcy pulled back from the kiss, her eyes closed.

"You sleep okay?" Casey asked.

Darcey moaned. "Yes," she said, pressing her legs together. She opened her eyes. "Except for the cold. What the fuck were we thinking?"

"Oh, man, we weren't." Casey looked for the sheets again. "Let me," she said, pushing herself up.

"No," Darcy said, holding Casey's busy arm in place. "I like it like this: a full view."

Casey dropped down, smiling, and they both shifted closer. "I think that's exactly what we were thinking."

Darcy brought her arm down between them and mimicked Casey's touch.

"Fuck," Casey muttered, closing her eyes. She pushed her hips forward. Arms, hands, bodies mixed. She had to pee but ignored the urge.

"What time do we have to be at the repair shop?" Darcy asked, her voice as soft as her touch.

"We start packing the truck at nine."

"Didn't Bill say he'd stay and take care of it?"

"You're right, he did." Casey raised her head to see over Darcy's shoulder. On the nightstand between the beds, an old digital alarm clock read quarter to eight. The bed she'd been using until last night was still made, its comforter and sheets tucked tight at the corners. "It looks like we have some time, then."

They shifted closer, kissing, with tongues and lips lingering. But Casey's mind raced again; her body stiffened. Suddenly she was back in the procedure room, confined and screaming, feeling unimaginable pain as her chip was turned on. She pushed the image from her head, but not before Darcy inched away, her brow furrowed with concern. "You okay?" she asked. "Did I hurt you?"

"No, don't stop. This is nice." Casey took her hand from between Darcy's legs and placed it at the small of Darcy's back, urging her closer. "I think the thought of going back there has made me nervous."

"That's understandable."

Casey thought about being locked up, about the rescue that never came, and about how alone she'd felt. Emotions welled up inside her. She silently cursed as she fought to keep them in check, but a chin quake gave her away.

"Hey . . . it's okay," Darcy said, removing her hand. She slipped her arm up and under Casey's, pulling her close. "It's different this time.

I'll be there with you." She leaned her head back, looking Casey in the eyes. "No one's going to pull any shit on my girlfriend."

Casey smiled. "Girlfriend?"

"You have a problem with that?" she questioned with mock incredulity.

Casey kissed her, their lips barely touching. "Not one fucking bit."

3

The troops were massed.

Ludlow Garage and Car Repair, the makeshift headquarters for a makeshift Resistance, buzzed with life. Casey, dressed in her peacoat, hoodie, cap, and gloves—fresh from the hotel—stepped past the floodlights and into the brightly lit space. She pulled off her cap, its fibers clinging to her stubbly hair. She tugged off her gloves. At the far end of the garage, Bill passed boxes up to Greg, who was standing on the deck of the stolen box truck. They were dressed in matching white jumpsuits and white painter's caps. A logo for Trident Cleaning & Supply was on their chests and caps. It was the same logo—a three-pronged mop, brandished by a brawny, jumpsuit-clad man—that they'd plastered across the stolen truck. The plan was to go in Trojan Horse-style, and the official cleaning company of Todt Hill was their cover. Bill turned, armload in hand, and nodded, acknowledging Casey's arrival. She tipped her hat and gloves his way, then stuffed them into her coat pockets.

Off to her right, Darcy was running through today's plan. With her back to the room and with Lena and Jamal, two Park people, next to her, she pointed to a large screen with the blueprints for Todt Hill's gymnasium on it. All three were dressed in the white Trident Cleaning jumpsuits, the same as Bill and Greg. Casey moved toward them, hovering a few feet behind. The all-too-familiar gymnasium had its layout tweaked with a stage opposite the overlook conference room, and chairs set facing it. Today was a graduation day of sorts, with the latest group to reach Level Four surfacing. Thanks to the tap on the mayor's computer—he had been invited to attend—Dan had learned of the assembly and set his plan to deactivate the brainwashing chips around it.

Darcy turned from the screen. Seeing Casey, she smiled sheepishly.

Watching her new girlfriend, Casey realized that, in a weird way, Darcy reminded her of her mother. It was the way she held her shoulders back, more confident than stuffy. That was her mom. Casey sighed, thinking about her. It had been too long, and she had things to share: her father's truth for one, and her relationship with Darcy for two. She hoped that after today, a reunion would be possible; she brightened at the thought. If everything went well, Hargrove, Todt Hill, and his brainwashing scheme would all be exposed.

She turned to go and check on Bill. On her way around, she noticed Jennifer watching her through the cracked plexiglass window of the shop's waiting room. She was standing next to Dan, who had his back to the window, studying a trio of screens in front of him. Stan was there too, pacing the length of the room. They were all dressed in street clothes, as their roles in today's operation had them staying back, with Dan pulling the strings. Jennifer waved at her, squinted inquisitively, then grinned. *She knows*, Casey thought—she knows about the sex with Darcy. Jennifer always knew. Blushing, she gave her best friend the finger, then continued across the garage to Bill.

"Ninja," Bill greeted her, extending his oversized hand.

"You shouldn't encourage me," she said as they double-slapped palms, and fist-bumped hello. "How goes it?"

"This jumpsuit is riding me hard." He bent at the knees and wriggled a bit for effect.

Casey rolled her eyes. "With the truck, I mean. How goes it with the truck?"

Bill motioned to the open cargo box. Greg was inside, stacking shelves. "I think we're good," he said. "We got the temp down—should beat the sensor—but it'll be a cold few minutes for you guys," he smirked.

"Don't gloat."

"It's not my fault that I'm too big for that space."

The space Bill was referring to was a hidden compartment—a false wall, really—that they'd built at the back of the cargo box, behind the cab. With two people riding up front, the other four in back would have to hide. The cold part came in as a way to mask the extra body heat. They had rigged the truck's air conditioning to pump into the space. Casey stepped closer to the truck. "And Dan's tech?" she asked.

"Jensen!" Bill called up to Greg. "Show Ninja here the bins."

Grabbing a handgrip at the back of the truck, she hopped onto its deck. Taking up the majority of the truck's open space were four waist-high plastic bins. Each bin was filled to the top with Todt Hill Academy–branded towels.

"Ninja?" Greg questioned, lifting a box of bleach from a stack near the back of the truck.

"From our sparring," she answered. "I took him down."

"Who would've thought?" Greg said, slipping between the rear two bins.

"Certainly not me," she said as he joined her at the front. "And what about you? I don't think I've ever seen you work so hard."

"It's a phase."

"Well, it's becoming."

Smiling, Greg pushed the sleeves of his jumpsuit up, his new Resistance tattoo visible on his forearm, just above his wrist. He reached into the bin. From the center stack of towels, he removed a bunch to reveal a black plastic box with two rubberized antennae attached at its sides. At the top of the box was a screen, off for now, but ready to be activated by Dan once the bins were in place around the gym and a connection made to the brainwashing machine upstairs.

"Looks good," she said, touching Greg's shoulder. "Thanks." Turning, she hopped down. She saw Jennifer heading her way. "You have everything you need?" she asked Bill, leaning in Jennifer's direction.

"Everything."

"Excellent," she said, then turned away. Stepping over the flood-lights' wires, she met Jennifer halfway.

"You're late," Jennifer said. "He's getting antsy."

"Yeah." Casey looked over Jennifer's shoulder to the waiting room. Dan was still busy, and Stan was still pacing. She noticed Bart was there too, asleep in his bed under the desk. "We didn't want to walk in together."

Jennifer leaned in. "I can't believe you had sex."

Casey ignored her best friend's disbelief, wrapped her arm around hers, and led her back the way she came.

"You're practically glowing," Jennifer tried again. "What has it been, a year?"

"And two months," Casey whispered as they walked into the waiting room. "I don't know. Maybe finally having some answers about my dad helped."

Bart raised his head and yawned. Stan stopped his pacing and mock-saluted her.

Casey returned it as Jennifer studied her. "You do seem differ-ent," Jennifer said. "In a good way, not an I've-been-fucked-up-by-brainwashing way."

"Thanks," Casey said. "It's probably a bit of both."

Dan looked over his shoulder. On his center screen, paused, was Jennifer, shown from the waist up, in the manner of a news anchor. She was dressed semi-formally in a button-down shirt; her hair was pulled back. Next to her, paused mid-scroll, was a list of names. The list was drawn from the pool of brainwashed recruits who would be part of today's assembly. The recording served two purposes: first, to warn the recruits—hopefully softening the blow when their chips were switched off—and, second, to expose Jennifer's father. The recording, along with the packets of incriminating evidence Dan had worked on the night before, were to be streamed across the tristate area. It was a one-two punch, meant to cut off the flow of recruits and put Michael Hargrove behind bars.

Dan spun around in his chair. "You're late," he said, more tired than angry.

"It was strategic, trust me," Casey said.

Bart stood, stretched, then sauntered over to her. She knelt, scratching him behind his ears. He dropped for a belly rub. His fur was soft and free of the knots she had felt when she first found him. Casey looked up at Dan. His eyes were red, and the circles underneath were dark. She knew he was beyond tired, yet he kept on going anyway. "You promise to get some sleep tonight, right?"

"If this plan works, I'll get all the sleep."

"If?" Stan questioned.

"There are no guarantees," Casey said, wrapping up Bart's belly rub. "Something I know all too well."

Tail wagging, Bart headed to the corner of the room, past the row of chairs, to where his bowls were set up.

Getting to his feet, Dan frowned.

"Sorry," Casey said. She knew Dan still felt terrible about her botched abduction, and she hadn't meant to make light of it.

"It's the truth," he said. "Even the best-laid plans can go to shit."

"Great," Stan said, starting to pace again.

Casey moved to block his path. "We have a good plan," she said. "We'll be all right."

It was a good plan—she meant that—but there were lots of choke points where things could go wrong: the guards at the entrance, the hand scanners, or someone eyeballing them as out of place. That they were splitting up made things even more nerve-racking. With Bill leading the team into the gymnasium, it was up to Casey and Darcy to make the connection to, then promptly destroy, the brainwashing machine. That meant being near the conference room and next to the infirmary, and all the potential contact that came from that.

In Dan's hand was a small package, which he handed to Casey.

"They came?" she asked, eyes wide.

He nodded, smiling.

"I picked them up from the P.O. box this morning," Jennifer said.

Casey pressed the cardboard at the box's edge, then pulled its packing tape from down the center. Inside, cushioned by foam on all sides, were two hard-sided eyeglass cases. The glasses were of the spy variety and a concession for their having to split up. They would give Dan a bird's-eye view and let Casey and Bill keep in touch. "Do we need to sync them?" she asked, taking one case out and placing the box on the desk.

"Yes, and we need to make sure they're charged."

Darcy appeared in the doorway. Casey held the case up for her to see.

"They came," Darcy said, smiling. "Excellent. I'll get Bill."

Casey smiled back as Darcy spun around. She watched her go, thinking about their night together. Still smiling, Casey noticed Dan staring at her. "Say it," she said.

"It's not my business." He gathered the box from the desk.

"It's okay. Our business is pretty much each other's anyway."

He took the second case out and placed it on the desk's charging pad. An indicator on the case's lid held a steady green. "Well," he said, "as it relates to our shared business, you're about to face some serious shit." He picked up the case and handed it to her. "I don't want you preoccupied."

Casey looked at Jennifer, who raised an eyebrow in response.

"It's a bit late for that," Casey said, handing him back the first case. "But I hear you."

"I don't want to be out of line."

Casey inched closer to Dan as Bill and Darcy crowded into the room. "You're not out of line," she said. "I trust your instincts. My head will be in the game, I promise. It's kinda programmed for that."

Dan nodded, placing the second case on the charging pad. It, too, held a steady green and was ready to go. He handed it to her, and Casey held both up for Bill to see.

"They came," Bill said as Darcy moved to Casey's side.

"This morning," Jennifer said. "Early delivery."

Casey handed one of the cases to Bill.

Darcy leaned in close to Casey. "What was that all about?" she whispered.

"That was why we walked in separately," Casey said, opening her case. The glasses were plastic-rimmed and generally stylish. "He thinks I may be distracted."

"The way I'm rockin' this jumpsuit," she said, nudging her shoulder into Casey's, "you better be."

"Darcy," Bill interrupted. He handed his screen to her.

Her smile sagged as she read the opened message. "Shit," she muttered, looking at Bill.

"What?" Casey asked.

Darcy handed Bill back his screen. "Remember I mentioned that your father's partner at the Ninth is kinda our mole?"

"Sure," Casey said.

Dan stepped forward to make a foursome. "Detective Warren?" he asked.

"Yeah," Bill said.

Jennifer and Stan joined the group, settling in next to Casey.

"Well," Darcy said, "he says they're planning on raiding the park today."

"Shit. That's not good," Jennifer said.

"Not good at all," Bill said. "They're looking for the generators."

"You mean like that stack sitting out there?" Dan pointed out the waiting-room door.

"And more in the park," Darcy said, "waiting to be distributed."

"He wants us to bring what we have left to a drop-off point." Bill held out his screen. A map showed a pin dropped near Broadway, off Tenth Street. "He thinks if we can get them to him, he can throw the task force off our scent. If not, they'll be ready to overturn the park looking for them."

Stan broke from the circle, then paced behind them.

Dan checked his screen, grimacing. Lena and Jamal hovered near the doorway.

"My mom has one in her tent," Jamal said. His dark eyes, and even darker eyebrows, converged with worry. "What if someone is caught with one?"

Bill turned. "They'll be arrested, I assume."

"We can't let that happen," Casey said.

Dan tapped at his screen. "There," he said to Bill, "I sent the code for the car. Take it; load it up."

Bill checked his screen. "Appreciate that."

"Jamal," Darcy said, "you come with me. We'll gather what we can from the park and warn them."

"I'll come too," Casey said.

"No," Darcy and Dan said in unison, taking Casey back.

"We need to keep prepping," Dan said.

"Give us an hour, if that," Bill said.

Darcy turned to Casey. "We got this," she said. "You need to keep a low profile, especially if cops are involved."

"I'm about to walk into a lion's den of brainwashed soldiers. I think I can handle a few cops."

"Best laid plans," Dan said, stepping away and patting Stan on the shoulder as Stan paced past.

Bill stripped off his jumpsuit.

"Case," Jennifer said. "It's not about what you can handle. Let them go."

"We'll be fine," Darcy said, stepping out of her jumpsuit. "You're not going down there without me." She handed the disguise to Casey. "We will be back. I promise."

4

The hour Bill had asked for was up, and they were not back.

What was left of the team anxiously waited, fittingly, in the repair shop's waiting room. Casey, standing over Dan, watched as he scrolled through social media feeds. Whatever had gone down with her father's ex-partner must not have gone well, because the park had indeed been raided. The social media posts confirmed the worst. There had been beatings, and there had been arrests. There were photos of people—some bloodied, others bewildered, but most just hopelessly looking on. There was video of police in riot gear, marching and swatting their way into the park. Casey recognized some of the forlorn faces, but Darcy's and Bill's were not among them. She was beside herself. Pulling her screen from her back pocket, she chewed at her lip. For the third, maybe fourth time, she messaged Darcy.

"She's probably fine," Jennifer said, putting her hand on Casey's back.

"It's the 'probably' part that's the problem."

Dan looked over his shoulder at them. "We need to make a decision," he said. "Our window is closing."

"Why don't we go in?" Stan asked from the row of waiting-room chairs. "It's not like we all don't know the plan." His knee bounced as he spoke.

It isn't the worst idea, Casey thought. But it wasn't the best, either. Their plan of placing the bins in the gymnasium called for stealth, and putting two more Roosevelt Prep people in that gymnasium would double their chances of being recognized. She looked to Greg, who was standing in the doorway, still dressed in his jumpsuit. Bart was on a leash by his side.

Greg pointed to himself, then around the room. "Four in the gym, one upstairs. We have the numbers."

Casey looked at Jennifer.

"I got nothing to lose," Jennifer said. "It's not like I wasn't going to be disowned when the video went live anyway."

Casey looked at Dan.

"I don't think we have much choice," he said. "The tap could be gone tomorrow. We may not get another chance."

"I don't know," Casey said. "Shouldn't we go to the park?" She pointed at Dan's screens. "See if we can help them?"

"What could we even do?" Dan questioned.

Casey checked her screen. "Ten more minutes," she said.

Shaking his head, Dan stood up and stepped between Casey and Jennifer. "We don't have ten more minutes," he said, practically in Casey's face. He continued on toward the door. Greg and Bart moved out of his way. "It's now, or who-the-fuck-knows-when," he said on his way out.

Unfortunately, she knew he was right. He was right about this, and, she reluctantly admitted, he was right about her being distracted. She knew if it wasn't Darcy out there, she wouldn't be looking for more time. Her feelings had compromised her. She looked around the room. Greg was on one knee, unhooking Bart from his leash while looking up at her. Stan got up from his chair and was closely watching her. Jennifer nodded her encouragement.

Casey looked at Jennifer, then at Stan. "You're both sure you want to do this?"

"Sure as shit," Jennifer said. "I love jumpsuits."

"Same," Stan said. "But without the jumpsuit part."

5

Traffic to Staten Island was heavier than expected.

Their window to act narrowed with every stop-and-go. Casey watched their progress from the back of the truck, split-screen-like, on the lens of her spy glasses. The view was Dan's, from the driver's seat, beamed back to her from his pair of glasses. They were now on Todt Hill Road, only minutes from their destination. The closer they got, the more nervous Casey became. While never having experienced any kind of post-traumatic stress before her brainwashing, she thought maybe the sick feeling in the pit of her stomach, along with her escalating heartbeat, came close. Biting at her lip, Casey watched as modest two-story homes slipped by. She held onto a well-stocked shelf for balance, swaying with the truck's every turn. With the bins taking up most of the floor space, the crew kept to the outskirts, holding and rocking as well. Casey and Jennifer were standing on one side; Greg and Stan were on the other. It was like a high-school outing except with stolen trucks and disguises.

Casey eyed Jennifer, who was, in turn, studying her again. Jennifer, her hair tucked under her Trident Cleaning cap, was wearing Darcy's jumpsuit and was rockin' it as well as Darcy had.

"Are you okay?" Jennifer quietly asked.

"Yeah, I think so," Casey said. "Being here is different than just talking about being here."

"I'm sure. But you'll be fine. We'll be in and out in no time."

Casey raised her hand, her fingers crossed.

"Come," Jennifer said, turning Casey to face her. "Let me take a look at you."

She straightened her posture as Jennifer adjusted the wig under

214 | MARC DANIEL ACRICHE

her cap. "The blonde suits you," she said. "The glasses do, too. You got a Sexy Librarian thing going."

Casey gestured to her jumpsuit. "But I was going for Sexy Maid."

Jennifer smiled. "Then next time, we cut off the legs. Get some butt cheek showing."

"In your dreams," Casey said as the truck hit a bump, rattling supplies and people alike. She held onto the rim of the bin next to her. "And, you? Are you ready to be the face of the Resistance?"

"If it means stopping my father and getting Martin back, I look forward to it."

Always confident, Casey thought. She wondered what that must be like.

From the receiver in her glasses, Dan cut in. "It's time."

From Dan's view, she saw they were turning onto the road that led to the Academy. There was no turning back. "We should get in," she said, waving Greg and Stan closer. Turning to the false wall behind her, she tugged at a seam. A panel gave way, and she pushed it open, pocket-door-style, letting out a stream of icy air. She moved to the side, letting Jennifer in first.

"Chilly," Jennifer said, rubbing her arms with her hands.

"Just wait."

Jennifer stepped in, then scooched deeper, her back pressed against the wall. Stan followed, then Greg. Casey went in last, sliding the door back into place. The cramped space was dark, except for the little bit of light from the false wall's seams and the glow from the screen in her glasses. Pressing up against the cab wall behind her, she felt Simone's gun against the small of her back. It made her uncomfortable to be armed, but the guards had shot at her once, and with her friends now part of the equation, she was not going to be caught defenseless again.

Up ahead, the quaint red-brick guard booth and the Ivy-League-looking campus came into view. Dan waved down his window as he slow-rolled to a standstill. A barrier arm, striped red, stopped the truck from going farther. The guard in the booth, his bulky coat in camouflage, slid open his window and held out a screen. "Hand," he said, his breath visible in the air.

Dan laid his hand flat on the screen. After a moment, the guard pulled it back.

"You're a late addition," the guard said.

"Other driver got sick."

Next to Casey, Greg shivered. "Almost," she whispered. "We're almost through."

"Pull under there," the guard said, pointing to a canopy behind the booth.

Shit. They were going to be inspected. A chill ran through her from both the cold and the threat. A clock above the feed from Dan's glasses read 2:45 p.m. The assembly was scheduled to begin at three. The plan had them getting the bins in place before the assembly started. At best, that was a long shot right now.

Outside, the barrier arm went up. Dan drove through, making a hard left just past it.

"Are we through?" Jennifer whisper-asked.

"No," Casey answered. "Inspection."

"Shit," Jennifer said.

Dan pulled under the canopy—its white canvas shaped by a scaffolding frame. Attached at the corners and down the posts of the scaffolding were various cameras and sensors. The guard was now out of the booth with his screen in hand, waving Dan forward. He stopped him at the edge of a red line painted on the asphalt. The guard tapped at his screen, unleashing a grid of red lasers across the truck. With Dan having access to everything Todt Hill, none of this was a surprise, but, as the day had already shown, planning and execution could be two very different things.

"Hang on," Casey said as the grid retreated. "We're almost done."

The guard studied his screen, then looked at the truck. "Open it up for me," he ordered Dan.

Grimacing, Casey shook her head. They had been expecting the sensors and had shielded their equipment appropriately. But a human inspection was unexpected, and it left them vulnerable.

Dan jumped down from the cab. He walked around the truck with the guard leading him to the back. Casey's view jostled with each footfall. Dan unlocked the door, then rolled it up. Through

Dan's feed, Casey could see the wall they were hiding behind, and she thought it appeared genuine enough. She looked down the row of cramped friends. Everyone was wide-eyed and at attention.

The guard hopped up onto the truck. After glancing around, he slipped between the bins and toward the back. He was headed straight for Jennifer, inspecting the shelves as he went; his footsteps were audible on the metal floor. Jennifer eased back on her toes, forcing herself flat. The guard turned to the towel-and-tech-filled bins, his shoulder pushing at the false wall as he did. Jennifer looked Casey's way, her eyes wide and pleading. Casey nodded her acknowledgment. If the wall gave, the mission would end before it could really begin. Casey held her breath. She debated reaching around for the gun but didn't want to risk the movement. Then she remembered Nurse Kristof's tranquilizer in her jumpsuit pocket. She'd brought it along as a nonlethal option. Slipping her hand into her pocket, she palmed the tube, its metal casing cold to the touch. The guard inched forward, relieving the pressure on the wall and, for the moment, on them as well. Casey let out her breath, only to hold it again as the guard began to reach into a bin.

"Casey," Dan whispered through the glasses as he grabbed a handrail to hop up onto the truck too. "Be ready."

As I'll ever be, she thought.

But just as the guard began to dig, a horn honked impatiently back at the booth. Dan stood down as the guard looked past him and turned to see two black SUVs lined up, waiting to get in. *Probably the mayor himself arriving*, Casey thought.

"Shoot," the guard said, audible through the fake wall. He shuffled down the length of the truck, then jumped from its deck. "You're fine," he said to Dan, walking past. Dan turned with him. "Just put a back-up driver on the register when you submit in the morning. It'll speed things up."

"No problem," Dan said. He turned to the open cargo box and acknowledged his relief with an eye roll. "That was way too close for comfort." He grabbed the door's lip and pulled it down.

"Way too close," Casey said, pushing at the fake wall and sliding it back. The fresh air was as much a relief as the guard's standing down. She stepped out, then waited as her chilled friends followed.

Dan stood outside at the back of the truck, watching as the SUVs drove down a short incline and into the covered parking area. "Our mayor, I assume," he said.

"It's a good bet." Casey looked at Jennifer, who was warming her hands with her breath. "We need to hurry up."

6

Dan pulled to the curb in front of the Academy's service elevator. "Sit tight," he said. Up ahead, maybe sixty feet, the SUVs had pulled in too. Sitting tight and waiting to throw the cargo door open, Casey watched along with Dan as the SUVs emptied. Two large men, dressed identically in dark suits and dark overcoats, got out of the lead car. They did a brief survey of the parking garage, noting Dan, or at least the truck, with a head nod between them. When they were done, they met at the rear SUV, taking positions on either side of the passenger door. The bodyguard closest to Dan watched him intently.

"Shoot," Dan said.

"Don't sweat it," Casey reminded him. "You're allowed to be here."

"Right," he answered. Looking down at the dashboard, he tapped off the truck's engine. "I should get moving." He opened the door. As he hopped down, he glanced toward the SUVs again. The passenger door opened as the bodyguards stood watch on either side. A man got out from the back seat. Sure enough, it was Jennifer's father. The mayor was dressed in a suit but no tie, looking afternoon-assembly informal. At the same time, a harried aide had come around from the front to meet him. The aide had a bag hanging heavy from his right shoulder and an overcoat folded across his left arm. He offered the coat to the mayor but was waved off. Instead, the mayor turned to the open car door. Putting his hand out, he helped a woman from the passenger seat.

"Fuck," Casey muttered.

The woman was Simone—her dad's mole and the mayor's mistress. She wore modest pumps, a pencil skirt, and a fitted dress shirt, looking much like the banker she was pretending to be.

"You saw that, then?" Dan asked as he turned from the scene and made his way to the back of the truck.

"So much for going into hiding," Casey said. She looked at Jennifer, who was standing in front of her, listening to the one-sided conversation. Casey held a finger up to Stan and Greg, who were waiting by the back two bins, signaling for them to sit tight.

"Something must have changed," Dan said.

Jennifer scowled. "Simone?" she whispered.

Casey nodded.

"Fucking bitch," Jennifer said.

After reaching the back of the truck, Dan unlocked the door, then tossed it open. Grabbing a handle at the center of the truck's deck, Dan tugged, struggled for a bit, and then pulled the loading ramp out and down to the ground. He hurried back to the open cargo box, and Casey handed him a plastic caddy filled with cleaning and espionage supplies. He took the caddy by its handle and carried it to the curb. The mayor and his entourage were now on their way into the elevator. The bodyguard watching Dan followed last, giving him one last look before the elevator doors closed.

"They're in," Casey said, waving the Trident Cleaning crew into action. She rolled her bin down first, its wheels clanking on the metal ramp. Dan walked to the service elevator and placed his hand on the panel next to it. Casey navigated her bin up a curb cut and came to a stop next to him. The panel's indicator light showed green, and the elevator doors opened. "This is it," she said to him.

"Yeah," he said. "For a minute there, I didn't think it was going to happen."

"Because of them," she said, jutting her chin towards the SUVs, "or because I wanted to wait for Darcy?"

Dan raised an eyebrow as he stepped to the elevator. "Someone who was focused wouldn't have hesitated."

Huh. She was surprised he hadn't moved on. "You think that was about focus?"

He shrugged, putting his hand out to keep the elevator door from closing. "It wasn't a hard decision."

For you, she thought. That she kind of agreed with him was irrelevant at this point. Casey turned away as Jennifer rolled up. Greg came next, with Stan close behind.

Greg looked at Jennifer, who had a face on because of Simone. He looked at Casey, who was forming a face of her own over Dan. "Are we doing this, or what?" he asked.

"Doing this," Casey said as she led the way, past Dan, and into the oversized elevator car. At the other end of the car was another pair of doors. They packed the bins in as they had been on the truck: two deep and two wide. Casey waited for Dan to get in, then pressed B-1 for the procedure room and B-2 for the gym. As the doors closed and the elevator started down, she reached into her jumpsuit pocket, pulling out her screen. There was still no word from Darcy.

"Are you getting service?" Jennifer asked, still clenched.

"For now, yeah. I doubt for much longer, though, the deeper we go." She slipped the screen back into her pocket and looked at her best friend. "Forget about Simone," she said.

"I just don't get why she's here."

"Hopefully, it's Resistance business. She's on our side."

Jennifer scoffed. "Her only business is fucking my father."

"Your father abducts and brainwashes kids. How is it that his adultery has you so bent?"

"Her mother," Greg said from behind them. "They're disrespecting her."

Jennifer touched her finger to her nose, then pointed it at him. "He knows," she said.

And he did. As the product of an adultery-fueled divorce, Greg could relate.

"But she's doing it for a good cause," Casey said.

"Still disrespectful," Jennifer said as the elevator slowed.

"My stop," Dan said, lifting his cleaning caddy above his waist and shuffling between the bins. He settled between Casey and Jennifer with the caddy resting on the corner of the container. "For what it's worth," he said to Jennifer as the elevator doors opened, "I don't trust her much myself."

7

Dan left for the procedure room with little fanfare. "Get in, get out, no bull" was his parting advice. It was advice they all agreed on wholeheartedly, except maybe for the "bull" part, which Casey took personally. As the elevator continued down, she realized Stan hadn't seemed as wholehearted as the rest. Casey turned to him. "Are you okay?" she asked.

Stan tilted his head from side to side. "I guess I felt braver before."

"Yeah. It comes and goes. We'll be all right, though."

Casey watched as Dan arrived at the procedure room. Cautiously, he pushed open its swinging doors and stepped inside. If Casey's nerves hadn't been fired up enough, seeing the procedure room— even secondhand, from Dan's view—certainly stoked them now. Dan inspected the chair and its crown of confining screws. He inspected the black-box machine itself, pulling the chip-implanting needle from the sleeve along its side. Casey's mind reeled; she pressed her hand against the elevator wall to ground herself. Taking a deep breath, she rationalized that the procedure room was Dan's business now. She didn't have to deal with it, and that was a good thing. Ignoring the images, she squared her shoulders. *Be here now,* she told herself as the elevator stopped and the doors opened.

The wide hallway was busy, frenzied even. Kitchen staff, dressed in checkerboard pants and white shirts with mandarin collars, sped by, carrying supplies. Fresh produce in waxed cardboard boxes went one way, and empty industrial-sized pots and pans in need of cleaning went the other. Amidst the scurrying kitchen staff, Casey stiffened as she spotted an authentic Trident Cleaning employee pushing a mop and bucket. He was their clone, except in a better-fitting jumpsuit. Casey looked at Jennifer, who was side-eyeing her. The genuine Trident employee glanced in their direction. If he thought they were imposters, he didn't show it. He just looked away again, never breaking his stride.

"Friendly," Greg deadpanned. "Remind me not to sign his birthday card this year."

Jennifer chuckled.

Casey rolled her eyes but was glad for the cut in tension. "Come on," she said, waving them forward. The kitchen, along with the main elevators, were to the right. Their goal—the service corridor to the gym—was around the corner to the left. After checking both ways, she crossed the hall, pushing her bin in front of her. The comforting smell of fresh-baked dinner rolls filled the hall. Casey had liked the dinner rolls.

"Smells like they fed you pretty well," Jennifer whispered, pushing the next bin in the row.

Casey half turned. "Yeah. Brainwashing in the morning, and a nice meal at night. It made it all worth it."

Jennifer scoffed. "You always manage to find the good in things."

From Dan's feed, Casey saw he had settled behind the machine's console and was attaching a transmitter to it. Like the tech in the bins, the transmitter was shoe-box-sized, with rubberized antennae and a screen on top. Dan tapped at the screen, turning it on. After a moment, line after line of computer code scrolled by. From her own preparations, Casey knew the code was being copied from the console itself and that it contained the chip's kill switch. After the code was copied and all the chips were deactivated, the original would be erased, and Hargrove's brainwashing days would be done. That they were so close was hard to believe. She thought about her dad and about how proud she thought he'd be. She hoped that when all this was done and Hargrove was discredited and behind bars, the truth about her father's latest disappearance would emerge.

Up ahead, the hallway split, with a sign to the right directing them to the gym and laundry room. Casey made the right, bin first. At the end of the hall was a pair of swinging doors with GYMNASIUM stenciled above in black letters. She recognized the entrance as an exit from the other side, but she had never been down this hallway before. On her left, about halfway down, was another set of doors marked LAUNDRY CENTER. These doors were propped open, allowing the fresh smell of clean clothes to waft outwards.

Casey turned to check on her crew. Their four-bin caravan was in place, with Greg taking up the rear. *This is really it,* she thought, as she headed for the gymnasium doors. Passing the laundry room, she glanced inside. There were massive-looking washers on one side, matching dryers on the other, and a row of tables down the middle. About a dozen Trident Cleaning staffers were loading and pulling and folding throughout. Then, a short, stout woman pacing the floor saw Casey and waved to her. The woman had dark hair with gray roots and wore the same Trident uniform—minus the hat. Casey checked around to see if the woman could have been waving at someone else, but then the wave was followed by a stern march toward them. It was clear she was coming for them.

"Shit," Casey said, then urged everyone on.

"Hold it!" the woman barked as she reached the hallway. She put her hand on Jennifer's bin and called Casey back. "Who ordered these towels?" she questioned, pointing to the containers.

Jennifer stepped forward; Casey, Greg, and Stan exchanged glances.

Jennifer tilted her head and smiled. "Supply did, ma'am."

The woman grunted. "No. This has to go through me." She pulled a screen from her jumpsuit pocket while studying Jennifer.

Casey thought the woman was studying Jennifer a bit too hard, and she moved from behind her bin. Was Jennifer being recognized? And as what: mayor's daughter, or ersatz coworker? Either option sucked. But then the laundry lady ended her inquisition, looking from one of them to the next with equal skepticism. "I don't recognize any of you," she said. Squinting, she pointed at Stan. "And you . . . what are you, twelve?"

Stan, in his oversized jumpsuit and bowl haircut, pushed his glasses up his nose. She wasn't wrong. Stan's baby face could not be hidden, even by a pretty good disguise.

As the laundry lady tapped at her screen, Jennifer subtly waved Casey away. "You should have the order," she said to the woman. "Truck's upstairs, and the gate was notified."

The woman pursed her lips, her shoulders relaxing. "It's here," she said. "But they need to tell me this shit." Satisfied, the lady took a step back, waving them toward the laundry room. "C'mon . . . bring 'em in here. Gym's stocked, and they got their thing going."

No, Casey thought, coming forward again. There was no way these bins could be left anywhere but in the gym.

"Casey," Dan said in her ear. "The bins can't—"

"I know," she whispered, curtly.

"That's all right," Jennifer said. "We were told to deliver them to the gym."

"My laundry, my rules," the lady said, latching onto Jennifer's bin.

As Casey inched closer, Greg came from behind his bin. Casey reached into her pocket for the tranquilizer. She hadn't imagined using it on a civilian, but here she was. Casey checked over her shoulder: There was no one between her and the gymnasium doors. She checked over Greg's shoulder: People passed behind him in the main hall, but no one came their way. Casey gripped the metal tube, then slipped it from her pocket. She checked the laundry room to see if she had an audience, but the staff were unaware, busy with work. She checked herself and realized her anxiety was gone; it had been replaced by a wave of adrenaline.

The laundry lady was holding Jennifer's bin, pulling it behind her. She stopped, then turned and looked first at Greg, who was approaching her from one side, then at Casey on the other. "You can't just leave them in the hall," the lady said, her voice pitching higher.

Casey pressed the plunger on the tranquilizer, forcing its small needle to emerge from the other end. She stepped in front of the woman to block what she was about to do from the view of the laundry staff behind them. The laundry lady, her brow furrowed, tried to push Casey out of the way, but Casey held steady and stuck the needle into her upper thigh. Gasping, the lady went limp almost immediately. Casey grabbed her arm to keep her upright, and Greg put his arm around her back, balancing her weight against his chest.

"That was close," he said as they gently lowered her to the floor.

"Yeah, too close." Casey checked over her shoulder. Now the staff were paying attention. "Help!" she called out to them.

Soon they were in the middle of a scrum, being pelted with questions about what had happened. Casey answered that she had no idea what happened, that the woman had just collapsed. Casey grabbed the nearest person's arm. "You should get her some help," she said, standing and urging the stranger forward. Across from her, Greg stood and urged action as well.

Satisfied with the level of care they had shown, Casey side-stepped from the scene, meeting Greg behind the scrum.

"What was that?" he asked, pointing to her closed fist.

Casey flashed him the tube. "Tranquilizer," she said. "It's strong, and, unfortunately, I've had the pleasure—twice."

"Fuckin' nuts," Greg said, then returned to his bin.

Casey passed Jennifer on the way to her own bin. "I didn't like doing that one fucking bit," she said, disgusted with the violence, nonlethal though it was.

"Well," Jennifer said as they got back to business, "hopefully she's the last of our troubles."

8

After passing through the gymnasium doors, the ostensible Trident team emerged at the back of the gym. They were facing the stage. Behind them, a few stories up, the conference room loomed. Using the running track as their guide, Casey directed Jennifer and her bin in first and off to the left. Stan and Greg circled to the right. The recruits, in camouflage shirts and caps, sat down the middle. There was a large screen centered over the stage. Below it, eight officer-looking types sat, four to a side. A woman—Sergeant Collins, if Casey remembered correctly—was at the microphone, center stage, praising the surfacing recruits for their tenacity in getting this far.

Sticking close to the outer edge of the track, Casey followed Jennifer. She searched the rows of recruits for her old group. She wanted to see them but felt conflicted all the same. That they probably thought her a traitor was part of it, but, in reality, she didn't want to acknowledge the good feelings she'd had for them. Lara had been great; Brian was always upstanding. But those good feelings weren't real; they had been programmed. Either way, from behind, the sea of buzzed napes and squared shoulders all appeared the same. It wasn't until Sergeant Collins asked for the group leaders to stand and be recognized that Casey spotted Brian. His broad back gave him away. He was about halfway down, standing at an aisle seat on Casey's side of the gym. He was armed, which was weird since the group leaders had never been armed when she was a recruit. She thought that perhaps her escape had something to do with the change in protocol. Next to Brian sat Lara and Martin; they were looking at their colleague, beaming. It was inconceivable now, but Casey knew that if her chip had not malfunctioned, she'd be there beaming too. After Brian sat down, Lara touched his leg, letting her hand linger for a moment. *Finally together*, Casey thought. She was glad for them but repulsed by the institution that had brought them together.

Gauging her progress, Casey stopped. Their goal was to place the bins lined up with the first and last rows, thereby containing as many recruits as possible between their four corners. Jennifer was in place at the front. Casey checked on Greg and Stan. They were in position, waiting on her. "We're good down here," she said to Dan.

"Copy that," Dan said. "I'll need a few more minutes for the download. Get everyone upstairs, and I'll meet you at the truck."

From Dan's view, Casey saw the screen attached to his device was still running through the code. "Sounds good to me," she said. Looking to Greg and Stan, Casey tilted her head back the way they'd come. She turned to Jennifer, who was distracted, looking not at her but at the recruits. Casey followed her stare. Jennifer was looking at Martin, who was staring right back.

"Shit," she said, marching towards her wayward friend. Jennifer saw her, snapped out of it, then hurried her way.

Casey checked on Martin. He was still watching Jennifer, craning his neck for a better view. Casey met Jennifer halfway, then about-faced, matching Jennifer's long strides in the other direction. "What the fuck were you doing?" she questioned.

"I don't know . . . I'm sorry. I didn't mean to see him."

"Just keep walking."

"Fuck," Jennifer muttered, her head down and her hand up, casually touching the side of her face.

"Yeah."

Up ahead, Greg and Stan waited by the gymnasium doors. Coming around the track's curve, Casey glanced back. Brian was now standing up and was following Martin's stare, a stare that led right to her. They locked eyes. Despite the wig and the glasses, it was clear she had not been able to pull off the disguise. Casey snapped her gaze away, her heart in her throat. "Brian," she said. "Fuck. He made us."

"Casey," Dan cut in. "What's going on?"

She waved for Greg and Stan to get out. They understood and rushed through the doors. "Our former classmates know we're here," she said, brushing the wig's bob forward to cover her face.

"That's not good."

"Not good at all." She glanced up.

It got worse.

Jennifer's father was standing at the conference-room window; his focus was not on the stage, but at a point closer. Casey turned to see that he was looking at Brian, who was now heading in their direction. She peered back up only to be greeted by Hargrove's glare. Casey swallowed hard. "C'mon." She pulled urgently at Jennifer. Together, they sprinted the last forty feet to the doors.

"Dan, do what you got to do, then get the hell out," she said, checking over her shoulder. Taking measured but quick steps, Brian had his hand on his gun and was pulling it from its holster. Martin was on his feet too, climbing over Lara to get out.

After bursting through the doors, Casey and Jennifer stopped cold.

Shit. Her tranquilized victim was strapped to a stretcher and being pushed through the laundry room's propped-open doors. Casey didn't recognize the nurse doing the pushing, but the one walking next to the stretcher was Nurse Kristof, her ambivalent nurse and almost-helpful hostage. Kristof had his back to Casey and his hand on her victim's shoulder. Despite their bursting through the gymnasium doors, Kristof didn't turn around or even seem to notice them, which was good. But they still had nowhere to go.

To Jennifer, Casey whispered, "The nurse next to the stretcher— he knows me."

"So does Brian." Jennifer tilted her head behind them. "And he has a gun."

"Right," Casey said, unzipping her jumpsuit to the waist. "But so do I."

Casey reached behind her back and pulled the gun from her waistband. Armed or not, they still had nowhere to go: The stretcher was blocking the tight hallway as it turned from the laundry room. Behind them, the gymnasium doors swung open. They turned to see Brian stepping through, his gun aimed at them. Martin was right behind Brian, his face twisted and confused. Casey pointed her gun at Brian while glancing over her shoulder for options, but the fucking stretcher was still in the way.

"Drop it!" Brian ordered.

Martin, ignoring the standoff, stepped past Brian. "Jennifer?" he questioned.

"You're not going to shoot me," Casey said, holding her gun steady, their barrels only feet apart.

"No," Brian said, his chin jutting out. "But they will."

Casey glanced over her shoulder.

Four soldiers with Military Police armbands were rushing down the hall. They had their guns drawn and were shouting for people to get down and out of the way. They split up, two by two, around the stretcher. Nurse Kristof turned. He was unfazed by the commotion and grinned when he saw Casey.

"You shouldn't be here," Martin said to Jennifer.

Casey raised her arms, letting the gun dangle from her trigger finger.

"We were trying to help," Jennifer said, moving toward him.

A hand from behind jerked the gun from Casey's finger. Another pair of hands chopped her arms down as her feet were swept from under her. She was pushed forward, landing on her knees, then her face. Sharp pain accompanied both landings. Casey's glasses bucked up hard against the bridge of her nose and came to rest askew. Her cap and wig tumbled from her head. A moment later, Jennifer was lying next to her. They were facing each other, cheeks to the floor, as their wrists were bound with plastic cuffs.

"You think your father will be in a forgiving mood?" Casey asked.

"Sure," Jennifer answered. "Maybe he'll take us for sundaes."

9

There were no sundaes, but the conference room did have a spread. A credenza laden with finger foods and beverages greeted Casey and Jennifer as they were escorted in. Their hands were still bound, and a soldier apiece guarded them. Hargrove, jacket off and sleeves rolled up, paced beside the floor-to-ceiling windows opposite them. His bodyguards were at either end of the room. Simone, standing at the far end of the conference-room table, watched them warily. She was joined by Dr. Marshall, Stan's dickish and evil dad, who had his arms crossed in front of him. Behind them, the mayor's aide hovered, tapping at a screen in his hand. As they entered, Hargrove stopped his agitated pacing to glare at them, red-faced, from across the table. In the gym below, the assembly had seemingly continued uninterrupted.

Side by side, they were jerked to a stop in front of the credenza. Casey rolled her shoulders, trying to relieve the tension. The soldier behind her marched to the table, placing her cap, wig, and gun on it.

"I want the recruits, too," Hargrove snarled at the soldier, waving him toward the door.

After a moment, they were joined by Brian and Martin. The pair had been trailing Casey and Jennifer and were told to wait in the hall. Both recruits now stood at attention, their eyes focused on a spot somewhere above Simone's head.

Hargrove stepped up to the extra-long table, grabbing Casey's cap and wig. "Tell me why you're here," he said, holding the disguise in Casey's direction.

"Bullshit him for a bit," Dan said through the feed. "I'm almost ready."

From Dan's point of view, Casey saw the brainwashing machine's code was still downloading. She looked at Martin, then at Jennifer. "C'mon, Mr. H.," she said, purposefully personable. "Jen wanted to see her boyfriend. That's not a crime."

"No," Hargrove said. "But breaking into an ICP facility, armed, is." He turned to his daughter, thrusting the disguise in her direction. "Don't tell me you'd really go through all this trouble just to see your boyfriend."

Jennifer's posture stiffened, her eyes narrowing. Casey knew that look: It was the look of her best friend ready to unload. "Trouble?" Jennifer growled. "You fuckin' kidnapped my boyfriend, put a fuckin' chip in his head, and for what? To keep him from me? To protect your election? How much fuckin' trouble was that?"

Hargrove slammed the disguise down on the table. Its embedded screens flickered under the impact. Casey watched Martin for a reaction, but he had none, even with the story coming directly from Jennifer. On the other hand, Brian did seem to crack a bit, the sharpening crease between his eyebrows giving him away.

Leaning forward with his hands flat on the table, Hargrove's eyes tightened just as Jennifer's had done a moment ago.

This should be good, Casey thought.

But before the next round of fireworks could begin, there was a knock on the conference room door. The bodyguard closest to the door went to answer it. Grunting, Hargrove turned from the table as Casey and Jennifer exchanged glances. The bodyguard, after a brief back-and-forth at the door, moved aside, and Stan and Greg appeared at the threshold with their hands bound behind their backs.

"Fuck," Casey whispered as they were ushered inside. She had hoped they'd made it out.

Stan walked into the room with his head down, while Greg kept his defiantly raised. He had a welt across his cheek and a cut on his forehead.

Across the room, Dr. Marshall's arms had come uncrossed and his face unglued. "Stan?" he asked meekly.

Stan raised his head; his bowl haircut slid back into place. He didn't look worse for wear, but something was still off. Then Casey realized it was his glasses—he wasn't wearing them. They must have been lost in whatever tussle had brought them here. Undressed, his eyes looked small. "Dad," he said, squinting. "I can ex—"

But, before he could get more out, the embedded screens in front of each seat at the table switched on. The Resistance symbol, its circle and bars in red against a black background, was seared across all of them. In the gym, the large screen over the stage repeated the same. After a moment, Jennifer's public service announcement began playing. Looks were exchanged throughout the room. If Hargrove's face could possibly have turned a deeper shade of red, it did. His eyes flitted among the table's screens before turning to the big screen over the stage.

At over a story tall, Jennifer loomed over the gym, and, effectively, over her father.

"Recruits of Todt Hill Academy, my name is Jennifer Hargrove," the recording began.

"Here we go," Dan said.

This was it. The device that had been downloading the code now had a DEACTIVATE icon flashing at the bottom of its screen. Dan's index finger hovered over it. He would wait until Jennifer's recording was done to deactivate the chips, but there was no stopping the packets of damaging data being sent with the feed. The whole city, including the families of the unwillingly recruited, were about to know exactly how their mayor had risen to power and how he intended to keep it.

Casey cracked a small smile. She thought again of her father, hoping he was somewhere watching and appreciating what was happening. She looked at Simone, who had the same reserved smile on her face. They locked eyes and nodded to each other. Only then did Casey realize that Simone's time undercover with Hargrove would be coming to an end too—an unintended but hopefully appreciated consequence of his exposure.

Across the room, even Martin had lost his authoritarian posture, melting into something more human as he watched, slack-jawed, the recorded version of his girlfriend on the big screen.

Hargrove turned to the live version of his daughter and scowled. "What is this?" he spat, a vein protruding down his forehead.

"Your comeuppance," she said with smug satisfaction.

He turned back to the window. "Somebody cut this feed!"

But it wasn't clear that anyone in the conference room could.

"If your name appears on this list," Recorded Jennifer continued, raising her hand like a meteorologist at the names scrolling next to her, "then a chip has been implanted into your brain by my father, with the help of Dr. Marshall and others."

"This is nonsense," Stan's father said. "We're helping these kids, giving them purpose."

Stan bristled. "Dad, don't try to justify this," he said.

"But, son—"

"No!" Stan yelled, his lips tight and his eyes wide. He pointed to Martin. "He was my friend, and he had all the purpose in the world before you put a chip in his head!"

Dr. Marshall withered, leaned back, and said nothing.

"That's what I thought," Stan said, losing his attack posture upon his father's silent admission.

On the screens, the scrolling list of names ended. "Consider this an intervention," Recorded Jennifer continued. She explained that their chips were about to be turned off, and that they should expect some discomfort and disorientation. She announced that their families had been told where they were located and to come get them.

Brian stepped from Martin's side and next to Casey. The soldier behind her put her arm up between them. "Is this true?" Brian asked, ignoring the barrier. "They did this to you?"

"Recruit!" Hargrove bellowed. "You don't talk to her!"

Brian looked at him, then raised his index finger, putting Hargrove on hold and making his defiance clear.

Casey's heart swelled. If the Resistance had managed to reach Brian, then there would be more to follow.

232 | MARC DANIEL ACRICHE

She answered Brian. "Yes, they did this to me, and to Martin." She nodded toward the assembly below. "And to a lot of them, too." At least half the recruits were now standing, some looking back quizzically at the conference-room window.

And then, as if a silent bomb had exploded, recruits started dropping.

Some fell to their knees, some seemingly passed out cold, and others held their heads while sitting in their chairs. The recruits not affected appeared totally bewildered. In the conference room, the scene repeated. Martin fell to his knees, howling, and, much to Casey's surprise, so did Hargrove's bodyguards and the two soldiers. The soldier behind Jennifer fell forward, bumping into her on his way to the floor. The one on Casey's side collapsed backward onto the credenza, then slid down its front, dragging a tray of food with him to the floor.

On the other side of the table, Hargrove stomped over, arms flailing, to Dr. Marshall. Leaning forward, he got in his face. "Stop this!" he yelled.

The doctor cowered, seemingly at a loss.

"Casey," Greg whisper-shouted, jutting his chin toward the gun on the table.

The confusion was their chance.

Casey looked at Simone—the only ally in the room with her hands not bound—for help. After eye contact was made, Casey tilted her head toward the gun. Immediately, Simone understood. On the window side of the table, she bolted down its length, swinging chairs out of her way, and grabbed the gun. It had been hers to start with, so it paired green and unlocked right off. Hargrove turned to see what his mistress was up to but did not protest—that is, until she aimed the gun at him.

"Are you kidding me?" he questioned, as Casey and Jennifer tiptoed over the downed soldiers to join Martin, Greg, and Stan on the other side of the room. Brian, on the other hand, stood frozen in place.

"Not kidding," Simone said, backing up to keep Brian in her sights as well. "Drop the screen," she said to the aide. "Arms up, all of you," she said to the rest, waving the gun. As they complied, she looked at Casey. "Can we trust him?" she questioned, gesturing at Brian.

Casey grimaced. She thought maybe she could, but she wasn't sure, and there was too much at risk. "I don't know," she said.

"You," Simone said to Brian. "Your gun . . . on the table. Unlock it, and slide it over."

"Recruit!" Hargrove shouted. "Do not obey!"

But Brian did obey. Slowly he lowered his arm and, with his thumb and forefinger, slipped the gun from its holster. Raising the weapon up and out in front of him, he placed it on the table. He tapped at its grip until the lock-light on its base turned green, then slid it across towards Simone.

Hargrove scoffed, lowering his arms. "I'm not—"

Simone took a step closer, aiming squarely at his chest. "What part of 'not kidding' don't you get?"

He studied her. "I don't know what this is," he said, slowly raising his arms again, "but I hope you've thought it through."

"I've had years to think this through," she hissed. Stepping back, she grabbed Brian's gun, stuffed it in her waistband, and then hurried around the end of the table, stepping over a downed bodyguard and soldier as she did. "Go!" she said, waving Brian over to the other side of the conference room.

Brian did as he was told, stepping over the other soldier as he went. He looked back at Casey. "You could've trusted me, you know?"

"I'm sorry," she said, meaning it. "But I couldn't be sure."

Through the lens of her glasses, Casey could see that Dan was dismantling parts of the brainwashing machine and placing them into his cleaning caddy. In front of her, Simone, while keeping her gun aimed at Hargrove's end of the table, eyed the credenza. From a tray of utensils, she grabbed a plastic knife. After another look, Simone tossed the knife aside and instead pulled a carving knife from a small slab of rare roast beef. "This will do," she said, waving Casey to her.

"Thank you," Casey said as she was cut free. She rubbed her sore wrists.

"No problem." Simone reached into her waistband, then handed Brian's gun to Casey. "Whatever you guys did, it was amazing. Good work."

"Yeah—kinda worked better than we thought," Casey said as Simone went to free the others. Casey tested the weight of the gun in her palm, then pointed it at Jennifer's father.

"Go ahead," Hargrove said. "I expect nothing less from a terrorist."

Casey just shook her head; Jennifer, rubbing her freed wrists, moved next to her.

"What does that make me, then, Dad?"

"Confused, sweetheart . . . very confused."

Jennifer scoffed.

At their feet, Greg and Stan were swarming the soldiers, gathering and unlocking their weapons. After a moment, Stan handed Jennifer a bunch of plastic cuffs. "Would you like to do the honors?" he asked, tilting his head toward the mayor.

"No—that's all yours. I have a boyfriend to take care of."

As Jennifer walked away, Simone and Greg began herding disoriented bodyguards and soldiers to the other side of the room. Before Stan could walk away, Casey turned to him. "You okay?" she asked, touching his forearm.

"No," he said, looking at his father. "I was kinda holding out hope he was innocent, you know? That maybe he just got caught up in it all."

"I'm sorry it came to this," she said.

"Yeah, so am I," Stan said. Then he joined the collaring and cuffing that was going on at the other end of the table.

With her gun still trained across the room, Casey stepped back. Jennifer had Martin on his feet and her arm around his shoulder. He looked at Casey. His eyes were red and wet. "I'm sorry I didn't believe you," he said.

"No harm," she said. "You weren't yourself."

Switching her attention to Dan's view, Casey saw that he had finished packing and was on the way out of the procedure room. "I'm coming to you," he said, pushing past the room's swinging doors. He wasn't far from where they were, which was good, as they could all navigate their way upstairs and out together.

With everyone secure, Greg and Stan rejoined the group. Martin thanked Stan and Greg, letting them know it was good to see them. Simone, however, hovered about mid-table, a pile of screens and guns and the aide's shoulder bag next to her. Casey moved to her side. "C'mon," she said. "We should get going."

"No," Simone said. "I'll be okay. I have a way out. You go get your father."

Casey did a double take. "What?" she questioned, her head cocked. "My dad's here?"

"Yes," Simone said, a bit too nonchalantly for the gravity of the news. "Has been for weeks now. I assumed you were here to rescue him."

10

Plans changed.

Casey split from the rest of the team—she needed them to be safe more than she needed their help to rescue her father. Dan had held out the longest, being close to her father and all. Still, Casey had insisted she go alone. "Alone" was a relative term; the hallway outside the conference room was anything but lonely. Recruits, either on their own or with help, were streaming through it. They were headed toward the infirmary at the end of the hall. Having stripped off her Trident overalls to the more recruit-appropriate attire she wore underneath, Casey blended in with the flow, feigning distress like the recruits around her. She had borrowed Martin's cap, and she wore it low on her head so that its brim touched the frame of her spyglasses. Brian's gun was stashed in her waistband. Its steel was cold against her back.

The closer Casey got to the infirmary, the denser the crowd became. On her toes, she saw the logjam up ahead; Nurse Kristof was directing traffic at the infirmary doors. Anyone not affected was ordered away while the rest began forming a line to the right of the door. Some stood, more leaned, and others sat against the wall, their minds apparently, and appropriately, blown.

236 | MARC DANIEL ACRICHE

Casey was sympathetic, that was for sure.

As her progress continued to slow, she saw that Dan's had improved. He'd taken the crew in the opposite direction, toward the main elevators, elevators that had been feeding the flow to the infirmary but were now freed up. "Can you pinpoint him?" she asked Dan, whispering so that the recruits around her wouldn't hear.

Dan glanced at a screen in his hand; the schematics for the Academy were on it. He tapped for more detail. "It looks like he's in number three."

Cell Three had been her cell. She thought about her time there: the cold, the hunger, the sleepless nights, the fear. She hoped that her dad was faring better. "Can you unlock the cells?" she asked.

"On your word, yes."

"Good," she said, now only a few feet from the flustered Nurse Kristof.

She watched him from between the heads and shoulders of the recruits in front of her. With the hallway splitting, she needed to make a break. She slowed, letting the recruits behind her pass in front. She waited. The nurse's eyes were everywhere, following the chaos around him. As the flow of recruits broke between those affected and those not, she used one of the bigger recruits as cover. Her head down, she turned with him, following close behind as he lumbered towards the end of the ever-growing line. Then she slipped from his wake and continued on her way.

Casey took a deep breath; she picked up her pace. The hallway in front of her was clear. The elevator that would take her down to her father was up ahead, its hand scanner jutting from the wall. "You sure my print will work?" she asked Dan, remembering her brush with this particular scanner on the night of her escape.

"You've got full access," he assured her.

But before she could answer, she was interrupted by someone calling her name.

It was Lara, she was sure, but there was no way she was going to engage. She kept her head down and her feet moving.

"Casey Parker!" Lara tried again, her agitated voice getting closer. "Don't you fucking ignore me!"

Casey closed her eyes. She hemmed and hawed, then stopped and turned to see Lara marching toward her. "I can't," she said. "Not now."

"Can't what?" Lara asked, getting in her face. "Be my friend? Explain yourself?"

"I am your friend. I just don't have time right now." Casey turned away.

"You're no friend," Lara snapped after her, a quiver in her voice. "A friend wouldn't have used her friend's screen and then left her alone to pick up the pieces."

Casey turned back. "What are you talking about? What I did—my leaving—had nothing to do with you."

"Didn't it?"

"I used your screen . . . that's all."

"They thought we were working together!" Lara yelled. "They thought I was a traitor, like you."

"I'm no traitor," Casey said, annoyed. "This," she said, pointing around her, "is the problem. If you can't see that now, I don't know what to tell you."

"You know," she said, "I didn't believe them—but I should have. You're a disease, and I'm not going to let you infect us anymore." Lara turned, raising her hand.

Hell no. Friend or not, having Lara snitch on her was not how this was going to end.

Lara scurried away, looking to get someone's attention.

But Casey wasn't having it. She reached behind her back and pulled the gun from her waistband. There would be no shooting, but a whack on the head was not out of the question. With a compact swing, she cold-cocked her friend. Lara collapsed to the floor in a heap. Casey slipped the gun away again while kneeling next to her. "Sorry," she said, gathering her from the floor. "This is all too important."

Holding Lara under the arm and around the torso, Casey dragged her to the end of the growing line for the infirmary. She lowered her down gently, leaning her against the wall. The recruit next in line turned around, looking down at them. His eyes were unfocused, his expression pained. She did not know him, and even

238 | MARC DANIEL ACRICHE

better, he didn't seem to recognize her. She didn't need another setback. "Take care of her," she said, standing up. "And yourself, too. It will get better. I promise."

Turning, and with no more time to waste, she sprinted down the hall.

||

The hand scanner proved not to be a problem.

Casey was in the elevator, heading down; at the same time, Dan and the Resistance crew were heading up. She stood at the doors, shoulders squared and gun drawn, ready for a fight. The gun had a speck of blood on its grip. She assumed it was Lara's but did not care: the time for remorse was over. If there were feelings to be had, if there was a reckoning for who she had become, she'd deal with it later. She had a father to rescue, and if that involved violence, so be it.

The elevator slowed to a stop. Casey crept to the side. She kept the gun raised in front of her, holding it with two hands. The doors slid open; the short hallway was empty. She stepped out. There was an open door to her left and a closed one to her right. The hallway ended with two swinging doors; it was past those doors that she would find her father. Staying to her left, she crept along the wall toward the open door. With her back flat against the wall, she peeked around the open doorway. The room was some kind of office, but it was very much empty. There was a desk, maybe five feet in, facing the back wall. On the desk was a bank of screens—six screens in all, stacked in two rows of three.

After checking the hallway, she walked inside and to the desk. The screen at the center top was cut into eight squares with views from each of the cells in them. They were all occupied. Her father was in the third cell, as promised. He was lying on the bed, feet toward the door, staring at the ceiling. *Shit*, she thought, he didn't look well. His beard was way longer than when she'd seen him last, and his frame was absolutely gaunt, swimming inside the

Academy-issued T-shirt and pants. Casey teared up, hating that this is where he had been, and for so long.

Wiping her eyes, she stepped closer to get a better look. She picked up a scent. It was of a man's cologne, or aftershave, or something. It was woodsy and familiar. *The guard*, she thought, taking a step back. The room smelled like the creepy guard—the one who had roughed her up and watched her undress. Gross. She took another step back, not wanting to be anywhere near the desk.

"It's a full house down here," she said to Dan as the crew was nearing the surface.

"I see that. If you can get them up, there's room in the truck. Just don't get bogged down."

She turned from the desk and stepped to the door. "I won't," she said, checking the coast.

"Just give me the word," Dan said, "and I'll open them up."

The hall was still empty, but for how long? Judging by the guard's lingering scent, he had to have been around recently and would most likely be back. She sprinted from the office to the swinging doors. "Okay. Unlock 'em," she ordered, pushing through.

Locks clanked as she ran past a pair of cells to the third. She pulled the heavy door open. Her father was up on his elbows, watching. After a moment of registering the situation, a weary smile emerged through his heavy beard.

"Dad," she said, rushing to the bed, her tears pooling. "We have to go."

"Case—how are you even here?" His voice was weak.

With the gun in her right hand, she stooped, lacing her left arm around his back to help him stand. Up close, his nose looked broken; he had bruises under his eyes and dried blood in his beard.

"It's a long story," she said, trying to push past her dire feelings about his physical state. "But you have Simone to thank in the end."

He chortled. "Funny . . . I thought she was why I was here."

"You're not the only one," she said, taking his weight against her. "Can you walk?"

But before he could answer, the woodsy scent from the office wafted in.

Orders for her to drop the gun, to put her hands up, and to step away from the bed followed.

She cursed the poor timing of it all.

In the doorway, the asshole guard loomed, his gun raised and pointed at her. Resigned, she slowly placed the gun on the floor and inched away from the bed.

"It's you," the guard said, sauntering into the cell. "I remember you." His creepy smile returned.

Casey said nothing. Instead, she sized the man up. Sure, he was big, but he was not Bill big. If she could handle Bill, surely she could take this guy.

The guard strutted towards her; the scent of his cologne up close made her stomach churn.

"I haven't seen talent like yours in a while," he said, dragging the barrel of the gun under her chin.

"Enough," her father said, struggling to get into a seated position.

The guard looked at him, then pushed him back down.

Incensed, Casey saw her opportunity and took it.

She grabbed the guard's gun hand by the wrist and pushed the barrel away from her head. Not letting go, Casey turned her back to the guard and trapped that same arm in the crux of her elbow. She squeezed as tight as she could, adding her free hand into the mix. Leaning forward, she pounded his gun-gripped hand into her bent knee. All the while, the guard struggled against her, pulling and pounding on her to free himself. The blows fucking hurt, but Casey persevered. After a bunch of quick strikes against her knee, his gun fell to the floor. Freed from the threat of gunfire, she kicked behind her, smashing her heel into the guard's knee. He dropped onto his good knee while grasping at the injured one. Casey turned, whipped her leg around, and planted her foot into the side of his head. He fell over, using the hand that was nursing his bad knee for balance against the floor, then managed to get to his feet and stagger away. However, in the confines of the tight cell, he could only go so far. Casey was on him again. As he stood, she slammed her hand up and under his nose with the base of her palm. Blood splattered from what she hoped was his shattered face as his head hit the wall. From there, he slipped to the floor a disoriented mess.

"Talent, huh?" she mocked, adding one last kick into his side for good measure. "You should show some respect, you fucking asshole."

At the doorway, a few of the freed recruits with the wherewithal to leave their cells looked on. They appeared to be as run-down as her father. She thought she recognized one of them from Roosevelt Prep. She stepped toward the doorway. Huffing and puffing, she apologized for her language and reassured them that she was here to help. Satisfied, she ordered them to gather those who couldn't gather themselves. She told them there was a truck on the surface, waiting to take them to freedom.

The recruits' relief was palpable.

Turning around, Casey cursed. The guard had dragged himself, belly to the floor, to the back of the cell. "Stop!" she yelled, marching toward him.

But when he rolled over, the equation suddenly changed: He'd managed to corral his gun underneath him, and it was now aimed at her.

She stopped short, frozen in place, terrified.

Then, before anything else could register, a gunshot blast erupted through the confined space.

Much to her surprise, she wasn't dead or in pain—though a heart attack wasn't out of the question. It was the guard who had taken the bullet. He was laid out, bleeding, his gun down by his side. She turned to the source of the gunshot, and there was her father, hanging off the side of the bed, Brian's unlocked gun in his hand. Her ears ringing and her body trembling, she rushed to him. She gently took the weapon from his hand.

"I had no choice," he said.

"No choice," she said, her voice cracking. "You saved me."

In the corner of the room, the guard continued to bleed out and seemed very much dead.

"Can you walk?" she asked, reaching around her father's shoulders to help him up.

"I think so."

Together they stood. Casey held him for a moment as he got his feet under him. She used the same moment to get a grip on her frayed nerves. Slowly, they ambled from the bed. She glanced back at the guard, not entirely convinced he was dead. But with the color drained from his face and the rest of him unmoving, he looked as dead as dead can be.

Entering the hall, she nodded to the prisoners gathered there. The girl she thought she knew from school stepped forward. "Jasmine, right?" Casey asked.

"Yeah," she said. "We tried the elevator." She held up her hand. "But it didn't work."

Casey flashed her own hand. "This one will."

"Dan?" her father asked.

"Yes," she said. "His handiwork."

"Good. I'm glad he's all right."

12

The elevator from the prison level had direct access to the surface. Dan had moved the truck and was waiting for them. Other than Jennifer's father and the people Simone had under control in the conference room, it seemed no one was aware that the rogue cleaning crew was responsible for the chaos below. Casey, though still shaken from the shooting, felt lighter. With her dad's arm around her, she absorbed the thanks and well-wishes from the escapees. At the same time, she was focused on the image from Dan's feed. He was in the idling truck, facing forward, with a view of the Academy's guard booth. "Dan, am I seeing what I think I'm seeing?"

At the booth, a number of cars—maybe ten and counting—were parked, or in the process of parking, along the side of the road. Casey assumed that these vehicles belonged to families of the brainwashed. Their occupants were piling out, bundled up for the cold, and streaming into the garage.

"Yeah," he said. "It's quite something."

"Could they really have made it here so fast?"

"If they're from around here, then sure."

Amazing. She looked up at her dad. While it had been her hope that the forces unleashed today would lead to families being unified, seeing some of them here, and now, floored her. Casey realized that dedicating herself to right a wrong—to a cause much larger than herself—had paid off not only for her but for them as well.

From inside her pants pocket, her screen vibrated. Surprised by the service, she hoped it was Darcy. Casey fumbled for the screen, pulling it from her pocket; it was indeed a message from Darcy. She closed her eyes, relieved. Darcy had been arrested, but she was out now and wanted to help. "No worries," Casey typed. "We're on our way back." She glanced up at her dad, then continued typing. "We have my dad with us too." Casey smiled as she slipped the screen away.

The elevator doors opened. A few feet in front of them was the idling Trident Cleaning truck, its cargo door open, with Jennifer on one side and Greg on the other, waving them on.

"Jennifer's part of this?" her father asked.

"A big part, yeah."

"Is that Greg? Punk-ass Greg is a part of this too?

"Yeah," she said, smiling. "They're your new team."

He gave her shoulder a weak squeeze as they exited the elevator. She led him to Jennifer's side of the truck, then helped him up. Once there, he gave Jennifer a hug.

As Greg corralled the last person, Casey stepped away from the truck. She gave a thumbs-up to Dan in his side-view mirror. The families, closer now to the truck, looked distraught and optimistic at the same time. She hoped they had done a good job of giving them some answers. After her father's long absence, she knew the not-knowing part was the hardest thing to bear.

Jennifer hopped down and stood next to her. "Is that blood?" she asked, pointing to Casey's pants and shoes. "What happened down there?"

"We'll talk about it later. I think I'd rather focus on this." She lifted her chin toward the arriving families.

"You did that," Jennifer said. "They're here because of you."

"I don't know," Casey said. "I'd say it was more you. If you hadn't harangued me about helping you find your boyfriend, none of this would have happened."

"You could have told me to fuck off."

"Never," Casey said. "I would have told you to piss off. Language, you know."

Laughing, they turned together and walked back to the truck. Jennifer hopped up first, then reached out her hand to help Casey. Once steady on the deck, Casey pulled the door closed.

"Take us home," she said to Dan, then turned to face the others.

As the truck started to move, she held her hand flat against the door for balance. That she had called the garage "home" was not lost on her. She soaked in the sight of the people around her. On her left was her dad, sitting on the floor along with the other more seriously injured prisoners. They had their backs against the shelves. Stan and Greg hovered among them, making sure they were all okay and comfortable. On her right, Jennifer and Martin held onto each other and the shelving behind them. Martin seemed lost, but appropriately so. His world had just been torn apart; on that point, she could relate. Jennifer caught Casey's eye and smiled. Casey smiled back.

Sure, her friends were part of her father's new team, and downtown was their new home, but it was more than that. They were family now, having chosen each other and a greater cause. This held for herself too, she thought, surprised by her own lack of cynicism. For the first time in her life, she truly belonged. She was part of something bigger, something outside herself, and for that, she felt happy.

EPILOGUE | SISYPHUS RULES

THE ABANDONED SHIPPING CONTAINER made for good cover.

The rusted-out hunk of steel sat etched into the asphalt on the condemned side of Fourth Street and across from Martin's apartment building. In her peacoat and cap, Casey sat with Jennifer, who was bundled in her parka, at the container's open end, waiting for Martin to come down.

"It's good that he gets to have a life," Jennifer said, her head turned, peering through the crack between the hinged door and the body of the container.

"We will too," Casey said, her chin up soaking in the afternoon sun. "It's just a matter of time."

Jennifer nodded. But the truth, which they both knew, was far from that.

It had been three weeks, three long weeks, since their mission at Todt Hill. And, with each passing day, accountability for Jennifer's father looked less and less likely. Facts, or what they had thought were facts, were spun so far from reality that their origins blurred.

Jennifer was labeled disgruntled and misguided.

Brainwashing? That was just "enhancing brain function."

As for the abductions, well, they'd been nothing more than training exercises.

While there were wins coming from that day—the Academy

being shuttered, the brainwashing machine dismantled, families reunited—in the end, Dan had been right: Exposure begot misinformation, and the misinformation drowned out the facts. It was disheartening for sure—mostly since Casey had thought that revealing the truth would lead to her seeing her mother again. That was the life Martin had as a former recruit rather than an accomplice, and it was something Casey and Jennifer both pined for.

From down the street, footsteps rustled the cracked pavement. Casey stood up, putting her hand on Jennifer's shoulder for leverage as she stepped from the container. She saw Bart first, off his leash, strolling their way. He was happily smelling the ground and wagging his tail. Darcy was a few feet behind him, a broad smile on her face as she approached. Casey, kneeling to scratch Bart's head, enthusiastically returned the smile.

"My father let you walk him?" Casey asked as Bart dropped to give her his belly.

"What can I say? He trusts me," Darcy answered.

Darcy had been by Casey's dad's new place—an abandoned building in the condemned zone—to drop off supplies. Casey, worried for his wellbeing, was glad he'd taken to Darcy. While she respected her father's choice to be alone, she still wished he was staying at the hotel with the rest of the crew.

After a few belly rubs, Casey stood, then sauntered up to kiss her girlfriend. She closed her eyes, appreciating the spark between them. After letting their lips linger, they reluctantly separated. Casey took Darcy's hand—their fingers intertwining as if by wellworn habit—and led her to a seat next to Jennifer.

"Martin's not down yet?" Darcy asked Jennifer.

Jennifer turned, greeting Darcy with a smile. "No," she answered. "He said something about the power and helping his mom empty the fridge."

"We need to get them a generator," Darcy said.

"I tried," Casey said, sitting. "He wasn't having it. He said others needed them more."

They all nodded in agreement.

Bart, who had gone exploring inside the shipping container,

appeared between Darcy and Jennifer with a stuffed bear, well-worn and filthy, in his mouth. After dropping the raggedy stuffed toy on Darcy's lap, he looked at them, pleased with his find.

"Good boy," Darcy said, scratching him behind the ear.

"He's here," Jennifer said, jumping up and disappearing around the container's door. She came back, draped around Martin.

Martin, smiling, held on to her with one arm. Under his other arm he carried a small stack of poster boards. "Sorry about the wait," he said. "If it helps, I made us some signs." He let go of Jennifer, rifled through the cardboard statements, and handed one to Casey. "This one's for you."

The sign, in bold block letters, read: ELECTRICITY IS A RIGHT. SCREW YOUR PRIVILEGE. Lightning bolts adorned the corners.

"You know me so well," Casey said, getting to her feet. "Thanks."

"Do we have time to drop Bart back?" Darcy asked, extending her hand for a lift.

"Sure," Casey said, helping her up. "We don't start marching until three."

The march, informally sponsored by the Resistance, had been called to protest the mayor's latest blackout regulations; regulations that were only enforced downtown and had grown harsher since his position as mayor came under threat.

Together, they headed east to her dad's place. Darcy took Casey's hand. Bart, walking a few feet in front, carried his newfound toy in his mouth.

"We should probably wash that," Darcy said.

Casey smiled and squeezed Darcy's hand. "I don't think they make a detergent strong enough."

Darcy nudged her playfully. Casey smiled wider.

Maybe, she realized, she'd been too harsh when assessing their losses. The dent they had made in Hargrove's armor mattered. And, while she wasn't living the life she'd imagined, she was living life unstuck, and that's what counted.

ACKNOWLEDGMENTS

I'D FIRST LIKE TO THANK YOU, the reader. Thank you for letting Casey Parker and her friends occupy a small bit of space in your heads. It means so very much to me that she is out in the world and people are enjoying her story. Thank you.

My next big thank you goes to my longtime girlfriend, Dina R. D'Alessandro, and my best friend since forever, Ted Leibowitz. Thank you both for being the first to read and shape *Drained* into the book it would eventually become. Thank you to author Kat Howard. Your edits took *Drained* to a level I never thought possible. I am a better writer today because of your insights. Thank you to cover designer extraordinaire, David Litman. Your cover art absolutely blew me away. You could not have captured the feel of the book and of Casey Parker any better. And thank you to filmmaker Laura Jean Hocking for reading a late version of *Drained* and helping me add some of the smart finishing touches.

Finally, thank you to all of my cheerleaders—family and friends alike—especially my parents, Yvonne and Joseph Acriche; my sister, Lisa Ben-Aderet; my nieces, Sivan and Tobey Ben-Aderet; my aunt, Loretta Mallah; and my cousins, Sophie Sabat and Robin Mallah. Without your ongoing love, support, and encouragement, *Drained* would not exist.

ABOUT THE AUTHOR

AUTHOR MARC DANIEL ACRICHE is a hardcore native New Yorker who currently lives in a tiny apartment in the East Village of Manhattan with his girlfriend, Dina. Drained is his debut novel (unless you count the one he wrote about dinosaurs in the first grade). Aside from writing, Marc watches way too much television and spends way too much time yelling about politics on Twitter. You can learn more about him at www.acrichewrites.com and on Twitter (@ acrichewrites).

DRAINED | DISCUSSION QUESTIONS

1. How does the book's title work in relation to the book's contents?
2. At the beginning of the book, Casey is in her own head, worrying about her father's absence, her mother's new relationship, and her tanking grades. How does that affect her relationship with Jennifer?
3. When Casey's father comes back suddenly, she is reluctant to forgive him, but then regrets doing so. Do you think that she should have forgiven him sooner? If so, why or why not?
4. What are your thoughts on Casey's realization that she's been in denial about her parents' relationship after first seeing Bruce and her Mom together in the kitchen and then watching her Dad and Beth share a sweet moment in the headquarters?
5. Discuss the role that sacrifice plays when Casey agrees to be chipped by the Resistance and abducted by the ICP. Similarly, how does sacrifice play a role in Jennifer's decision to become the face of the Resistance?
6. The themes of friendship and found family occur throughout the book. In your own experiences, describe how friendship, and the surrogate families found through them, affect your own life.
7. Describe the ways that privilege and status influence each character's experiences.
8. Which quote or scene affected you the most?

Made in the USA
Coppell, TX
28 December 2021

70337393R00152